★

A VIEW TO
DIE FOR

A VIEW TO DIE FOR

★

SHEILA BARRETT

Sheila Barrett [signature]

POOLBEG

Published 1997 by
Poolbeg Press Ltd,
123 Baldoyle Industrial Estate,
Dublin 13, Ireland

© Sheila Barrett 1997

The moral right of the author has been asserted.

The Publishers gratefully acknowledge the support of The Arts Council.

A catalogue record for this book is available from the British Library.

ISBN 1 85371 689 8

Cover design by Poolbeg Group Services Ltd
Set by Poolbeg Group Services Ltd in Goudy 10.5/13.5
Printed and bound in Great Britain by
Cox & Wyman Ltd, Reading, Berks.

A note on the Author

Sheila Barrett was born in Dallas, Texas. A graduates from Vassar College, she came to Ireland to live in 1969. *Walk in a Lost Landscape*, her first novel, was published in 1994 by Poolbeg.

Acknowledgements

I would like to thank Superintendent Bryan O'Higgins and all at the Garda Press Office for their patient, courteous responses to my questions; and indeed all those members of the Garda Síochána, past and present, who have been so kind. I'm also indebted to Tim Barrett, Gene Carolan, Gerry Gregg, and Helen and Des Murray.

Renate Ahrens-Kramer, Niamh Barrett, Dermot and Mary Brady, Mary Rose Callaghan and Phil McCarthy read the book in draft form and made many helpful comments, and Alison Dye, Cecilia McGovern, Joan O'Neill and Julie Parsons have been supportive throughout. I'd also like to thank Michael Gallagher for sharing his vast knowledge of crime-writing, the Arts Council of Ireland for giving me a travel grant to the Bouchercon conference in Nottingham, and Michael Simonds, for permission to quote from *Irish Varieties: A Victorian view of the histories of Dalkey, Kingstown, Killiney and Bray*.

Heartfelt thanks to Jonathan Williams, for his continuing good care; to my wonderful editor, Kate Cruise O'Brien, and to Philip MacDermott and all the fine staff at Poolbeg.

And to John Barrett – more than I'll ever be able to express.

For Niamh, Bronwen, Denis,
Tim, Michael and Grace

Dalkey is a real place. I like to think that Thorn Crest and Thorn Grove and Granny's Wood might easily exist there; in fact they don't, though a "view to die for" might be seen from almost any high point, and there are wild areas among the houses on the north side of the hill.

All the people in the book except Grace O'Malley, or Granuaile, are entirely fictional. Although Granuaile's activities in Dalkey Sound in 1575 are well-documented, we do not know if she ever set foot in Dalkey itself.

And now, at this day, what is the proud position of Dalkey? Let the value of land for building purposes attest. The "common" covered with magnificent villas and stately mansions; the rocks themselves bear witness to the march of improvement and the advancing tide of civilization, supporting the noble and numerous structures wherein reside the wealthy citizens of our metropolis seeking health and relaxation in the pure air, amid the romantic and unrivalled scenery of the surrounding country.

– Irish Varieties: A Victorian view of the histories of Dalkey, Kingstown, Killiney and Bray

"Yes, thou art like those dim sea caves –
A realm of treasures, a realm of graves!
And the shapes through thy mysteries that come
and go,
Are of wealth and terror, of power and woe."

from "Etty Scott, The Beautiful Dreamer
of Secreted Treasures,"
        Irish Varieties

Chapter One

Briege O'Neill had an affinity with the number three, and that was why she was worried. Before, three and its multiples had been seductive and reassuring in her life. It was only now, at the age of fifty, that she was asking herself why.

It was only a sort of numerical heresy, a mild enough form of rebellion for a person who was both reasonably religious and a banker. But over the years it had penetrated Briege's way of thinking, and in the end she noticed configurations of three whether she wanted to or not.

It was this superstition that had made her sure from the outset that Dalkey, in south County Dublin, was the right place for herself, her brother Séamus and Séamus's baby daughter Talulla. As Séamus coaxed his Mini on to the roundabout at Sallynoggin, the three hills had materialised in front of them like three dark green, sleeping hedgehogs. That day twenty-three years ago, they learned that there were three beaches on the other side of the hills. There were three castles and three convents in the environs and, in the little village itself, three chemists. At least Briege learned all this: Séamus wasn't interested at the time.

It also happened to be Briege's ninth year in the bank, which meant that she qualified for the low mortgage interest rate. Lastly, she had just celebrated her twenty-seventh birthday, though "celebrated" wasn't the right word; it was a muted affair because of Séamus's situation.

Séamus's wife Hope, an American, had abandoned him and Talulla. In the words of one shocked nurse, "She was out almost before the afterbirth," but that was an exaggeration. Talulla's premature arrival had sabotaged Hope's escape plans only temporarily; she was on her way to Dublin Airport when the taxi-driver, an old hand, decided to deposit her at the National Maternity Hospital instead. The porter enticed Hope out of the car before the waters broke ("You'll not be let on that plane anyway, Missus"), and Talulla was born an hour later.

Hope saw her daughter once. She gave the frail scrap in the incubator a dull look, then turned and shuffled back to her bed. The next day she was gone. "Two babies having another baby," said the Sister, shaking her head, for the staff felt sorry for them – Séamus, who was twenty-one, with a child to rear in a country with no divorce; Hope, twenty, a failure despite her beauty; and Talulla, abandoned and peculiarly-named. That was another story.

When Briege leaned over the incubator and saw the sad, spidery little form, her breasts tightened with yearning. For a moment the unfocused blue eyes seemed to meet hers, and the tiny hands trembled and moved pitifully towards the mouth.

Briege's conviction that Talulla was hers to protect and love never wavered from that day. She told Séamus that he wasn't to bring the child to the flat: she deserved a house, the best they could find, and a proper education. That meant an established neighbourhood and good schools.

"Will we put down money for the wedding as well?" asked Séamus. "And the funeral?" He was drunk.

"You and your funerals! Do you want your ears boxed or what?"

"Do what you like," he said, indifferent. Miserable as he was, he was a "fine thing", with his blue eyes and his thick brown hair. Briege wanted to shake all six feet of him.

By the time they found the house in Thorn Crest, Séamus had begun to rally and be more himself. He teased her for agreeing to buy a house with no "three" in the address. "There's a 'three' in the price," was her rejoinder.

"Very lucky, so. Does this mean we can't ask them to knock it down to eight-two?"

"We're lucky to get it at all."

They were. It wasn't a very big house, being a nineteen-fifties semi, and it was exactly the same as the others in the small cul-de-sac; anywhere else, it would have sold for much less. But they could see the bay from their back bedroom windows, and Dalkey was lovely. It was off the beaten track. The village with its narrow street of shops and little stone castles, one ruined, one the town hall, was a sleepy, intimate place in those days. The three hills were wooded parkland; the three beaches were open to everyone. Best of all, the houses on their side of Thorn Crest backed on to a wilderness called Granny's Wood.

They had good steady jobs, Briege in the bank and Séamus in the Garda Síochána; kind neighbours in the cul-de-sac and interesting neighbours in the big house beyond; even a legend. "Granny's," they were told, was a corruption of "Gráinne's." Granuaile, the Pirate Queen, was said to have walked through the wood to dine with William Travers when she was on her way home from her meeting with Elizabeth I in 1575.

So what if Briege, after a few near misses, had never married? Or if Séamus had never recovered from losing Hope? Watching Talulla grow, they had lived for the day that was in it. Three promotions at the bank; three in the Garda. Then, just as Talulla reached twenty-two, it started to go wrong, like some malevolent fairytale.

The minute Séamus told her his bad news, his terrible news of lung cancer, a voice in Briege's head said, "One." It took him a year to die. Then, a bare fortnight after his death, came "Two," when Talulla was injured in a freak shooting in the centre of Dublin. Briege was half-tempted to walk under a bus: that, at least, would take care of "Three." She knew, however, that Fate does not relinquish her own rhythms.

Chapter Two

Briege slipped down to White Rock beach on dry mornings before she went to work at the bank. She preferred to walk there than in Granny's Wood. For all its commanding view of the bay, Granny's was somehow claustrophobic and too near home. Perhaps it was just too near the past: Briege's worries from Talulla's childhood were snagged on the branches there, reminding her of hundreds of grazes and scraped knees, anxious searches, tricky bonfires, cigarettes and finally poor Emma Morrissey and her pregnancy.

White Rock had a brooding intimacy about it that pleased her. Sorrento Point and Dalkey Island to the north obscured Dublin entirely from view; to the south, far beyond the long, flat strand at Killiney, Bray Head leaned out to protect even quieter vistas beyond in the Wicklow mountains. Briege shivered, thinking of what had been happening along those lonely roads.

At White Rock, as always, she felt secure. The granite retaining wall soared confidently towards the railway line, the lot resting easily on the solid thrust of the hill and made from it. Raw rock pushed out from its covering of gorse and trees like the uneven knees and shins of old men or women bared to the sun, like Briege's own knees and shins would look before long.

Flung on the shingle were drifts of soft-coloured, sea-smoothed stones and pebbles. Briege liked the thought that many of them came from far away, small hitch-hikers on glaciers before there was a sea. They reminded her of the people in Dalkey, who were all sorts from all over.

She had started coming to the beach during Séamus's illness. When words, however well-meant, were a hindrance instead of a comfort to her, the slow scrape of the waves on the shingle calmed her. Today was different. It didn't matter how she scolded herself for being rigid, a compulsive planner and a worrier to boot; each soothing rush and fall of the water seemed only to erode her defences against the welter of memories that weighed on her.

All those years, she had expected, indeed hoped, that Séamus would fall in love again and remarry. Perhaps that was what drove her so hard at work – all along, there had been a possibility that she would lose her precious Talulla to another woman. When Hope obtained her American divorce three years after she left Séamus, Briege's heart had quailed; at the same time, she prayed that he could start a new life. Surely he would try again? He wasn't particularly religious; Catholic scruples wouldn't stop him from remarrying. He was a young virile man, and he liked women and they liked him. And would he settle? Not at all. That was what Hope had done to him.

Briege sighed and recollected herself. In her reverie she had stopped short, as she often did these days, and the late October morning was cold. There was a brisk breeze off the sea and a lot of wrack and debris on the strand. Briege hated to see the twists of sodden clothes among the seaweed; they were unutterably mysterious and sad. She half-dreaded that one day she might find clothes with their owner still in them.

Wrack and debris. Twenty-four years ago, Séamus, herself and their sister Tessie had been sharing a flat in Upper Pembroke Street. Those were great times. It didn't matter that the wall in the tiny sitting-room changed colour when it rained, or that the ancient black cooker in the alcove belched alarmingly when the gas was turned on or off. She and Séamus were working, and Tessie was in First Arts at UCD. They were a stone's throw from the Green and Grafton Street, which meant that they'd a stream of visitors. They'd students and bankers and young policemen, never mind their relations from Westport and Belmullet. Five marriages began in that flat, and Séamus's was the first.

It was the night before the All-Ireland, and the tiny sitting-room was packed. Jack Murphy, Séamus's best friend, was there with his girl, and three shy cousins from Belmullet were sitting in the corner on the bed-rolls they'd brought with them. A couple of Tessie's college friends were there as well, teasing the cousins unmercifully – there was one wedding out of that – and then, all of a sudden, the talk stopped.

Briege thought it was the landlady up to complain, and she cursed herself that she hadn't stowed the cousins' belongings out of sight in the bedroom; but when she looked up, it was Séamus she saw in the doorway, Séamus with an extraordinary-looking girl. Briege noticed everything about her at once. The girl seemed to slip into her consciousness entire, like a ghost or a fairy seen with an inner eye. Briege did not believe in ghosts or fairies, but she knew trouble when she saw it.

The girl was slim, almost frail-looking, and she

had long dark hair that waved softly on to her shoulders. Her skin was as pale and pure as any Irishwoman's, though Briege could see immediately that she was not Irish. Her eyes were the most arresting thing about her; they were enormous, and very dark grey. Her eyelashes were black, long and natural. There were blouses and skirts a little like hers in the Dandelion Market, but this girl's loose blouse, though made of cheesecloth, had been painstakingly embroidered and smocked. Her long, green skirt was of the finest wool, and the silver rings on her fingers were heavier than the norm. One – the lightest – was a claddagh ring.

Séamus beside her was very pale, as he always was when anything momentous was happening, and his eyes glittered. The word "exalted" came into Briege's mind. Suddenly she saw her brother as a stranger might; he was very handsome, with his dark hair and blue eyes. He was also vulnerable. She felt a sudden pang of grief for him. He was only a lad, after all, responsible and shrewd in the work he loved, but emotionally an innocent.

The girl stood close to Séamus, uncertain. He put his arm around her and said, "This is Briege, my big sister. Briege, this is Hope."

"Hope, you're very welcome. Bear with these

people now, you've arrived among a gang of lunatics. Séamus will have told you about the All-Ireland, will he? We've a roomful of hurling fanatics here, let that explain everything."

"I'm glad to meet you," the girl said. "I've heard so much about you." She flushed a little as she spoke.

"I'm Tessie," announced a voice behind Briege, and Tessie poked her hand past her.

"The *little* sister," Briege said. Tessie loomed over Briege, who was only five foot two, but plump.

"Yeah, I've heard about you, too," said the girl with a nervous, happy laugh. Then, to Briege: "You're 'Cherub.'"

Briege stiffened. Séamus was telling this girl the family nicknames? "Boston?" she asked coolly.

"Yeah – yes. I guess you've heard the Kennedys talking."

"And are you staying here long?" Tessie asked. The cousins from Belmullet had crowded up behind her, their eyes gleaming with interest. Briege glanced over her shoulder and saw Jack Murphy still sitting on the sofa. His expression was pleasantly neutral.

"Until the end of the week," the girl said. "My friend wants to leave then, anyway, but –"

"We're going to see about all that," Séamus said. His hand tightened on her shoulder. Over her head, he gave Briege an odd look, almost challenging. Then everyone was talking at once and Séamus and Hope merged with the others. All the same, the air was electric. They had brought something imperious and volatile into the room with them.

Briege remembered that night in terms of movement, of sensuous fluidity of gesture, subtle nuances of posture. In later years when she was less naive, though still inexperienced herself, she reckoned she had witnessed the beginning of a sexual passion that bypassed all reason. Together, Séamus and Hope seemed to glitter; when they became separated in the room, their bodies inclined towards each other with mute longing. At the time, Briege remembered, she had only felt that Séamus was about to make an eejit of himself.

"Where'd you find your wan?" she asked him the next day.

"My wan?"

"Your visitor friend."

"My visitor friend?" He gave Briege a very direct look. She was a little taken aback, but she hadn't the sense to stop.

"Hope. What's the story on her?"

"What do you mean 'what's the story on her'? She's a girl I met." He opened the door as he said it.

"Are you sure you met her?" Tessie called from the sofa. "Are you sure you didn't just fall over her out in the hall?"

"Will you eff off, both of you," Séamus said, and left for work.

"Why'd you call her 'your wan'?" Tessie asked Briege when the door was shut. "That only annoyed him."

"I suppose you didn't annoy him yourself! Tessie, he's not able for that girl."

"What do you mean, he's not able? Sure, she's gorgeous, but she doesn't suffer from intellect. Séamus could take her out and lose her."

"Well, I wish he would."

Tessie had her rebellious look. "You don't give Séamus any credit at all."

"I certainly do give him credit! Where do you think she got that ring?"

"The claddagh?"

"Wasn't it light-years cheaper-looking than anything else she had on? She'd never have bought that herself."

"You should have been the detective, Briege. Well, so much for love."

"Tessie, I've seen love, and this is something else. Let's pray she leaves when she says."

They were busy that week. Tessie was studying for exams, Séamus was on a night shift and, on the

Wednesday, the manager of Briege's branch collapsed on the fifth hole at Elm Park. Briege assumed that the girl had gone back to America. When she found out the truth, it was too late. Too late for what? she wondered now. She could never have influenced Séamus, not in the state he was in.

Hope's mother, Mrs Campbell, flew over from Boston when she realised that something was up. Hope was starting her third year in college; she was to be a debutante. Mrs Campbell reminded Hope of all this over dinner at the Mirabeau, Dublin's most expensive restaurant. She invited Séamus as well, probably in hopes that he would be churlish and embarrassed in such a setting, but if this was the plan, it backfired. Mrs O'Neill had reared her son well, and he was afraid of nobody.

Mrs Campbell had no intention of having Séamus as a son-in-law, but she was quite charmed with him until Hope, who could not finish her *coq au vin*, explained with a sleepy look that she thought she might be pregnant. "Then I guess we won't have dessert," said her mother.

Séamus, describing the scene to Briege much later, admitted that he had been as surprised as Mrs Campbell. "There was I, trying not to clatter the cutlery, and didn't I nearly swallow it."

Mrs Campbell brought Hope back to the

Shelbourne with her that night and threatened and pleaded until they both were exhausted. Finally she offered her an abortion. Hope was already hysterical, and this was the last straw.

She banged on the door of the flat at four o'clock in the morning, and Briege woke and let her in. Her heart went out to Hope that night – she had run all the way from the hotel, leaving her coat and her bag behind her. The next day, she went with dragging feet to collect her things and confront her mother again. The coat and bag were parcelled up and waiting for her in the care of the porter. Inside her bag was an open ticket, good for a year, for an Aer Lingus flight to Boston. Mrs Campbell had gone.

Séamus, both enraged by Mrs Campbell's behaviour and grateful for it, persuaded his uncle Anthony from Westport to marry them.

Chapter Three

The Campbells were great for dramatic departures. They were great for drama, end of story. Briege had often thought of this with dread as Talulla was growing up. She knew it was old-fashioned to speak of "bad blood," but anyone who behaved like the Campbells had something amiss. This private fear of hers intensified when Talulla entered her teens. Briege confided in their neighbour in Thorn Crest, Leila Cummings, whose youngest child was Talulla's age.

Leila had been Briege's mainstay when she first moved to Dalkey. They were comfortable with one another from the beginning. She and her husband John Joe were from Mayo, first of all; second, a Belmullet cousin had been at school with one of Leila's younger sisters, and third, John Joe had once bought a torch in the O'Neill's shop in Westport years ago, just before Mr O'Neill started concentrating on electrical goods. They learned all this when Leila stopped to welcome Briege to Thorn Crest, though it was actually Aidan, Leila's son, whom Briege met first.

She had brought two suitcases of clothes to the house. It was the first day she had the key, and although she was still troubled by Séamus's indifference, she couldn't help but feel excited. She went out into the back garden, which was dappled with bright sunlight and cool shadows from the trees in Granny's Wood. There was a little stile at the back wall; she hadn't noticed it when they looked at the house. The air was wintry, carrying with it a smell of damp, clean wood off the hill.

Briege climbed the stile and perched at the top of it. The quietness of the trees on the other side flowed out to meet her; a blackbird sang, his clear voice rising and falling amid shy rustlings of leaves and branches. Two gulls drifted high above. She could just glimpse the bay, a faraway dazzle of blue, which seemed to be trying to poke fingers of colour through the gaps between the trees. It looked cold.

There was an explosion of laughter and scuffling. Three little boys rushed towards her, pushing each other and shouting, only stopping when they were almost at the wall. When they saw Briege they skidded to a halt, eyes wide.

For a moment nobody said a word; then Briege burst out laughing. The tallest of the three, a thin boy with blond hair and chapped, cold-looking legs, seemed taken aback but the other two grinned at her. One had light brown hair and a round, mischievous face, while the other boy was much darker. It was he who spoke up. "Are you the new neighbour?"

"I am," said Briege, and held out her hand. The boy took it and they shook hands. The round-faced boy giggled, and the blond boy gave him a severe look. She reckoned they were all about seven years old. "And what are your names?"

"He's Aidan Cummings," the blonde boy said suddenly. "He's Peter Lawless (this was the round-faced boy) and I am Gareth Travers." His accent was slightly anglified, unlike the other boys'.

"Well, I'm Briege O'Neill. Do you live around here?"

"He lives in Beaulieu," said the dark boy, Aidan, nodding at Gareth Travers. Aidan had extraordinary eyes, blue with a touch of green in them. Briege was trying to remember the name of the colour when all three started to scuffle again.

"Those two live in Thorn Crest!" said the blond boy, Gareth, breathless.

"Well, we'll see you again, so," Briege said. Aidan acknowledged this with a smile that lit his face and then all three of them darted off, shouting mysterious instructions to one another, disappearing in a moment among the trees in Granny's.

The next person who spoke to Briege was Leila Cummings, Aidan's mother. She was wheeling a pram along the footpath as Briege was locking the hall door. She waited, smiling, for Briege to come closer and then introduced herself. Leila had the bulky, rather stooped appearance of a woman who has just had a child. Her wide eyes, which were the same aquamarine colour as her son's – that was the word, "aquamarine" – were gentle and trusting, her heart-shaped face a bit worn. Briege liked her at once.

The baby's name was Lara, and the moment her mother uttered it, she started to howl. Her tiny face reddened alarmingly; huge tears spurted from her eyes, and her fists appeared like two angry rosebuds at the top of the heaving coverlet. Briege stared at her, uncertain. Leila rolled the pram back and forth. "Wouldn't you know it?" she said. "The moment I thought I was finished, this little surprise package appears in the world, roaring. Have you any of your own?"

Briege explained that she was helping her brother with her niece, and Leila shook her head in wonder. "Aren't you very good? If you want any help at all, tell me. I've six. Lara's my last – I think! You've moved to the right place, anyway, for playmates. Mary de Burca's little boy is six months old now – you know the big Victorian house just past the cul-de-sac? His family's been there forever; she's from Clare. Mary's a pet, you'll like her. And there's a little girl in Thorn Grove, just a month old. Morrissey, that's their name."

It had all seemed so simple, Briege thought. Ready-made playmates. Three of them: Lara Cummings, Alan de Burca and Emma Morrissey, babes in arms the lot of them. And her Talulla.

Where on earth had the time gone? "Sure, kittens grow to be cats," Leila would say years later, during the hard times, when Briege would take refuge in her kitchen on a Saturday morning. They usually had the place to themselves except for Aidan, who liked to get up early on Saturdays when he wasn't working. Briege noticed that Aidan registered other people's conversations just like Séamus did, which both amused and annoyed her.

"I think thirteen's too young for them to be going to a disco," Briege said.

"Well, it depends, you see, Briege. Aidan," Leila asked her son, who was making the coffee, "do you know anything about that place?

'Muggins'? The disco over in the hotel, you know the one?"

"That one with the white slave traffic? Made for them."

"Aidan, are there drugs at it!"

"Nothing that'll improve Lara."

"She ransacked his tapes yesterday," Leila told Briege out of the corner of her mouth. "One of them broke in her recorder. He's incensed."

"All the same, Leila, I wish Talulla had someone to fight with besides me."

"You don't, Briege. She'd fight with you anyway, and you'd have to listen to all the other fights."

"I suppose it isn't their fault that Emma and Alan are allowed do absolutely everything."

"It isn't." Leila sighed. "Poor Alan . . . The thing is, if we let them go to this one they'll probably want to go to all the others."

"Maybe not. It might be a bit tough, you know, going to those. Sometimes nobody wants to dance with them." They brooded a little, thinking of their awkward, spotty children. "Mind you, I'm only afraid someone *will* want to dance with Talulla." Even at thirteen Talulla, flat-chested and with a spot on her nose, bore an extraordinary resemblance to Hope. Briege wondered what other resemblances might develop.

Leila knew where her thoughts were heading.

"How many times will I tell you, Briege, it's their age? Nothing hereditary here, pet. Or if there is, it's worldwide."

"Lara's problems aren't hereditary," Aidan said, looking hard at the kitchen door. "They're evolutionary."

"Thanks a bloody lot," said Lara's huffy voice from the hall. Footsteps thudded on the stairs and a door slammed above them.

"Aidan, you shouldn't wind her up," his mother said.

Aidan put two mugs of coffee on the table for her and Briege, and he smiled at her. His rather sullen good looks were transformed. Aidan Cummings was a heartbreaker. He was twenty; there was a seven-year gap between him and Lara, the baby of the family. Briege sympathised with him. John Joe Cummings had died from heart disease two years before and Aidan, who was the oldest child left at home, took on many of his responsibilities. He had given up the place he had won to study Arts in college, to join the Garda Síochána. This meant he was away from home for long periods, but at least he was costing his mother nothing. Indeed, he sent her everything he could.

Briege sometimes felt that, if she could discern the pattern to all the thoughts and memories she had during her walks on the beach, she would know what she was meant to do from now on. She had become obsessed with the past. It seemed only yesterday that Talulla was thirteen, and she and Leila had sat complaining in the kitchen. A lot had changed. Talulla, Lara and Emma were all twenty-three now; Aidan was thirty. Briege had no doubt that he was still helping Leila, though he hadn't lived at home for some time. Aidan was a bit of a puzzle. She wouldn't have thought that he could reach thirty without getting married or at least partnered, but there he was, a detective sergeant with good prospects and looks to die for, and no sign of a wife or long-term girlfriend. And he wasn't gay, either.

He was certainly good to Leila. Her life had not been easy over the years. Briege felt that she had neglected her in recent times. She had just been so busy at the bank, and then there was Séamus's illness. She wondered if Leila would have been so drawn to prayer meetings, to signs and wonders, if she had made more time for her. Now she was well and truly marching to the sound of a different drum, and Briege worried about her.

Leila had gone a bit uncanny. She lived alone, though Aidan's flat was close by in Dalkey. Lara had got halfway through an Arts degree, thrown it up, taken a secretarial course and migrated to

London. Leila attended a prayer meeting every week now. She claimed her asthma had improved, which was good, but she was also entertaining some very odd thoughts, which wasn't.

Briege recalled her meeting with Leila in Dalkey on the previous Saturday. They had bumped into one another in front of the delicatessen counter in Super Valu. Leila had seemed to be in another world, and it saddened Briege to see her old friend looking so drawn and pale.

"Leila, I haven't seen you for days. How are you?

It seemed to take Leila a moment to recognise her. "Briege!"

"I asked *how* you are, Leila. Should I ask *where* you are?"

Leila laughed, but her blue-green eyes were very dark, as they tended to be when she was worried. She had never made any attempt to tint her brown hair, and Briege felt that it had got much greyer in the past fortnight. "I couldn't tell you where I am, Briege – I don't know whether I'm coming or going. And I'm sorry. I should have been in to you. How's poor Talulla? Aidan was asking me only this morning."

"She's getting on very well. Her tutor there at Cabinteely – I can never remember that guard's name, and she's very nice. I'm a disgrace – well, she says Talulla can come back after the bank holiday weekend."

"This day week?"

"Exactly."

"And what do you think?"

"I don't know, Leila. If I did, it would make no difference."

"Isn't it true. I don't know, either, Briege. It's hard to. They are under attack, but I suppose they must go on as always. They must."

"'Under attack?'" Briege murmured, on her guard. This sounded like Leila's "charismatic" talk. Briege was prepared to take on harmless superstitions about the number three, but not personalised attention from the devil.

"Aidan hasn't been the same since he's been involved in that awful case. It's undermining him now."

"At least nothing's happened for a while."

"Something's about to," Leila said, so quietly that Briege could scarcely hear her. "Something's about to happen, Briege, I'll stake my life on it. There's just – " She shrugged, looking hopeless.

Briege drew her aside so that a woman behind them could buy salami. "Leila, you're making yourself sick with this nonsense! You look dreadful. You've taken on the worries of the world, and you don't even know what they are! I wouldn't mind, but you've always been so sensible." Briege smiled at one of her customers, who was passing with a loaded trolley (more on the overdraft). "Leila, I know it's none of my business, but those meetings – !"

"Briege, I know how you feel, " Leila said, putting her hand on Briege's arm. Briege had felt like crying.

All her certainties were being taken from her. She had lost her infuriating and most-loved brother; she had nearly lost her Talulla and now, in some way, she was losing her warmest, most reliable friend. Perhaps Leila had been more like an older sister than a friend. Now she was moving into areas where Briege couldn't follow her.

Briege considered the menopause. It didn't explain Leila's behaviour, but it might be the cause of some of her own anxiety and gloom. After all, the Wicklow Strangler – Aidan's "case" – was a solitary nutter roaming the country, not some diabolical manifestation of an entire era.

Séamus had died of cancer, but Talulla had survived the shooting. A painful graze. A scar. A narrow, almost miraculous escape it had been from terrible injury, even death. But Briege's hopes were fading that Talulla would be frightened out of pursuing her training in the Garda. Why wouldn't

Talulla see that she wasn't right for that life? Hadn't Séamus himself said it? Perhaps this was what had her down at the beach in all weathers, she thought; her attempts to get to grips with the fact that Talulla was making her own decisions and there was nothing she could do about it.

She loved this life, she thought, kicking at a milky-white stone, then picking it up. Who could have predicted all the things that would happen? When she started in the bank as an eighteen-year-old, girls were taken in hand by Miss Jamieson in the Green and told how to groom themselves and dress like ladies. Everything was slow except the *craic*. There were few transactions, because there was little money; the banks and the tax officials would never know how much had lined the mattresses and chimneybreasts around the country in those days.

Now the skies over Ireland tingled with numbers and conversations that bounced all the way to China, and the reedy growls of printers drowned the whispers of hands and pens. And along with this new era came young men with shotguns and sudden, intolerable needs. One of them panicked outside the bank in O'Connell Street just as Talulla was passing on her way to meet a friend. Not all the changes were good.

Oh, stubborn little devil! Talulla was just like Séamus. Show her an obstacle and she squeezed her eyes shut and charged it. Who could live with either of them?

Briege drew a long breath. Talulla was all right. She was fast asleep at home, not a bother on her. Her skin was pearly with health, and her hair, still summer-streaked, was gleaming on the pillow when Briege peeked in at her before leaving the house.

Things could be much worse: look at poor Emma Morrissey, only twenty-three like Talulla, but with a two-year-old child of doubtful provenance and a husband who beat her. Talulla had a BA in English Literature and no child, no husband. She had a short scar on her belly. She had a future.

So why did Briege's beloved beach fail to comfort her? She glared at the sea. The breakers were monotonous and distant. Bray Head behind her had dimmed. There was a mist coming down, and suddenly she was bitterly cold. As she trudged up the endless flights of steps to the railway bridge and the road, she felt her nose start to run. She took a last look at the long vista, which was quickly disappearing behind its grey mantle. "Bloody three," she muttered, and went to work.

Chapter Four

Talulla's pain-killer was like a fog. Little penetrated it, and what did had strange proportions. She snuggled beneath her duvet, snared in a dream. The sound of the banger going off in Minogues's next door had sizzled past the window in slow, spiky waves, from left to right. The faint movement of her shoulder against the bedding was like a whisper-shadow of her breathing, and now there were hollow, billowing thuds from downstairs. Declan James was after Emma again. He was nailing her to their back door by her hair so she couldn't get away and Talulla, being only a child, couldn't get out of bed to help her. Dad would come, though – he would save Emma again.

Talulla struggled from under the covers. The back door. Someone really was pounding on it, and her father was dead. She was out of the bed in seconds, her mouth dry with alarm. Crisp October air darted into the room when she flung open the window. It was Emma Morrissey below on the patio with her little daughter, Iseult, but both were calm. They peered up at Talulla.

"Emma, what's wrong? Are you all right?"

"Oh, feck! Sorry, Talulla, I didn't mean to wake you. I was hoping to catch Briege." Emma rubbed her nose vigorously, which she was inclined to do when thwarted. The breeze teased at her long, black hair and flowing skirt.

One of the few people who could scrub at her nose like that and still look beautiful, Talulla thought. She herself felt frowsy and too soft from the bed. Her hand strayed to her abdomen, which was stinging after her quick lurch to the window. "It's all right," she said. "What time is it?"

"Only eight. And listen!"

The revs and crashes of heavy machinery, out of sight behind the trees in Granny's Wood, creased the air. The bare branches of a young sycamore quivered against the dark green of the hill. "Emma . . . it looks like a tree's going down over by de Burca's."

"Murnaghan's broken into Granny's," Emma said briskly, and Talulla got her wits about her and went downstairs to let her in.

"Look, Tully. Can't you arrest them?" They had climbed over the stile at the end of the garden, struggling a little with Iseult, who wanted to dive-bomb into the leaves on the other side. Now they picked their way along one of their faint childhood routes through the trees, aiming for the wider track that straggled up from Thorn Road all the way to Beaulieu, the big house beside de Burca's.

"We're not meant to make complete eejits of ourselves. I'd do just that if I tried to arrest Murnaghan."

"But surely this is rubbish?" Emma waved the letter she had got in the post that morning. It was a form letter from Jason Murnaghan's solicitor, saying that he was going to pave the right-of-way through "the waste ground" between his property (de Burca's old estate, where Murnaghan was building town houses) and Thorn Road.

"Probably, but I don't know. They don't call him the 'Non-stick Prick' for nothing, Em. He usually gets his way."

Emma paused. "He mustn't, Tully. I couldn't bear it. Think of it, cars through here. Isn't it bad enough everywhere else!"

As if to support her point, the machinery fell silent for a moment. Delicate woodland sounds, small rustlings and flutterings and a sudden soft rush of wings eddied around them.

"This is where she stopped to look back at the bay," Emma said softly.

"What?"

"Granuaile! On her way to Travers's. Smirk all you like –"

"I never smirk."

"– I believe she was here," Emma said. "I promote all legends of strong women."

They had reached the grassy path on which Murnaghan wanted to base his road. Where the trees parted, layers of light hung in the washed air and Dublin Bay, today a deep, sharp blue, stretched before them like taut silk. Dublin itself meandered to the northern and western horizons, the faraway buildings strangely like rubble in the morning sun, and only the railway line seemed to prevent the vast clutter from sliding gently into the sea. It was so clear that the chimneys of the Pigeon House at Ringsend gleamed like two wires – like a two-fingered salute to Dalkey from the rest of Dublin, Talulla thought.

Nearer, the grey church spires at Dún Laoghaire caught the light, pinning the southern suburbs in place where the land rose towards Dalkey and Glenageary. The car ferry, gleaming like an enormous white cake, was sliding past the long arms of the harbour.

"God, of all of them why'd we get Murnaghan? He won't be able to do this, will he?"

"We'd want to get a move on. Briege must have

gone off on one of her blasted beach walks. We should have phoned someone on the committee."

"Sure, won't someone else hear and do something?"

"Maybe," Talulla said. She wondered what they would do if Murnaghan's men got aggressive. People had claimed to be intimidated by him or his workers over the years, and then the court cases seemed to fade away. She had never heard of Murnaghan or one of his minions being sentenced.

The machine spluttered into action again, nearer now. Emma picked up Iseult and they hurried on their way. For an instant, Talulla was reminded of all the other times they had rushed through Granny's, dodging through the brambles, shouting or hiding. "Are you all right?" Emma asked her, pausing so suddenly that Talulla ran into her. "Are you able for this?"

"Able for it! I'm bored rotten."

"When are you going back to work?"

"Tuesday, I hope," Talulla said.

"Hang on, I'm caught."

Talulla held Iseult's hand while Emma unhooked her skirt from a trailing bramble.

"I was so sorry about everything, Tully, your Dad, and then the accident. I've hardly seen you since. How are you, really?"

"I'm good. You've enough on your plate, Em. I should have been round to you, only I've been in such a stupor. Any news?"

"He hasn't been around." They both gave Iseult guarded looks, but the little girl shuffled at the leaves, oblivious, her fair hair lifting on the breeze. "The court date's set for February."

"That's over three months!"

"Quite fast, considering I've got the barring order. The solicitor says I should be delighted. Aren't men very strange?" Emma asked this with a curl of her lip. "Declan hates me now, and he's no time at all for –" she nodded towards the child, "but he won't let go." She kicked at a stone in her path and Iseult, laughing, ran after it. "He won't be happy till he has me pulped, but at least if he does come back . . ." She shrugged.

"Wouldn't you move in with us for a while?"

Emma shook her head. "Thanks, but my parents would be mortally insulted if I went to you and not them. And believe me, the war of nerves with Declan is a bagatelle compared to the war of nerves with Ma."

Talulla's answer was drowned by sudden, deafening roars from the JCB. Just beyond a clump of trees, whose garlands of ivy shook as the earth reverberated, the huge yellow machine roared and bucked as if furious. Iseult whimpered and clung to her mother.

There was a jagged breach in the stonework of de Burca's old garden wall, and an ugly clearing of ravaged earth and crushed roots had already been made outside. The sycamore Talulla had seen from her window leaned at a mad angle, part of a tangle it had formed with other trees as it fell, its roots poking sideways like reproachful fingers.

Deep inside the site, which was now exposed by the break in the wall, a second yellow monster, bucket swinging, tumbled the old house on to its foundations. Dust rose like incense; but its smell, caught on the wind, was of age and dry rot. There were all sorts of distorted smells, Talulla thought, disturbed smells of things opened or stressed – the earth, forced, breathing cold and outrage; a dusky chill from the broken stones; the acrid defeat of the old house crumbling and, over it all, the hot oily aggression of the machine. She shook herself to attention. Emma was about to stir the pot.

Chapter Five

The digger stopped. The driver, a slight, nervous-looking man, got out.

"Do you know that you're trespassing on a listed area?"

Talulla wondered what a "listed area" could be, but at least Emma had the man distracted. What they needed were reinforcements, and she wished Briege were there with her residents' committee cap on. The menopause was making Briege unreliable as hell. She was down at the beach in all weathers each morning before work, pacing up and down, wondering whether to take early retirement. "If you do, warn me – I'll need to start looking for a flat," Talulla had told her, joking. "You can start looking for one right now if you like!" was the rejoinder, and Talulla, amazed, had flounced out of the conversation.

Afterwards she was sorry. Briege too was

devastated by Séamus's death, and Talulla's "accident" was the last straw. Briege had always felt so responsible. Now, as she said herself, she was in the throes of her second adolescence, just "without man or acne."

There was a rustle behind her and Talulla turned, hoping to see a neighbour, anyone who could phone the others or simply plunk themselves in front of the JCB. However, it was "Charlie" (for Charlotte) MacDevitt, whose family had lived in Thorn Crest for about a year. Charlie was dressed for school in a new-looking green uniform that was about three sizes too big for her, making her look like a small, blonde turtle. She stared at the destruction, awed. "Will they tear down all the trees?"

"Not if we can help it, hey?"

The child smiled a little and shook her head, but the look she cast around was anxious and possessive. She slung the heavy schoolbag off her shoulders and sat down on it.

"Eh, Charlie – !"

"I just want to see what happens. It can be part of my nature project," Charlie said. Her eyes sparkled with collusion.

Talulla suddenly remembered what it was like to be ten and an only child, and she smiled at her. "Just as long as you're down at the school on time,

Charlie. Tell me . . . do you cut through here other mornings on your way to school?"

"Talulla!" Emma shouted.

The workman was climbing back into the cab of the JCB. Emma, Iseult in tow, promptly struggled into the vast scoop where it rested on the ground. The workman got down again. "Oh, now, Missus!" he said, distressed, glancing back over his shoulder. Another man was approaching from the site.

It was Talulla's first chance to see Jason Murnaghan – "The Golden Fleecer" or the "Killer from Killiney," depending on which tabloid he was suing at the time – at close quarters. He was tall, thin and rather stooped. His dark overcoat was immaculate and his shoes glassy with polish. His look at Emma, perched in the scoop like a rumpled Lady Lavery, was purely supercilious. Bertie Wooster with a hatchet, Talulla thought. You could almost admire him.

"Problems?" he asked his workman, who simply spread his hands.

Murnaghan approached the scoop, walking carefully, almost daintily to save his shoes. "Not the best place to mind a child," he told Emma. His voice was light and almost pleasant, his accent Dublin with the corners knocked off it. If you were talking to him on the phone, you'd be seeing in your mind's eye a man who was both honest and civilised. The reality was a very cool customer, indeed. He reminded Talulla a little of Chief Superintendent Murphy. She must have smiled to herself, because suddenly Murnaghan's eyes were upon her, with a gleam of interest that was brashly male. Fifty, if he was a day!

"I'm sure that, being an intelligent person," he said to Emma, "you'll realise we've a schedule to keep to here."

"I am intelligent," she replied, "so I know that's bullshit."

The look he gave Emma then was straight from his past. Talulla moved forward. "This is commonage," she said mildly. "It's enclosed, too. You can't run a road through it."

"Jason Murnaghan," he said, putting out his hand.

"Garda O'Neill," Talulla said.

"'Garda O'Neill'! I'd want to be careful where I put my hand then, wouldn't I?" he said, drawing it back with mock alarm.

"Your hand or your digger, Mr Murnaghan." Oh, he was doomed! She'd get him for that, the dirty so-and-so. They smiled at one another.

"Well, thank God!" said Emma. She was speaking to a new arrival in the clearing. It was Gareth Travers.

Gareth Travers, who was now thirty, had attracted a number of nicknames over the years. "The Lard of the Manor" dated from a brief puppy-fat phase in early adolescence which the girls, being seven years younger, could scarcely remember. The older generation sometimes called him "The Angel Gabriel" because of his fair hair and chiselled features, and Aidan Cummings, his best friend in the neighbourhood, teased him with "Hew-ige Lord Fauntleroy" because of his height. Mind you, you could hardly describe Gareth as being "in the neighbourhood": Beaulieu was a small world of its own.

Gareth smiled at Talulla and nodded at Murnaghan, but it was Emma he approached.

"Good thing you're here," she said shortly, squinting up at him. "Have you seen this?"

"Nice to see you too, Emma." He took the envelope she held out. "Talulla."

"This is Mr Murnaghan, Gareth," Talulla said. "Mr Murnaghan, Dr Travers owns Beaulieu."

The two men appraised each other. They were both tall and slim, but there the resemblance ended. Gareth, fair-haired and ascetic-looking in the dappled light, was very much the Angel Gabriel: Murnaghan, lean, long-coated, made a good Lucifer.

Gareth scanned the letter. He must have just

got back from England, Talulla thought. There had been some talk of his being on sabbatical from his university, but she had forgotten about it. She must have said her prayers without knowing it.

Now he handed the letter back to Emma, raised his eyebrows and waited for Murnaghan to account for himself.

Murnaghan, with a streety twinkle in his eyes, raised his own immaculate brows in return.

Gareth sighed. He turned back to Emma. "Keeping well, Em?"

"When'd you get back?"

"Last night. How's Talulla?" he said, turning his blue eyes on her. Talulla remembered that she could only be in Gareth's company for three minutes before she stopped admiring him and began to feel patronised.

"I'm grand."

"She's not 'grand,' she's been shot," Emma said.

"Shot! Shot? My dear girl!"

"Very British," Emma muttered.

Before Gareth, blushing, could reply, Murnaghan said, "I hate to break up this little gathering, but I'm afraid we must let Mr Evans here earn his crust." He nodded to the operator, who climbed back into the cab without a word.

"I'm sure," said Gareth, "but only where he's legally entitled."

"Would I allow him anywhere else?" Murnaghan seemed bigger all of a sudden. Talulla found herself wishing that Charlie MacDevitt, who was watching, round-eyed, had gone on to school.

"You already have," said Gareth. "You're on my property. See those stones there? They're the foundations of my wall."

Murnaghan achieved an interesting stillness.

"I want this off it immediately."

"My apologies," said Murnaghan. "Evans! We've trespassed. We mustn't go back the way we came, so . . . if this charming young lady will take her 'babby' out of the scoop . . . ?"

Gareth took Emma's elbow and helped her up. As she gracefully shrugged him away, pulling Iseult, who was half-asleep, on to her shoulder, Talulla had a rare sense of *déjà vu*. Then they all stood back as the great machine coughed into action.

Chapter Six

As they huddled together, watching Mr Evans carefully manoeuvring the machine, Talulla felt nauseated. Ever since the shooting her body, having found out where the adrenalin was stored, simply lashed out the lot of it on any excuse. Either that, or she was a creeping, grovelling, sweating coward. If that was the case, she would have to leave the Garda Síochána, end of story. She'd be no good to anyone. Emma was shouting something again. Talulla longed to go back to bed.

Gareth was holding Emma back. She had lunged towards the digger, and she was on the operator's blind side. Furious, she tried to shake Gareth off. "The rowan! He'll knock down the rowan!"

"That tree's within the law, dear," Murnaghan shouted over the noise. He motioned to Evans, and the machine plunged towards the rowan and the gap behind it. For a moment Talulla thought

Gareth would climb into the cab and grab the controls himself, his face was so set and staring, but he could not let go of Emma. The great toothed digger continued to chuck the ground, savaging the earth around the tree that soared, chalice-shaped, between it and the broken wall.

Iseult put her little hands over her ears and buried her face in Emma's shoulder. The growling and clanking reached a crescendo. Someone tugged at Talulla's arm. Charlie. The child's lips moved noiselessly. Her grasp tightened, urgent, and she pointed at the wrecked ground around the tree. The earth shuddered, cascaded, and Talulla saw.

She ran towards the machine, waving frantically. Evans, catching her expression, stopped it. Murnaghan approached.

Talulla stood uncertain, aware that her body had gone clammy and that everything looked too bright. This might be not a true glimpse but some hallucination brought on by the painkillers. She could not really have seen that – emptiness – that had been a face, the lower jaw slack and falling as if to scream?

Charlie, her eyes huge, still clutched at her arm.

Murnaghan had been too engrossed by Gareth's attempts to restrain Emma to see anything, and he raised his hand to signal to Evans to continue. Evans did not register it. He stared at the tumble of clay in front of the digger.

Although the JCB's engine was still running, Talulla's later impression was one of silence. There were some small, broken movements: Emma stood Iseult on the ground near Charlie and moved out of sight behind a tree. The little girl toddled after her, whimpering. Gareth followed.

Talulla approached the mound of earth that was still sifting back into the cavity beneath the rowan. The faintest smell drifted out, hardly more than a difference. She could not bear to poke at the soil with her hands, and she looked for some small branch or stick she could use. The thing they had seen had been covered again; there was only the dark woodland humus and the rowan's roots which, gashed and trailing, seemed to flinch in the bright air.

She grasped a brown stick that protruded from the soil and pulled. It came with some difficulty, then eased as it parted from something deeper. Talulla dropped it. She wiped her fingers on her jeans, then, frantically, on the damp grass nearby.

"What is it?"

Talulla turned to face Murnaghan: "What do you think? No – don't touch it!"

He stood back again, his face inscrutable,

almost professorial. Talulla heard retching noises. Gareth, who had picked up Iseult, offered Emma his handkerchief. Charlie stood alone by her schoolbag, transfixed.

Murnaghan started to laugh. He ran his hand over his slick thin hair. "Who'll I ring first? The guards or the archaeologists?" He reached into his coat and produced a mobile telephone. Talulla put out her hand and, after a second's hesitation, he gave it to her. She phoned the station in Dalkey.

"Looks a bit ripe to be the Wicklow Strangler's, doesn't it?" Murnaghan said, when she had finished. He nodded at the fretwork of rib and the scraps of sodden fabric that had been exposed when Talulla pulled at the stained shard she had thought was a stick. There was a pale sprinkling of finer bones further down. A hand, ruined and scattered by the machine?

"The Strangler." Surely not. But she had better phone Aidan Cummings.

"What do you think?" Murnaghan asked, when she returned the phone to him. "Will we have a plus or a minus for property values?"

Talulla stared at him, amazed.

"We'll soon see," he said, enjoying her reaction, "whether it's true that 'any publicity is good publicity'."

"That's your problem, I'm afraid." She

motioned to Evans to turn off the digger. Murnaghan did not argue when she asked Evans for the keys, but his expression darkened and became abstracted, and Talulla reckoned he was totting up how much the delay would cost him. Good enough for him, she thought. The pitiful bits and pieces at their feet seemed no more than an unexpected pipeline or drain to him.

Emma took Iseult over to the fallen sycamore and found a place to sit on its smooth trunk. Charlie lifted her schoolbag, then put it down again. She went over beside Emma, her finger in her mouth. She had not said a word since she first saw the skull nod and topple out of the earth.

Gareth produced a pack of cigarettes from his pocket and lit one. Then he remembered to offer them to the others. Everyone declined except Emma, who didn't smoke. She dragged on her cigarette unsteadily, her face so white that Talulla was sure she would be sick again.

Talulla could not understand her own feelings at all. Her mind couldn't hold the implications. She wanted Aidan Cummings to be there. At the same time she felt furious at him, as if this were somehow all his fault.

Aidan had been so good to Séamus during his last illness, dropping in several times a week, telling him everything that was going on in his investigations. Séamus loved discussing the developments, or lack of them, in the cases, especially the "Strangler" inquiries. The memory of their voices rumbling upstairs in Séamus's bedroom made Talulla feel hollow with loss. What was it? she asked herself, incredulous. Did she somehow believe that Séamus's and Aidan's desire to discover every iota of evidence was so powerful that it had summoned this thing out of the ground? Sure, she was jealous, too. Séamus had told Aidan things about police work that he had never told her.

"This thing." The travesty of a face, glimpsed and then lost again under the earth. Her hand rose; she blessed herself. Surprisingly, Murnaghan followed suit.

The little group settled itself to wait. Murnaghan had been busy with an elegant calculator, and he asked her how long she thought his JCB would be out of action.

"Sorry," Talulla told him. "We won't know until we've examined the site."

"We," she thought. She liked that. Maybe she would be all right after all; get her nerve back, and go on being "we" with the other guards.

A breeze stirred the trees around them, and leaves drifted on to the ground like belated tributes.

Chapter Seven

Aidan Cummings was deeply attached to places where he had been happy. From the age of six until he was almost grown, he had spent the summers running wild on his uncle's farm in Mayo, and he had felt restless in cities ever since.

Aidan had even older place-passions however, and these were de Burca's and Granny's Wood. De Burca's was being obliterated: only the gable wall of the old house still stood, and the sitting-room wallpaper, which he had traced with a small finger when his mother visited Mary de Burca, was quickly fading in the unfettered sunlight. Already in the levelled corner near the gates there were two stiff scrawls of concrete blocks, beginnings of the pinched-looking foundations for the new town houses.

He almost never arrived at a crime scene on his own but Talulla's message, coded as it was, had given him the opportunity to respond as if her call were personal. "Tell him his friend may have left something in Granny's Wood."

His "friend." That's what he and Séamus had called the Wicklow Strangler – "our friend." They had a tacit understanding that Séamus did not want the name brought into the house. One disease was enough to be going on with.

Now it was as if the destruction of de Burca's and its wall had opened a breach in their defences; the circle around their childhood had been broken.

It was incredible to Aidan that Alan de Burca would sell the house to a developer like Murnaghan. Alan had loved the place. He and Emma Morrissey, being more dragged up than reared, had almost lived in the garden and in Granny's. Maybe that was why Alan had done it: you never reject anything as fiercely as what you've loved and betrayed.

Or perhaps it was just a case of "out of sight, out of mind." Alan had left for England almost three years ago and, later, news came that he was out in Australia. People can change a lot between the ages of twenty and twenty-three. But Aidan, looking at the almost lunar devastation before him, felt the sale of the fine old house to Murnaghan was more a sign of despair than indifference, and he wondered how Alan was and if he had ever found out about Iseult. Alan had not come back to Ireland even for his father's funeral, never mind the sale of the house.

"Your friend may have left something in Granny's Wood." Which friend, that was the problem. Talulla didn't seem to have thought of that. Again, maybe she had. It was hard to know sometimes, with Talulla. The way she had looked at him when he visited her father. Shifty. Cross. The way she hardly looked at him at all when she was visiting her best friend who, for his sins, was his younger sister Lara.

Still half-hidden in the shadow of the gate, Aidan looked at Talulla where she stood with the others far across the site. She too was partly in shadow, but the crisp morning light caught her long, soft hair. He averted his eyes, willing away the insidious onset of desire. Gareth was beside her! When had he got home? He was leaning attentively towards Emma, who held Iseult in her arms. Emma seemed scarcely to hear him. While Gareth was speaking to her, she shifted the child on to her hip, saying something to her as if Gareth had not even been there. Emma didn't have to be such a bitch.

Aidan's gaze fell next on Detective Inspector Jimmy Meagher, his immediate superior. Jimmy, ferociously dapper as always, was chatting to

Boyle, the sergeant from Dalkey, beside the cavity that had been the basement of the old house. How had Jimmy got the call so quickly? Aidan could have done without Jimmy's sharp eyes and shrewd insights for a while longer.

Work on the site had stopped. The men assembled beside the Portakabin held mugs of tea. Their foreman hovered nearby; he was quietly seething, for all the good it would do him. The lads from Dalkey had already made preliminary markings-off. The sergeant, obviously aware of the number of children in the area and the residents' territorial assumptions about Granny's Wood, had instructed his men to extend the tapes far into the trees.

Aidan watched with interest as Murnaghan approached the sergeant and Jimmy. Murnaghan could have been ambling through the Shelbourne lounge. His pose was elegantly offhand, but it was plain that he did not like the outcome of their brief conversation. It was only the slightest shift of his head but, never mind the cashmere coat, you would always know if Murno was "looking at you."

That was his plan, a typical one for Murnaghan: in and out like a bandit, and new access to the site that transformed it from a cramped cul-de-sac off Hillview into an exclusive enclave at the end of a park. Aidan reckoned that corporation houses would have thicker party walls than the structures

Murnaghan was about to put up. Whatever about that, the town houses would be selling for over £100,000, and this for little boxes with free "stereo" – the neighbours on either side – and an economical solution to furniture – none fit. Murno should install a complimentary social worker under each breakneck flight of stairs; and still, Aidan would buy his own little box in a flash if he could live on the hill again. Not if they opened up Granny's, though. He couldn't live with that.

The technical team arrived in their blue, unmarked van. The sergeant looked at his watch. The men got out of the van and stood chatting, waiting for Dr Samantha McQuaid, the state pathologist, to come examine the remains and issue her instructions.

There was a rasp of metal on stone. The gardaí on the site turned, grinning. Dr McQuaid had arrived.

Until that moment it had not seemed real to Aidan. Now, seeing the familiar silhouette in the long, dark car, he wished he could make everything stop and go back again. He raised his eyes and saw Talulla watching him. She stood fully facing him. Her left hand held her right elbow; her right hand played nervously at her cheek, her lips.

What does she know? he asked himself. Poor Tully, what does she know?

Chapter Eight

McQuaid, a glare of spectacles behind the windscreen of her brown Volvo, veered away from the stone pillar with a curt wrench of the wheel. She stopped beside the broken steps of the old house, effectively trapping the JCB beside it. The foreman's frantic efforts to get her attention went unnoticed.

Aidan held the door while she heaved herself out. "What are they doing here?" she growled, indicating the workmen. "And what are you doing here?" She peered at him closely for a moment, then gave one of her barking laughs. "I hope our remains look better than you, Detective – or is it you I've been called for?"

"Tactless," he murmured. "Will I be the first to complain about your bedside manner?"

"After me husband," she said briskly, waving at the technical crew. "Keep your distance when you're talking to me, anyway; that's no hangover, it's flu coming on. It's in your eyes. Now, Detective, the other corpse: think it's one of yours, do you?"

"I doubt it."

"Good. So do I. Too enclosed, I gather. But who knows? This could be the beginning," she said cheerfully. "I rather like the idea of the Wicklow Strangler hailing from Dalkey, don't you? So middle class."

"Us," Aidan said.

"What?"

"Us. Me Ma lives over there," he said, broadening his accent and motioning over the trees.

McQuaid raised her eyebrows. "Anyone missing?"

He nodded.

"Not belonging to you, I hope."

"No."

"Good." She sighed. "Well. Some old leftover monk or Celt, with any luck. So. Will you and the Inspector want me little snapshot?" She meant her first impressions, if she had any worth noting.

"Please."

"Right." She steamed towards the others.

Aidan walked across the site to the little group beside the wall. They looked shaken, with the exception of Charlie MacDevitt, whose face was alight with impatience.

Talulla said without preamble, "Charlie's mother isn't at home and Charlie wants to go on to school."

"Sure, why not? Can you wait a few minutes, Charlie?"

"Yes." She blushed. "I want to get there before it's on the radio."

"We'll do our best." Aidan turned to Gareth. "So how long'll you be around?"

"Till Christmas, anyway. I was hoping till May, but if this lot is as noisy as I think they'll be . . ."

"Aidan, I've got to go home. The child's bum is in ruins," Emma said. Iseult writhed in her arms.

"I thought so," Aidan told her.

"Well, right. I'm going. I'll have to walk round the front now, won't I?"

"Let me carry her for you," Gareth said.

"It's all right. Really. No, Gareth. Thanks. Bye." And Emma was gone, striding quickly towards the gate. When she reached the large metal bin beside it she stopped, pulled at Iseult's little trousers, removed a disposable nappy with a swift, wiping flick, threw it into the bin, restored the trousers and was off again.

Talulla grinned at Gareth, who had watched this manoeuvre intently. "It's not all in books, Gareth," she said with a wink at Aidan.

"What do you mean, Talulla?" Gareth asked her politely.

"Life's finer arts – like salvaging babies' bottoms." Talulla smiled, but Aidan saw she was pale, and she continued to rub her right hand against her leg.

"Could I drift off as well? I was unpacking when . . ." Gareth shrugged.

"Just mention it to the sergeant there, Gareth. Boyle's his name. Look, Talulla, this road scheme's a disaster. Is the residents' association going to get a solicitor or what?"

"That was a quick change of hats, from detective to outraged house-owner!" she said.

"Just defending my inheritance, girl. Murno and Co. will still be here when the crime team are gone."

Gareth gazed at him appreciatively. Aidan had accomplished what he wanted. Talulla looked less shaken.

"Briege'll have the solicitor's number, *boy*," she said. "I'll phone her at the bank. The committee will want to meet right away. Gareth, will you come? It concerns you. Your Dad's on the committee, too, isn't he, Charlie?"

Aidan watched them move off.

Talulla walked up to one of the fellows with Boyle. He wasn't a recruit, Aidan thought, so not a classmate of hers. Could they be an item? No. Wrong body language. She turned and met

Aidan's look. He felt himself blushing like an eejit. Tully O'Neill. He raised his hand. "Goodbye."

He hung on, chatting with various gardaí and Boyle, the sergeant. Finally Dr McQuaid re-emerged. It was strange to see her stumping out of Granny's Wood. She and Aidan had been at four such scenes together during the past few months, but this was much too close to home. She trod through the rough gap in the wall like a figure in a dream, gesticulating with her strong hands and issuing instructions to the technical team.

"Still standing, are you, Detective?" she said when she reached Aidan. "Bloody digger made an absolute hames. The mess is terrific. The skull's quite presentable, believe it or not. How, I don't know. I'm interested in the teeth. Anyway. Take it we've a woman. Young. Medium height? A little under?" She sighed. "No flesh; the odd tendon. Well over a year. Could be much longer, I'm afraid. I saw a button. One of those coppery ones, probably off denims." She stared at him, frowning. "I'll let you know. Yourself or Inspector Meagher. Think 'teeth', dear. And go to bed."

"What do you think?" Aidan asked her. He wished she would stop referring to his health. He had noticed nothing wrong with it.

"Is it our man? No way to tell. But it was

shallow, and there's no sign yet of a handbag or purse. Amazing the animals hadn't more of a go. I'd have thought she'd be everywhere. I'll be in touch."

"Thanks, so."

She waved, plunged into her brown Volvo and, as men scattered, she was gone.

Aidan leaned against the cool, rough wall. Opposite where he stood, there had been a beech hedge and a small opening with a wicker gate. All that was gone; all the divisions and enchantments were gone, like Mary de Burca, Alan's mother, who had disappeared twenty years ago. Oh please, please, he said silently, let it be Mary de Burca.

Chapter Nine

Ever since the shooting, Talulla had craved junk food. Briege, intent on building her up again, brought home fruit and free-range chickens and strange, beige cereal-like substances in small packets. She inserted their contents into whatever she was cooking, which promptly turned to lead. Talulla couldn't stop her.

Once Briege was safely at the bank, Talulla went for walks, walks that brought her to McDonald's. She would take a long route to Dún Laoghaire, wandering down to Thorn Road and then Knock-na-cree. She would stop at Coliemore, watching the fitful activity at the little harbour for a while, then on past her old school to Bullock.

At some stage it had occurred to her that much of this coastline was presided over by women: the Carmelite nuns at Bullock, the Loretos at Dalkey and the Sisters of the Holy Child Jesus at Killiney.

There was a long tradition behind them. St Begnet established her foundation in Dalkey in the seventh century, and later the Daughters of Léinín started theirs at Killiney. They must have been a hardy lot, Talulla thought. Tradition had it that Begnet, having got her monastery up and running in Dalkey, had sailed off to Wales to found another. She was said to have died there. The place wasn't empty of traditions before the Christians got there, either; up in the graveyard at Begnet's in Castle Street was a stone whose carved concentric circles predated the cross that had been scraped in later on. All these stories had been told to them as children by their neighbour Mr O'Toole.

Talulla didn't know why her mind turned to this today. Perhaps it was because she was frightened. No, "frightened" was too strong; "confused" was more like it, though it was a queasy kind of confusion. The scene in Granny's Wood earlier that morning seemed unreal. Talulla kept going over it in her mind so that she could remember everything that had happened and then believe that it had happened at all. Standing at the harbour below Bullock Castle, with the wind whipping at her jacket and tossing her hair, she felt a strange affinity with the poor creature they had found. It seemed so abandoned; why had no one come for it?

Oh, God, if it was Mary de Burca . . . Talulla could hardly remember her, they were all so small when she left. She recalled feeling excited and rather awed and a tall, slender woman stooping to speak to her – the printed dress she wore, dark hair, pale face – her *scent*. After she left, Talulla always thought of Mary de Burca standing in a field of flowers somewhere. And – she had forgotten this – she used to imagine that Mary de Burca was with her mother, that women who left their children went to the one place.

She had never seen a photo of her mother. Once, when she was fourteen and Séamus was away at Templemore, she had gone through every one of his drawers, scoured among the shoe-boxes of old notebooks under his bed, even lifted the carpet. Séamus was furious: he was very protective of his notebooks, and he saw immediately that they had been moved.

"Not one picture of my mother!" Talulla screamed at him. "Did you ever think about me? Oh, no!"

"You went through everything I possess, Talulla, without so much as a by-your-leave –"

"I'm not going to run off and find her, Daddy, or anything like that!" Talulla said, weeping. "Auntie Tessie's after telling me I'm the image of her, and I know nothing about her. I'm her daughter, and I know nothing!"

"Why didn't you ask me, Talulla?"

"You hate her. You won't talk about her."

"You never asked," her father said. (This wasn't true.) "Anyway, I don't have any pictures of her. I'm sorry."

Talulla ran upstairs to her room. After a while, Séamus knocked on the door. It was such a timorous knock that she felt sorry for him and let him in.

"I'm sorry, Tully," he said. He sat down on her wicker chair, looking so weighted with care that she had visions of it breaking under him. "Ah . . ." He put up his hand as if protecting his eyes. "Auntie Tessie's right, though I could wish she'd keep her mouth shut. Miracles might happen," he muttered. "Anyway . . . yes. She was lovely. Your mother. Looked like you when she cried, too. She cried a lot. The year we were married."

Talulla held her breath so he wouldn't stop talking.

"She didn't mean to leave you. You were premature. She was on her way to the airport. Otherwise, she'd have had you in Boston. You'd be a US citizen, Tully. But I'd have brought you back here. Somehow." His face darkened.

"And is that all you ever heard of her, Daddy?" Talulla asked, after a short silence.

"Her mother – Mrs Campbell – phoned up a

63

few weeks after she left. She said they were prepared to look after you. They would see that you got the best education, everything laid on. You'd never want for a thing. Well, I asked her why Hope wasn't arranging this. What had Mrs Campbell to do with it?" He sighed. "'Oh, Hope isn't very well,' she said. 'Where is she?' I said. 'She's in River Lawn.' 'And what and where is River Lawn?' 'Hope's resting there, ah . . .' She could never pronounce my name. 'She's had a little breakdown.' 'And you're asking me to send my child to her?' I said. I asked how she was, and Mrs Campbell said she would be fine now that she was home. Meaning 'in her clutches', the old – bat."

Talulla sensed he was reliving it, his eyes were so fierce, and she shrank back a little.

He saw this and smiled at her. "That was that, Tully. Maybe I was wrong. You'd have had more opportunities over there."

"Oh, Daddy, you know I'm happy here. I just wonder . . ."

"Sure you do, love. I'm sorry. You are like her, too. She was lovely, Tully. We'll have to look out for fellas, now; they'll be beating a path to the door."

"Does nobody hear me?" came Briege's voice up the stairs. "I've cooked this lot, come and eat it!"

"Briege doesn't know about that phone call," Séamus said, getting up. "She was always afraid they'd come for you with a brace of solicitors at the ready. So I said nothing."

It was sad, Talulla thought, the way her father spoke of Hope as if she were dead. He always spoke of her in the past tense.

She wondered why, today of all days, she ended up thinking about Hope. On the other hand, it was becoming habitual. Hope had been weak, and Talulla was beginning to believe that she might be weak, too. Flighty. Even before the shooting, she had been restless. It had never hit her in Templemore, but one day in the station she had the queerest sensation in the world: she was looking down at herself in her uniform, sitting straight and alert, listening to her tutor's instructions about a door-to-door survey they were conducting, and she heard her own voice saying, "Poor thing . . . poor thing!" She must have gone white, for her tutor, Sergeant Janet Whelan, asked her if she was OK. It was scary and infuriating, but she was beginning to suspect that Briege and Séamus were right about her suitability to be a garda. And yet – she had liked it this morning, feeling in control and getting Murnaghan's telephone off him.

She forced herself around Sandycove Point and

past the Forty-foot for punishment. There were men's voices below. There would be two or three swimming as they did all the year round, mostly in their pelts, mercifully out of sight of passers-by. Going in each day, they never felt the cold. They lived forever. Briege called them and people like them "guardians"; they were the coastal people all around Ireland, land people who had to have the sea in their lives. They were a canny lot. You didn't hear of them drowning.

Past the martello tower, the tiny beach and its peculiar shrubby park, and on to the seafront. A long line of Edwardian houses; the enormous granite harbour: stability. Safety. "And now," she said out loud, "McDonald's!"

Going there was a way of taking control of her life. So what if it was childish? If her body was going to be ruined, it would be ruined and resculpted by herself, thanks very much, not by some trigger-happy eejit in the middle of O'Connell Street. A Quarter-pounder she'd have, and a chocolate shake. And yes, fries. And coffee. And apple pie.

"You'll wear your bikini, don't you worry," the nurse in the hospital had told her after the shooting, peering at the wound. "It's healing a treat!"

"You'll wear your bikini – !" What did she

know? The pellet had ricocheted across Talulla's abdomen like a tiny comet, leaving its indelible message: "Perishable. Damaged." What did that nurse know about bikinis? Hadn't she said she was married with two children? The scar on Talulla's belly was ugly. It would always be ugly. She wasn't sure why she was so upset. If someone really loved her, the scar wouldn't matter. "Someone." Ha. That was her next problem: something ridiculous had happened. She punched at the chocolate milk-shake with her straw. Everything was so intractable. Everything was so *weird*.

The garda station in Dún Laoghaire was only around the corner from McDonald's, and twice during the week Talulla had seen Aidan Cummings pass by. She looked up from her book, and there he was. Her eyes were drawn to him before she even recognised him: dark, dark hair, the set of his shoulders which was determined but a bit diffident, the way he was just a little bigger, a little brighter than the space he was in. There was a likeness between him and his sister Lara, her best friend – it was their colouring, mainly; dark hair, blue eyes and sallow skin. While Lara was disposed to be plump, however, Aidan regularly got too thin. Didn't look after himself. Hadn't discovered McDonald's. Hadn't been propelled there by the love of a good woman.

The morning's events had made Talulla late for her junk session, but she couldn't have stayed home. It was as if she had to keep things the same. That was all very well: in fact, she'd done a flit. She couldn't bear being in the house by herself where Briege could phone her, and she didn't want to go round to Emma, either. She wondered how she could face them. "Face them" – strange, as if she, Talulla, had wronged them. Well, she had, in a way: treacherously, she had doubted them or wanted to hide things. In her mind's eye she saw Emma again beside the digger, her face desperate, as if she knew something could be found. And Briege? Briege's radar would pick up Talulla's uneasiness immediately. Talulla did not like hiding anything from Briege, and yet Briege herself had always been full of secrets, protective sorts of secrets.

She could not stay long in Dún Laoghaire because Briege was up to high doh about the residents' committee meeting that evening. "For heaven's sake, Auntie-Mum, they've got more to interest them than the state of the carpet!" But Briege worried on the phone about the hoovering and the downstairs toilet, so Talulla promised she'd get started in the early afternoon. The rooms were as neat as always, but that wasn't what Briege was really fussing about. Normal, normal, normal.

Get everything back to normal and then coat the
lot with polish, so that Briege's number three –
whatever it might be – would just skid on them
and ricochet into someone else's life.

There! There was Aidan, hurrying past with his
friend the Inspector. Jimmy Meagher, that was his
name. Talulla couldn't eat any more. Some nerve
in her body had followed his progress right across,
like the bullet from left to right, except that it was
slow warmth instead of pain. Horrified, she
realised she was about to cry.

If only Lara weren't in London. Talulla was
close to Emma, but closer to Lara. They had
finally become best friends years ago when Emma
ditched them to go around with Alan all the time.
It didn't mean they didn't love Emma; they were
just more alike, that was all, always a bit behind
where Emma was concerned. She'd phone Lara
before Briege got back. Lara was the only other
person who would understand how serious things
might get.

Chapter Ten

Briege could not concentrate on her work at the bank. The news had penetrated all of Thorn Crest and Thorn Grove by mid-morning, and the neighbours would be gathering like crows on a telephone wire. She longed to be with Talulla and to know what everyone was saying. Talulla had been quite offhand on the phone, and that puzzled Briege and disturbed her.

The rest of the country heard it on *News at One*.

Gardaí are investigating the discovery of skeletal remains in a shallow grave in a wooded area of Dalkey, County Dublin. First reports suggest that the body is that of a woman.

A look like a touch flew among the women at the bank. It was as if, out walking, they had crossed the clawed spoor of a predator.

The man the press named "The Wicklow Strangler" had evaded the gardaí for over a year. The women he attacked had only two things in common with one another: they were trusting, and they were all from south County Dublin or from Wicklow. His four known victims had ranged in age from thirty-two to sixteen. None had been raped; all had been strangled. There was nothing to suggest why it was these and not others. They were simply in the wrong place at the wrong time.

When he was finished with them, the "Strangler" dumped their bodies. He had left his first known victim beside the railway line in Sandycove, between Dalkey and Dún Laoghaire. He abandoned the others in remote parts of County Wicklow, always beside some road or lay-by as if he wanted them to be discovered. He made only the most casual attempt to cover them, no more than a gesture in most cases – Vinnie Ruane, the third victim, had a mere scatter of leaves thrown over her. The gardaí thought that this was a tease, not a gesture of remorse or a desire to help their families get on with the funeral.

Early in the investigations, Aidan and Séamus had remarked in Briege's presence that they didn't like the Strangler at all.

"You don't like him?" Briege had echoed, sarcastic, setting down the tea tray she had brought them with a crash. It was a Saturday.

"We don't believe he's astray in his wits,"

Séamus said. He was having a good day sitting up in the bed, but then he loved Aidan's visits.

"We think he's as sane as you or me, Briege, just a nasty piece of work," Aidan said, smiling round at her. Not for the first time, Briege thought what a good-looking family the Cummingses were.

"Not even a psychologist could excuse him," Séamus agreed.

"I see. Well. How about you guards getting the finger out?"

"Any helpful ideas you have will be appreciated," said her brother, "politely stated, of course."

"Right, then." Briege stared at them solemnly. "When you find a man in Ireland who doesn't like women – you'll have him!"

"Now, lad. Across the street!" Séamus said to Aidan.

"It's not women Brendan O'Toole dislikes: it's dogs," Briege remarked, while the other two laughed. There had been a flaming row between the two neighbours opposite when Mrs Blakeney's Jack Russell dug up Mr O'Toole's winter cabbage.

"What did he want with winter cabbage in a garden that size, anyway?" Séamus asked, and the conversation moved on to Brendan O'Toole's eccentricities, which were legion.

Briege had cause to think of Brendan again later in the day. He phoned her at the bank to discuss the night's meeting. He was fairly sober, a good sign. Poor man, Briege thought, wondering could she ever finish up and go home. Brendan was never so odd when his wife was alive, and most of his outbursts were due to drink. It was sad to see how the children no longer trooped after him like they had in Talulla's time. She and Emma and Lara had been like bees around a honey jar, pestering him night and day to tell them his stories. They loved hearing about Etty Scott, "the gold dreamer of Dalkey," whose career as a visionary was ended by two cats, but most of all they loved him telling about how Granuaile came to see William Travers.

Brendan O'Toole was enraged by Murnaghan's incursion into the wood. He was far more upset by that than the finding of the body. "Think of the attrition on that hill," he said, scornful. "That could be anything. Half Dublin camped here for centuries to avoid plague; some of them would have brought it out with them. Graves all over the place. Sure, that's how we got the Traverses." It was Brendan O'Toole's affectation that the Travers family were mere sixteenth-century "blow-ins" to Dalkey.

Brendan even suggested that the skeleton might have been planted by Murnaghan himself.

"It would be just like the man. He's known to have a grotesque sense of humour. A Hallowe'en prank that will have the upstarts in Thorn Grove baying for spotlights and tarmacadam – I wouldn't put it past that fellow for a minute!"

That was all very well but Talulla, when she phoned earlier, had told Briege that they had spotted a shred of fabric and what might be a coppery button in the loose earth. Briege tried to remember whether she'd ever seen Mary de Burca wearing denims all those years ago. You'd remember most things Mary wore. What a tangle.

What a day! she thought, rubbing her temples. Bodies and builders at home, bastards at work. She'd spent the morning soothing one of the branch's most valued customers, who had over-extended himself to the point of transparency by opening two new restaurants. She wouldn't jack up his loan or his overdraft, and at one point she wondered if he'd have a go at her. It was all she could do to stop herself telling him that the whole of Dalkey knew his girlfriend was bleeding him dry while he rained gifts on his wife to keep her in the dark. Briege doubted very much that his wife was in the dark; in fact, it was likely that her husband's financial troubles were about to double. This was a small source of comfort, though. By the time that slimeball stormed off the premises, retirement had never looked so good.

Mary de Burca had the most beautiful clothes you could imagine, and you could hear her husband screaming across three counties every time the bills dropped through the letterbox. That time years ago, when he came down to take out a second mortgage on the house, his signature was like an old man's. Mary left soon after.

Brendan O'Toole phoned again at three to say that he'd an appointment set up with the solicitor for the morning. He'd also contacted the members of the residents' association committee and told them to meet in Briege's house at eight. "Always my house!" Briege wanted to say. "Why not Mrs Blakeney's?" But Brendan, of course, would not set foot in Mrs Blakeney's because of his mutilated winter cabbages.

Briege congratulated herself that with everything else going on, she remembered to do the grocery shopping and go into the church to arrange Séamus's "month's mind." As she emerged into the church carpark however, even this frail sense of satisfaction collapsed. At first, she couldn't believe her eyes: it was as if time had hiccoughed. Emma Morrissey and Alan de Burca were standing together in the doorway of the Queen's, directly opposite. They were unmistakable. Alan had

Emma by the arm; she tossed her dark hair and tried to pull away from him. He leaned over her, talking persuasively, gesturing with his other arm. They went inside, Emma stumbling a little at the door.

Alan de Burca, back in Ireland. How could he? Numb, Briege gathered her cakes and groceries and went home. Séamus's death; Talulla's shooting; and now, Alan de Burca was back from Australia. Somewhere in the events of this long, extraordinary day, Briege sensed the dreaded "three" imperfectly hidden, waiting to be discovered.

Chapter Eleven

After leaving the others that morning, Emma had bathed Iseult and dressed her in fresh clothes. Then she phoned her mother.

"It's not a good day, dear," Mrs Morrissey said in a fretful voice.

"I never ask you, Mum. By the way, it's not just for today; I need you to take Iseult for the weekend."

There was a stunned silence.

"Mum?"

"Until Tuesday? Do you mean for the Bank Holiday weekend? For Hallowe'en?"

"Yes."

"What's wrong?"

"Um."

"Are you crying, dear? Has Declan hurt you? Emma?"

"No, Mum." Emma wiped her eyes and pressed the "silent" button while she blew her nose.

"You're crying. That's it! I'm phoning the solicitor – no, the guards –"

"Mum, turn on your radio."

"How you could marry that –"

"Your best friend's son? Mum. A body has just been discovered in Granny's – a skeleton."

"Oh, my God."

"So, if you wouldn't mind . . ."

"You come too, darling. Please."

"I'll stay here. I really need to be alone, Mum."

The silence was very long this time. "No foolishness, Emma."

"Promise."

"I'll be over."

Emma refused to discuss anything with her mother when she arrived, and Mrs Morrissey had to be content with her beloved granddaughter and a bundle of clean clothes and nappies.

Mr and Mrs Morrissey gave Emma the family house in Thorn Grove when her marriage broke up. They still owned it and had left it to Iseult in their wills; that was to keep Declan James from ever claiming a share of it. Indeed, Mr Morrissey maintained that the only thing of his that Declan James would enjoy would be the sole of his boot.

Emma loved her house and Granny's Wood behind it. They sheltered her while she slowly recovered from the disaster her life had become almost three years ago. Her parents' move to a comfortable flat in Sandycove gave her the necessary solitude as well and in February, finally, she would be as free of Declan as the law allowed. That didn't mean she could be easy about him. As long as he drank, he would be dangerous.

Last New Year's Eve, he had kicked the back door open and given her the beating of her life. At the time she had been too frightened even to feel the pain. She didn't remember getting out of the house, only running through Granny's with him after her like some huge animal crashing against trees and brambles that she knew to avoid. It was only when she climbed over the stile into O'Neill's that she realised there was something wrong with her arm.

Séamus O'Neill had sorted him that night. Declan's family solicitor kept him out of Mountjoy, but Mr O'Neill informed Declan that he considered Emma one of his own, and Aidan Cummings would, too. After that, Emma knew Declan would never attack her while in his right mind, but when he got drunk . . . she was careful not to do anything to fuel rumours or cause him to be jealous.

And why would she? She had found a kind of peace. But when she saw the staring horror in the earth that morning, peace was gone. It was as if she had opened the wardrobe and seen those hollow eyes confronting her, or gazed into the mirror to find them looking back at her.

That was why she believed she was imagining things when she found herself face to face with Alan outside the Queen's. She believed her mind had snapped again, but no, he grabbed her arm and his touch was real. She dropped the bag of groceries she was carrying, and he picked it up for her while tightening his grip. She pulled back, testing, but she knew he would not let go even if she made a scene. Alan didn't mind about scenes.

His skin was brown, like a cliché of a person who had emigrated to Australia, and it made his face look harder – Spanish, almost, and lean.

"Where is he?"

"Who?"

"Your fucking husband!"

Emma started laughing. She couldn't help it. She saw Briege O'Neill, who had just come out of the church, stop to stare as if she had seen a ghost. Emma thought, "Better you than me, sister," and that made her laugh even harder.

Alan hung on to her arm and virtually dragged her into the Queen's. Suddenly she was so angry that she felt giddy. "Let go!"

"Sit down. I'll get you something. Coffee. You still drink coffee? Sorry. Please, Emma. Please."

Emma flopped down on a chair. She watched him at the bar. She watched him take money from his pocket and then pick up the white coffee cups with his long, brown hands. She told herself, I will be all right when I get home.

Alan was back with two coffees. She could smell him. He smelled like himself, Alan, in new clothes. She wondered if he could smell her, too. He probably hadn't thought of her for three years.

"I got back now," he said. "This minute. Walked up Castle Street and saw you."

"Small town."

"Are you well? Look, everything sounds stupid after . . . I came back to see you. I wanted to meet in some proper place."

"This is all right," Emma said.

He gave her a hungry look, as if he still loved her. She longed to go home and get into her small bed and pull the covers up over her head, just pull them up and listen to the foghorns on Dún Laoghaire pier in the distance while the room got darker and darker.

" – only heard now," he was saying. "How old is she? Your child?"

"Two and a bit."

His eyes went opaque while he counted. They met hers again. Emma shivered.

"And Declan's gone," he said.

Emma thought of Declan, bursting through the door like a malign jack-in-the-box, all six feet two of him. "Mostly," she said. How would he arrive this time? In a tank?

"Emma."

"Sorry, Alan. I'm dreaming. I'm just so – surprised to see you."

"It's been a while," he agreed. His pupils always got huge when he looked at her, Emma remembered. And then he would unleash some thudding cliché – "It's been a while," like dragging a dead dog out of a kennel.

"So it has," she said. "There have been quite a few changes, Alan. Séamus O'Neill's dead, did you know? Talulla's joined the guards. And Aidan Cummings is a detective sergeant. The garda presence has been very handy for me, Alan. But not the very big yellow JCB out in Granny's, chewing the arse off my garden and making a road between Hillview and Thorn Avenue so that de Burca Close, or whatever he'll call it, will be posh. Sorry, have to go. Defend my property."

With this, she was able to slip around the small table before Alan could catch her, and then she was out the door of the Queen's and into the darkening air. She had always been able to stop Alan by giving him too much to think about all at once. When she had tried that with Declan, she had ended up halfway through the wall. Declan didn't think, he totted. Milo Higgins, his barfly friend who'd been glaring at her from his stool in the Queen's, just tottered most of the time. He was probably on the phone to Declan this very moment to inform him that Alan was back, and with her.

Emma moved so quickly that she was opposite the Flags before she knew it, but she decided not to take that venerable short cut up to Ardbrugh. Too lonely, too narrow, like her life closing in on her. She hurried on, gasping a little as the road rose, and she was almost home before she realised she'd left her groceries behind her in the Queen's.

She slipped into her house and locked it without turning on any light; unplugged the telephone; undressed and snuggled into her childhood bed in Iseult's room. She pulled her old teddy into the crook of her arm.

Alan didn't know about the body yet. That was clear. She should have told him. Now someone else would see his face when he heard it first. Warmth stole around her, and Emma curled tightly around her teddy, weeping.

Chapter Twelve

While the strands of Emma's life tightened in the Queen's, Aidan and Inspector Jimmy Meagher were attending a case conference in Dún Laoghaire. The Strangler's latest outrage had provoked a firestorm of criticism in the press. The victim was a sixteen-year-old schoolgirl on her way to a friend's house. Her bicycle was found, its front tyre flattened, just outside Delgany. Her body was discovered a fortnight later by a man who had got out of his car to ease the stiffness in his joints. He was a former soldier and had served in the Lebanon. There was no mistaking that particular odour, he said.

"There's enough brass here for the proverbial band," Jimmy Meagher remarked. Assistant Commissioner Fitzgibbon was visible down the corridor outside Chief Superintendent Murphy's office. At least three guards from the technical bureau were in the group milling into the conference room, and Aidan saw Lorcan White and Esmé Dunne, detectives from Wicklow, among them. They shared his obsession with the Strangler.

Jimmy saw them, too. "The other two Musketeers," he said, eyes glinting. Jimmy had become an Inspector at thirty-three through unremitting determination and care in his work, and he pounced on "volatility" in his minions. Volatility was the downfall of any detective. "Only camels can be convicted on a 'hunch'," he would say mysteriously, and "Find the line between 'fanatical attention to detail' and 'obsession' and stick to it."

Jimmy thought Aidan had strayed into the midnight marshes of "obsession" with the Strangler case. Aidan was aware of his glances as they listened to the newest developments – there were few – and a rehash of the well-worn bits of evidence that had been examined and polished so often that they were beginning to have the intractability of diamonds, without the value.

The Strangler's first known victim was Justina Martin. She was found beside The Metals on the way to Sandycove Station. The Metals got its name from the atmospheric railway that brought granite from Dalkey Hill to build the harbour at Dún Laoghaire, but all that frenetic activity had ended over a hundred and fifty years ago. Now it was a quiet footpath beside the rail line, getting quieter as women with handbags or boy cyclists with leather jackets became wary of using it when alone.

Aidan had barrelled up and down The Metals as a boy, speeding along on his bicycle without fear of cars, deriving a subliminal sense of the countryside where The Metals ran between the line and the back gardens of houses. The railway embankment below was a wilderness of greenery and hedgerow plants, and the gardens, most of them invisible behind shrubberies or walls, were full of birds. He had liked all but the one stretch of it, and that was the place where Justina Martin was found.

This patch, a wide triangle of rough grass between an Edwardian terrace of graceful houses and the line, had been untended for as long as he could remember, its wrought-iron fence broken and tumbled into the tall weeds. The sullen clump of trees and shrubbery in its farthest corner looked like what it was, a repository for used condoms and syringes. Children did not play on this "green space," and dog owners waited for their charges on the footpath.

Aidan had spent time in the inner city and in the great housing estates to the north and west. He had seen a homeless man curled frozen in a cardboard box, girls shivering and bleeding, young fellows in smithereens from their last "joy-ride" ever. He had seen men lying in their own blood outside pubs and people knocked senseless by hit-and-run drivers.

Nothing prepared him for Justina Martin. She was dragged into the ugly little grove and dumped there, invisible both to the thousands of commuters a stone's throw from her and the residents of the quiet terrace opposite. An early morning walker found her, when his dog ran into the trees and refused to come back.

Aidan could think of nothing but her loneliness. She lay partly on her side, her face turned away from them as if they had failed her and she no longer cared. A dirty sweet wrapper had lodged in her short auburn hair. "Loneliness," "desecration," were the words that came to him.

He and Jimmy interviewed Justina Martin's husband, who had been made redundant from his bakery job and was trying to fill the gaps as a night-watchman. He was at work when Justina walked out of their house in Cabinteely to go to the shops, leaving her children alone for twenty minutes, as she thought. They'd no phone, and the children were too frightened to call to the neighbours in the dark when she didn't return. The husband knew nothing until he got home at seven the next morning and found the three children, tear-stained and still in their clothes, asleep in their parents' bed.

Justina Martin's purse was never found, though her small plastic bag of groceries was flung rotting under the bush beside her. Aidan sighed, and felt Jimmy's eyes upon him.

The bleak résumé of facts continued. Two of the four dead women were known to have gone out with handbags, and the third, the schoolgirl, had her backpack with some homework in it. None of these items had been recovered.

There was no identification for the woman in Granny's Wood yet either, but the lads were digging around the area to see what they might find. People in the surrounding houses would be surveyed. Memories would be jogged, carefully assessed and compared.

This woman had been buried, that was the difference. She wasn't meant to be found like the others. She wouldn't have been, either, except for Murnaghan's clumsy invasion: she'd have been there forever, and they'd never have known.

Jimmy gave Aidan a nudge.

Monday's *Crimeline* programme on RTE had attracted some telephone calls about the Strangler case, they were told: a woman walking home just outside Rathdrum had been offered a lift by a man in a red car. It was dusk, and she hadn't really seen him, but she wondered . . . This was worth putting on the map, because a red car had been seen driving slowly in the vicinity of Kilpedder on the day that Carmel Bermingham, the second victim, was murdered. Carmel Bermingham was on her way home from a friend's. Her body was dumped at Djouce Woods on the road to the Sally Gap, only a few metres from where the schoolgirl's had been discovered months later.

"I don't think we need to include the caller from Wexford on the map," Garda Williams was saying, resting his pointer on the desk. "The last phoned response we got was from a woman who reported seeing a man who drove a red car gazing fixedly at young women each evening in the Spinnaker Lounge. Our investigations revealed him to be a local politician, whose regular habits in this direction provided him with an alibi for all four murders." There were some patient chuckles from the back of the room, and Garda Williams sat down, his face a bit flushed.

The map was fine, all the same. The last appearance alive of each victim was marked in red, along with known or suspected routes she would have followed; the place she was found was shown in yellow. All the victims had been found north of their homes, or the areas in which they were last seen. This suggested to Aidan that the killer was on his way towards Dublin when he struck, or – improbably, surely – that he killed on his way out of the city and unloaded his victims on his way home.

Vinny Ruane. Everyone who knew Vinny had been amazed. Though she was only twenty, Vinny was streetwise and tough. She was from Newtownmountkennedy, and had just got a job as a courier with a firm in Dublin. She had worked since she was sixteen to buy her Harley-Davidson 883, and her friends said she was "over the moon" about her new prospects. She was an experienced, resourceful girl. Her cropped hair and leathers had caused some comment in her community, but she was held in affection and regard by most.

Vinny's murder caused the greatest fear in Wicklow. It was the most brutal, for one thing – she had struggled hard – but the main reason was that people felt the Strangler must have the guile of the devil himself to have gained Vinny's confidence. It was after Vinny's murder on the eighth of April, almost a year after Justina Martin's death, that doors were well and truly locked, and women stopped going out at night.

There they were, a spatter of fallen stars on the map. And they'd so little. A scrap of flesh under

Vinnie's nails. A few grains of sand on Carmel Bermingham and the schoolgirl, Una Ivory. Three footprints, size eight, from a sports shoe sold by the hundreds in the chain stores. These were found beside Justina Martin. One deep impression in the soft earth might have been made by a person carrying a heavy weight, but there was nothing sure about that. There were a lot of dog tracks, too, some under the body.

There was a sour, mocking miasma over the whole series of killings. Aidan knew the Assistant Commissioner sensed it too when, summing up, he said, "We've a devious, cunning man on our hands, and any evidence that comes our way must be handled with the usual scrupulous care – and then some. I think you'll agree that his treatment of his victims – the contemptuous way he leaves them at the side of the road – is a very bad sign for us. This gentleman will not stop by himself."

Then it was out with the jobs book, and all the follow-ups were arranged. Lorcan and Esmé waved at him from the door; they were in a hurry.

It was almost a relief to Aidan when Sergeant Black appeared at his elbow and said, "Alo Devlin's stealing bicycles again."

"How's his mum?"

"Nothing on at the moment. Probation."

"Right." Time for another chat with Alo, who was nine. Aidan ignored his headache. After an afternoon of the Strangler's crooked spoors, it would be a positive pleasure to confer with Alo's mother in the immaculate flat filled with the fruits of her shoplifting.

Chapter Thirteen

Briege arrived home that evening in such a flap that Talulla refused to let her cook. She produced the two frozen meals from Marks and Spencer she had hidden behind the peas, and shoved them into the oven instead.

Briege had to have the kettle on and the tea bag in the cup before she felt able to tell her news. "Alan de Burca. With Emma. In the middle of Castle Street, for anyone to see. Going into the Queen's, for God's sake! Tully, what is she thinking of? Three months is all she has to wait – !"

"That means nothing, Auntie-Mum, and she knows it. A legal separation isn't going to keep Declan off her back."

"Everybody that fellow knows drinks in the Queen's. I'm surprised he wasn't there himself."

"Maybe he was."

"We'd have heard the sirens, girl."

"Emma must be in bits," Talulla said slowly.

"Poor girl. Yes, she must. I wonder did Alan know?"

"About what? Iseult?"

"I wasn't even thinking about Iseult. Do you know, Tully, I wasn't overjoyed when you went into the garda, but you never gave us worries like that."

And you don't know the half of it, Talulla thought to herself. "Well, what, then?" she said aloud.

"Murnaghan."

"Murnaghan?"

"Well – Alan might have heard . . ." she said doubtfully.

"Briege, Alan wouldn't fly back from Australia to plead with Murno on our behalf! Eat that, it'll put some sense into you."

"But –"

"How could Alan know what's going on here?"

"To tell the truth, Tully, I'm muddled."

"Do you know what? I'd say Alan hasn't heard about Iseult, or Declan's behaviour, or about anything. He certainly can't have known what Murnaghan's up to. Alan is here on his holliers, tidying up his three hundred and fifty thousand. That is the Alan we know!"

"You're a bit hard on him," Briege said mildly. "Aren't you eating that awfully fast?"

"No."

"Well, I pity him," Briege said. "I pity him that the day he arrives here, they've probably dug up his mother with a JCB!"

Talulla put down her knife and fork. "It's awful, Auntie-Mum – something about that makes me want to laugh."

Briege stared at her, wide-eyed. "Aren't you very hard?" Then, in spite of herself, she started to giggle.

Talulla laughed until she cried.

At seven o'clock, Talulla lit the fire in the sitting-room. She moved slowly. The day had finally caught up with her, snaring her in its shadows. Briege saw how drained she looked and sent her packing out of the kitchen, while she cleared away and made sandwiches for the meeting.

Talulla curled up in the wing chair and watched the fire as it started to take. The cat materialised out of nowhere and leaped on to her lap, arching his back. "All ready for Hallowe'en, are you?" she murmured to him, and rubbed his black chin while he purred.

It was dark outside. The late October mist had been collecting since mid-afternoon, drifting in from the sea, shrouding the back garden and reducing the trees in Granny's to faint sketches against the deepening, greying woodland of the hill. The fire burned brighter in the spotless room and the moving shadows, softly domesticated, seemed to stroke the walls.

The gardaí were finished in Granny's for the day, though the tapes were still up. Talulla had called over when she got home that afternoon. There were a couple of uniformed men in de Burca's keeping an eye on things; she didn't look into Granny's to see how many were combing and digging. She knew one of the lads outside a little, and he told her they'd found nothing except the bones and a few shreds of cloth, not even a shoe. In return, she told him that a woman from the neighbourhood had been missing for years, which he of course already knew. "Sure now, there'd never be just the one scandal in a place like Dalkey?" he asked, smiling, but with a shrewd look in his eyes.

"Most of our killings take place on the stock market, darling."

"Do tell," said the guard.

"Nothing this vulgar has happened since the Vikings."

"Quite."

"Whoever did this came from beyond the Pale."

"Yeah, Dalkey is the Pale, isn't it? Sure, it isn't Ireland at all," remarked the guard, smiling broadly when he saw his remark hit home.

Talulla, bristling, started to reply when she realised he was still teasing her.

"I wouldn't mind it myself," he said, "living a stone's throw from me idols."

"U2?"

"The same. And they say Greenman's looking at houses here."

"He'll have heard about the druids," Talulla said. Greenman, aka Albert Loftus, was a six-foot-three, one-hundred-and-sixty-pound Geordie who had discovered Nature. His mysticism was a bit fuddled, but his musical talent was formidable. He was quite a shrewd operator, or someone in his retinue was; he'd released a single, "*Samhain*," at the beginning of the month, its eerie lyric about supernatural love spot on for Hallowe'en. Talulla was familiar with it. It seemed to be a favourite of the Minogues next door.

"They all look at houses here. Blow-ins, the lot of them!" she said. The guard laughed, and she scuttled off.

The cat mewed plaintively on her lap. "Sorry, Moggins." She had hugged him too hard.

She could wish she were a cat, knowing things the way animals know them, sensing everything and then processing it: will it hurt me? Can I eat it? Play with it? Breed with it? It was a queer thought. Every animal in Dalkey, including Moggins, probably knew that body was there. Dogs, cats, foxes, shrews, rats, mice, badgers, insects – oh, stop. Only the fish were left out of it. But the dead woman was nothing to any of them; "it" she'd have been, a curiosity, a brief intensity of the smallest lives.

But before? Had she died right there behind their houses? Perhaps she had looked despairingly at their windows, lit like now and visible at night over the low walls, hoping that one of them would sense, see, hear, help her. What if it wasn't Mary de Burca? What if – what if it was someone young? What if she had children somewhere, wondering what had become of her, wondering what they'd done wrong?

The curtains, undrawn, framed a black square that suddenly shattered into pink and green swirls, followed by a tremendous explosion. The Minogue children, holy terrors, wasting their rockets two days before Hallowe'en. Talulla thanked them in her heart. In the moment before they demolished that darkness, she had realised that she couldn't approach the window. She could neither bear to look at it nor get out of the chair to cover it. She had just half-imagined, half-hallucinated herself, hand on the cord, looking into the eyes of someone on the other side of the glass; and the face wasn't the one she had expected, but another, more familiar and more strange. Holding back tears so that Briege wouldn't hear her, she sneaked upstairs and took her second-last pain-killer.

Chapter Fourteen

Mr O'Toole and Tom MacDevitt, Charlie's father, had drawn up an agenda for the evening. The committee would formally engage the solicitor and decide a date for an emergency meeting of the combined residents' associations of Thorn Crest and Thorn Grove. Then all hell could officially break loose. Talulla was glad they were coming. There was something reassuring about neighbours gathering around a fire to sort things out.

It was going to be a bit tricky, too. Much care was taken in the neighbourhood that Mrs Blakeney should not be burdened with very much information. She tended to take a negative view of events and the motives that precipitated them, and she was fond of passing on her interpretations to those who could appreciate them most.

The doorbell rang. It was Tom MacDevitt, looking pale, clean and dyspeptic. He had changed from his business suit to immaculate casuals –

slacks, cashmere jumper, windcheater, slip-on shoes. Briege always said he was "well turned out," as if his wife ran a cloth over him before each departure. Mist clung subversively to his hair and windcheater. "Rotten night," he said, wiping his feet carefully on the mat. Briege brought him into the sitting-room.

Mrs Blakeney arrived next, clutching her soft tweed coat about her. "Am I very late?" Carefully she removed the silk scarf from her hair, managing to leave every white strand in place. Talulla sniffed appreciatively. *Joy*.

"Sparky has me driven mad," Mrs Blakeney was saying. "Poor wee man. He loves his little patrol up and down Granny's, but the guards said 'No.' Mind, he might have come back with something a little too interesting this time! – I'm dreadful. I shouldn't make light of it, I just never knew Mary de Burca – it must have been awful for you – Oh hello, Tom – I'm sorry, Talulla, really – we're the early birds! Briege, isn't it dreadful. Do you know, Tom," she said, gliding into the sitting-room, "I worry a little about your Charlie and Kevin Minogue. He's such a mad scamp . . ."

Talulla saw Gareth Travers's silhouette in the glass before he rang the bell. He had a lonely outline. Maybe it was just arrogant; sometimes it was hard to tell. Gareth was Aidan Cummings's oldest friend, though they could hardly be less alike. Lara said Aidan never discussed him. Lara had suffered from what she called a terminal *grá* for Gareth since she and Talulla were about thirteen and he appeared at Aidan's twenty-first birthday party, shoulders erect and pimples cleared.

Tonight, almost ten years on, he looked abstracted and tired. Lara claimed that this was when he was most delicious, suspended in a sort of academic fog and vulnerable to the pounce, though not her pounce, unfortunately. It would kill her to see him now, in Angel Gabriel mode with the streetlight sparkling on his hair.

"Sorry I'm late."

"Everyone's saying that, Gareth, and three of them aren't even here yet."

"Will Mr O'Toole be coming?" he asked, handing her his coat.

"Mr O'Toole? With Murnaghan ready to pour tarmac on the footsteps of Granuaile? Too right he's coming."

"Good."

"So how's the house?"

Gareth shrugged. "Ah, could be worse. Nothing leaking. Tenant tried to do a clean-up before he left."

"Would you ever have in the cleaners? Not that it's any of my business, of course."

"Indeed and I would. And have. I just do the first few goes myself. That way, I know where everything is."

"Well, you're great," Talulla told him, feeling ridiculous the moment she said it.

"How are you, anyway, Talulla?"

"Back to work on Tuesday," she said briskly, and ushered him in to the others.

The light tapping on the door this time was Mr Lawless, who lived with his wife at the end of the cul-de-sac. He and Leila Cummings had arrived together. Mr Lawless was plainly ready for battle, but Leila, who was usually bubbly and sweetly daft, was subdued. She was wheezing, though not badly. Mr Lawless removed her coat and then his own with swift, surgical movements. Talulla had never seen him so upset.

"I hope that solicitor will have something useful to say, because I am prepared to do anything to stop that fellow!" Mr Lawless announced.

"I'd say his blood pressure is up," Leila Cummings whispered as Mr Lawless swept into the sitting-room. "We'd want to keep an eye on him. Tully, you're looking very well. Are you?"

"I'm grand. Any news of Lara?"

"Won't that be the day, when we get news of Lara? I believe three of them went off to Brussels for a weekend, but that was almost a month ago.

She was thinking of changing her job again." They both threw up their eyes. "Aidan said she could do what she liked, just not to come home."

"That was a bit mean."

"She gives him no peace over the Strangler, dear. Lara's got a bee in her bonnet about the Wicklow Strangler."

"Haven't we all."

"Well, there now, you see," Leila said vaguely. She gave Talulla a warm little hug and went inside.

Talulla opened the front door to see if Mr O'Toole was on the way and he was, marching along with a stiff, rolling gait like an animated teddy bear. He paused under the streetlight and rummaged in his pockets but, instead of the dreaded flask, he produced a large handkerchief and blew his nose. Papers, rolled into a cylinder, protruded from the other pocket. He raised his hat when he saw Talulla.

"Well, Guard!" he said, handing her his coat. "Which one of us do you suppose did it?"

"You're the first to ask. Anxious, are you?"

"Oh, ho! There's the girl. The thing is . . ." he leaned close. Whiskey, God help the meeting. "The thing is –"

"Is that Brendan I hear?" a voice from inside called out.

"It is," Talulla called.

"Now, why'd you give me away? I wanted to tell you –" he paused, searching again for his handkerchief.

"You'll hardly be let, they're dying to start the meeting, but if you know something, Mr O'Toole –"

"I do, but it's not that, not that. It's that bloody dog. She's here, is she?" nodding towards the sitting-room. "*La belle dame sans merci?* My little *pieris*? I'm not speaking to her about it again. I want to know –"

Briege appeared in the hall. "Brendan, stop flirting with my niece and come in to this meeting. We've got a corpse and a superhighway on our hands."

"Some old plague victim, I'll lay odds," he grumbled, but shuffled in after her.

As Talulla's pain-killer gathered momentum, the meeting took on a surreal atmosphere. It began on an anticlimactic note with Leila Cummings breathlessly reading the minutes, the high points of which were the committee's concern about the partial collapse of one of the footpaths after work by Dublin Gas, and the on-going problem of what was euphemistically noted as "dog dirt." Dublin Gas had repaired the footpath, but the "dog dirt" situation had not improved.

"We wouldn't be able to step out of our houses if that mongrel of Nealon's hadn't been run over," Mr O'Toole said. "As it is, the place is festooned with turds."

"Brendan, with respect, there are more important matters to discuss tonight. I suggest you move 'dog dirt'—"

"Please. Let us call this what it is."

Mr Lawless's face went bright red. Mrs Blakeney's was stony.

"Perhaps this could be first on the agenda for the next meeting?" Gareth suggested.

The others agreed quickly and Mr O'Toole, his point made, settled down.

Briege asked for the solicitor's report. Mr O'Toole produced his notes from their telephone conversation, which gave little joy. He hoped to find out more in the morning. A lively discussion began about property values, squatters' rights, injunctions, sit-down protests.

Outside, the wind was picking up, and Talulla, sleepy, half-dreamed that they were huddled around the fire, with nothing at all between them and the rising shadow of the hill. It was as if, instead of coming in, the spirit of the dead woman had called them out, saying "This is where I've been for so long." Granny's Wood had never seemed so lonely, or the hill so dark and high. Was she near, then, pained that her fate was less compelling than the felling of trees or an increase in traffic and the chances of being burgled? Talulla's dreams crept outward, sifting the darkness.

Chapter Fifteen

"I'm sorry?" They were all looking at Talulla. She had dozed off in her chair.

"Cup of tea?" Leila Cummings asked gently.

"Oh! Lovely. Was I asleep? Have I missed all the gossip?"

"You've only missed Gareth going out with a flask of tea for the guards over on the site," Briege said. "Go on to bed. That's where you belong!"

"I'll stay," Talulla said. The others, sipping their tea, seemed to approve. The business of the evening was far from finished.

"Perhaps it's my being a woman," Mrs Blakeney said, plainly continuing something she'd already started, "but I can't imagine how anyone can put a pair of hands around another person's neck and squeeze the life out of them."

"I don't think that's just to do with being a woman," Leila Cummings said. Tom MacDevitt looked pained.

"I think I could easily start with dogs and work my way up," Mr O'Toole remarked.

Mrs Blakeney gave him a look that Talulla thought was almost as good as a pair of hands.

"I think we should consider, realistically, who it was out there," Mr Lawless said. "It will have implications."

"What implications? What could it have to do with us?"

"It was there, Mrs Blakeney, it was there," said Mr O'Toole. "*Ergo*, it has implications for us."

"Only for whoever put it there, surely!"

"And that is exactly it," said Mr Lawless. "What do you think the guards will be asking themselves? 'Who is it? And who put it there?' We want to be ready for that. This neighbourhood is going to be turned inside out."

"How? We all know who it is," cried Mrs Blakeney. "And who put it there, too!"

"We think we do," Mr Lawless said.

"Well, do you believe – does anyone believe that it's *not* Mary de Burca?"

"All I am saying, Mrs Blakeney, is that there will be questions, and it might be well for us to be careful about starting any hares," said Mr Lawless, looking straight into her eyes.

"I'm sure we're none of us gossips or tittle-tattles here," Mrs Blakeney said, flushing.

"I think we can rely on Aidan and Talulla to pass on any information they feel is relevant from our quarter," Mr Lawless added, inexorable.

Leila Cummings leaned confidingly towards Mrs Blakeney. "If I say it myself, Maud, Mr Lawless is right. You know I'd be the very last person to be obstructive, with my own son a detective, but with the Strangler inquiry – you know, just anything mentioned would have to be followed up –"

"What would be mentioned?" Mrs Blakeney asked, wide-eyed.

"Well, nothing. Anything. It's just that any odd death gets particular attention just now –" Leila began to cough.

"Is that thing Mary de Burca or isn't it?" Mrs Blakeney demanded.

"It is almost certainly Mary de Burca," Mr Lawless said, "but because we have this animal causing mayhem up and down the country –"

"Well it seems to me that it would be preferable if that body was a victim of the same 'animal,' some stranger, and not Mary de Burca at all," Mrs Blakeney said stubbornly. "It doesn't look very well for the neighbourhood, even if it did happen all those years ago!"

"Indeed, but all the same –" said Briege.

"And what could any of us know about it? What would I know, or be mentioning to anyone?"

"*The lady doth protest too much, methinks,*" muttered Mr O'Toole.

"Brendan," Mr Lawless said, between his teeth.

"I apologise, Walter," Mr O'Toole said. His tone had changed, and now the others listened to him. "I know Gráinne's Wood as well as anyone. You could say I know it like the back of my hand." The others murmured assent. "And the behaviour of the gardaí suggests that this is no figment from Deilginis, from the distant past." He took his flask from his pocket and tipped it over his tea, but nobody said a word. "My wife and I used picnic a lot in Gráinne's," he said.

After a few moments, Mrs Blakeney seemed ready to speak, but Leila Cummings put out her hand to her.

"It was after Franny died, wasn't it, Brendan, that you stopped going there for a while?" she asked gently.

He nodded. "Three years ago. I missed all the – the goings-on." He sighed. "Bad timing, wasn't it? I might have stopped it."

"Young people will be young somewhere, Brendan," said Mr Lawless.

"That was the only time in the past thirty years that such a burial – such a desecration could have happened in that wood without my knowing it," Mr O'Toole said. "I'm almost sure of it."

"So . . . from Franny's death . . ." Leila said.

"A little before. Late summer. I thought . . . I don't know what I thought when I knew. Franny and I were very fond of Emma, you know. She was a wild little creature, but there was never any malice in Emma. Franny's death must almost have coincided with that child's conception; with that monstrous marriage!"

"So it mightn't be Mary de Burca at all," said Mr Lawless heavily.

"Not unless she came back," Mr O'Toole said. "I can understand how one could strangle another human being much more easily than I can understand a mother leaving her child and never coming back to see . . . Alan was so small when she left. How could she stay away unless . . . ?" He shook his head. "Now I think I am becoming 'tired and emotional,' to use the modern phrase. If I can get out of this chair, I'm going home."

Mr Lawless, visibly relieved, helped him up.

Talulla handed Mr O'Toole his coat in the hall. "Things are on the move," he said. "The two worlds approach each other. Don't look so uneasy, dear. I speak metaphorically."

"What two worlds, Mr O'Toole?"

"Did I never teach you a thing? Is it not appropriate, that just two days before *Samhain*, the dead return to make themselves known to us?"

"Um," Talulla said. The hairs prickled at the back of her neck.

"Thought for the day," Mr O'Toole said. "Good night, my dear. Take care of yourself."

Gareth, who was halfway up the footpath with the empty cups and flask, simply handed them to Talulla. "Will you wait a moment, Brendan?" he said. "I'll walk with you. The guards think they'll be on the site all tomorrow," he told Talulla. "After that, they don't know. Will you make my excuses?"

She watched them crossing the road, the ageing teddy bear and the Angel Gabriel, chatting amicably. It made sense: both were guardians of the past. Mr O'Toole held the history, and Gareth Travers held the house. A road through Granny's would open a gash across their memories, and Charlie and the Minogues would have to "look both ways" to avoid traffic instead of to catch a glimpse of Grace O'Malley's ghost. The children who would live in the new town houses would never know Granny's Wood at all. Not as she had. And what you don't know, you don't miss. Or – what you don't know, you don't know you miss.

Talulla phoned Emma when they had all gone, ostensibly to tell her about the meeting, but really to see if she was all right.

"Don't worry, I've all eighteen locks on the door!"

"Is it true Alan's here?"

"God, were they all talking about it?"

"They weren't. I don't think anyone from here has seen him except Briege. It was all the usual stuff – plus who was it, and how can we keep the gardaí – us – out of their – *our* lives and, last but not least, the Minogues's bangers."

"Kevin Minogue told me they were given forty pounds to take into Henry Street."

"Forty pounds!"

"More," Emma said. "Ciarán took some of his First Communion money as well. They'd better keep building their horrible nuclear stockpiles over in Sellafield, hadn't they? The Minogues are 'contenders'." She sighed. It was a frail, patient sigh.

"Well. If there's anything we can do . . . Emma, please phone, or come."

"Thanks, Tully." She rang off.

Talulla put the phone down as carefully as if it were Emma herself. Not a word from Emma about Alan. She sat on the side of the bed, thinking about them. All those years of being inseparable, and then – how could things have gone so wrong for them?

And what had Mr O'Toole said? *I can*

understand how one could strangle another human being much more easily than I can understand a mother leaving her child . . . Plainly it was easier for mothers to leave their children than Mr O'Toole thought.

That night, Talulla dreamed her father stood in front of the churned earth, the crime team behind him curiously still, like mourners at some Victorian graveside. "*Tá inigh mo ghrá ar ais,*" her father said. "My little Hope," and he picked up the button. Caught in it was a long, dark strand of hair. This, weeping, he wound round his finger. The button he put in his mouth and swallowed.

Chapter Sixteen

The wild-eyed woman in the bed clung to the young nurse, who clucked and soothed as if she were the older of the two. The registrar, white-coated and stethoscoped, leaned against the wall. This was the third time he'd glanced at Aidan, who was beginning to get annoyed. Detective Garda O'Hare was ogling the nurse, following her movements with large soulful eyes, and that annoyed Aidan, too.

"Dark-haired . . ." he prompted softly.

"It was so – no light inside the car. Kind of warned me – black, bushy – looked . . ." She tried to swallow.

"A wig, maybe?"

The woman cleared her throat. It sounded painful. "Yes. Could."

"Good. See his eyes? Dark? Light?"

"Couldn't tell. They . . ."

"Take your time."

"Deep-set. Small."

"Anything about his hands?"

Her own hand, bruised and swollen, went to her lips, which were swollen also. Little blood vessels had broken in her eyes, giving them an oddly speckled appearance. There were darkening marks around her neck and a long, evil-looking graze.

"Ring," she said hoarsely. "But . . ."

"Yes?"

"Smell. Smell off . . . hands. White spirit . . . ?"

"Good! Any other smells? Was he clean? Dirty?"

She thought for a long moment, mouthed "Don't know."

"And the car was red, you think a Toyota . . ."

"Sorry," she whispered.

"You've done great. Great."

Her face twisted and she started to cry, short, harsh sounds like a bird.

The registrar pushed himself off the wall. "Right," he said.

Aidan put his hand on the woman's. "Thanks. Well done. We'll be back tomorrow. Have a good, safe sleep; you've earned it."

The corridor outside was silent and dimly-lit. The last cup of tea had been wheeled round hours ago and the patients given their sleeping tablets.

The registrar came out with them. They could hear the young nurse's soothing voice as the door closed behind them.

"She shouldn't be by herself," Aidan said.

"She won't be. We'll contrive. We'd put her in ICU but it's full, and anyway, physically . . ." The registrar shrugged. "Why in the name of God do they get in the car with him?"

"There's not one of them yet who wasn't stranded in some way, or in a hurry. He spots 'em a mile away."

"I take it he'll have been ever so deprived," said the registrar fiercely.

"Oh, aye," said O'Hare.

"We'll look after her," said the registrar. "Not too early tomorrow, if you don't mind. We'll be running a few tests."

"Hate bloody hospitals," O'Hare said in the lift.

"Beats the morgue."

"It does that. Say it's our man?"

"Could be." Aidan rubbed his own neck. His fingers felt hot and awkward. "Oh, yeah, I think it's our man. She was so lucky. That's all it was. If that lorry driver hadn't been falling asleep –" He yawned.

"How is he?" O'Hare asked.

"Better than he deserves. He saw nothing; he only opened his eyes when she thrashed against the horn in the other car, and across the road and into the ditch with him. Gave her the chance to get out, anyway. Useless bugger. Pity he didn't wing them. We might have had the car then, and our man. Somebody should've breathalysed him."

"Well – tomorrow's another day," said O'Hare, glancing over his shoulder. "Will I come back with you tomorrow?"

"Do your nurse-chasing on your own time, O'Hare."

"What 'own time'?"

"'Sorry for ya'," Aidan said, but O'Hare, who was hard to ruffle, only laughed.

"Any news from McQuaid?"

"Said something would be 'on my desk' in the morning," Aidan said. He yawned again. "I don't know who she thinks is going to put it there."

O'Hare grinned cautiously.

"Go home," Aidan told him.

O'Hare went.

Aidan stood on the steps of the hospital. He felt strangely indecisive; it wasn't all that late. He could go back to the station for a while, catch up on paperwork. That wasn't where his restlessness came from, though.

For the first time, the Strangler had lost his prey. According to the woman's story, he had driven away from the scene untouched. Would he have been frightened off? Aidan doubted it. There was nothing to do but wait.

Chapter Seventeen

They had been talking, just chatting, waiting for the bus and then he got agitated. "I've forgotten something," he said with a dark look, and he pulled the shotgun out from under his jacket. He was a complete stranger, not an acquaintance like Talulla had thought, and she was cross with herself for making the mistake. If it had been a film it would have been slow-motion, but it wasn't. He fired the shotgun fast, before anyone could even turn away. The schoolgirl tottered on the kerb, her charity collection tin bouncing and clattering under the bus, and the man in the car put his hands up to his eyes. Talulla shouted, but she couldn't move; she was being stung by wasps travelling in prickles across her abdomen.

Briege shook her very gently. "I'll swing for those Minogues," she said. "I'll boil the kettle while you're in the bath." As she spoke, there was a second explosion.

"What time is it?"

"Nine. I'm phoning Jenny Minogue. It's too much!"

It was bright. The low autumn sun sliced through the curtains into the room. Half a morning slept away, if it weren't for the children and their infernal bangers. Tomorrow would see the end of it, at any rate; the Minogue boys were not hoarders.

Talulla had never been allowed to have bangers when she was growing up. After all, they were against the law. That didn't stop herself and Lara and Emma from pooling their pocket money and going into Dublin to buy them, the year they were twelve. They told everyone they were going to Dún Laoghaire for the afternoon and then, swarming with glee and guilt, they caught the Number 8 bus and were off.

The city had never been more magnificent than it was that day. It seemed to open itself to them: "Ah, so you're here." Everything had a scary sweetness to it. There was the Liffey, wide and full and slanting under its bridges towards the sea, the gulls more knowing than the ones in Dalkey; and O'Connell Street, the lovely buildings rising above the ground-floor tat of gaudy restaurants and arcades; and finally, Henry Street where the hawkers, with the same shrewd and cheerful glances as the gulls, spread their long, dark coats like wings to display their illicit treasures.

They misjudged the time and the vagaries of the Number 8 bus, so they were an hour late getting home. It was dark. They gave Emma all the bangers because she was the least likely to be searched, but Aidan was waiting for them at the terminus and that was that. None of them spoke to him for weeks.

Of course Mr Cummings, who was much older than Leila, had died the year before; and Aidan, as the oldest left at home, had huge responsibilities. This made no difference to the girls. Aidan was the arch-villain for years, with Séamus running a close second. Emma and Alan used to taunt Talulla and Lara about living in "police states", but even then Talulla had a lurking sense that Emma was running wild and Alan was neglected.

The bangers escapade was the last adventure the three girls had all to themselves. Soon after that, Emma and Alan became best friends. That's what Talulla and Lara called it then because, even though they teased them about their "romance", they didn't understand how they loved each other.

There was a little volley of popping noises, and Talulla went to the window. All three Minogues were in the garden next door, leaping and yelling like imps. Charlie MacDevitt was there too, a lighted match in one hand and a fat banger in the other. A little girl from Thorn Grove hovered near the kitchen door, hands poised at her ears. "One! Two! Three!" shrieked the Minogues. Charlie, her eyes huge with fear, lit the banger and threw it near the end of the garden. A flushed face appeared above the back wall and began to speak. The banger went off. The Minogues disappeared into the house in one fluid movement, leaving Charlie and the other girl in conversation with the guard.

Mrs Minogue sailed out, looking anxious and wiping her hands on a cloth. "Nice one, Jenny, good enough for you!" Talulla muttered under her breath. There was a brief exchange. The guard melted back into the trees in Granny's, and Mrs Minogue, looking rather huffily over her shoulder, shepherded Charlie and her friend into the house.

Now their own kitchen door slammed and Briege walked out with a tray. She balanced it on the stile at the end of the garden, leaned, called. A different guard appeared. His face brightened when he saw the tea. The other followed. In a moment all three were engaged in earnest conversation.

By the time Talulla had bathed and dressed, Briege had the tray wiped and a second pot of tea brewing. She shook the pot and poured out, then removed a plate from the oven.

"A fry!"

"You need it. There's not a pick on you."

Briege had the rashers just right. "And Hick's sausages!" Talulla said. "Must get shot more often."

"I'll give those to you not to get shot. They're about to take on new staff in the bank, by the way."

"Sorry, Auntie-Mum, I wouldn't be able for the excitement. What did the lads say?"

"Clear that plate and I'll tell you."

Talulla looked at her. She realised that Briege had been avoiding her eyes ever since she came downstairs. She put down her fork.

"What?"

"Nothing that's not in the papers, they say."

"Go on."

"Well," Briege said carefully, "the woman they're after finding in Granny's could be an American."

"An American."

"Teeth. Some kind of work we don't do here. Go on now, before that's cold."

"Was Mary de Burca ever there?"

Briege shook her head. "She actually talked about it. Wanting to go."

"So it's not her," Talulla said.

"No."

"Are you glad?"

"Yes and no," Briege said slowly. "It depends, doesn't it? God forgive me . . . if it's somebody who's nothing at all to do with any of us, then I'll be glad it's not Mary de Burca."

Talulla took a bite of rasher. It had a strange taste now, which was really no taste at all.

"That girlfriend of Alan's," Briege said.

"Yeah?"

"With the Irish name, well, she was American, wasn't she?"

"She was. But you can forget her, Briege. She was vast."

Briege did not seem to have heard her. "Something odd about her name."

"Ashling. Spelled 'A-s-h'. It's just not possible, Briege."

"Surely that's not why he came back? To, to move it in case – ?"

"Not like him," Talulla said firmly.

"No, it isn't."

"I can see Alan taking a punch at that girl, Briege. Did you never see her? She was the Amazon from hell, but hiding her and burying her and sneaking around? We'll never see Alan with a spade in his hand. He'd throw her in the boot of his dad's car and dump her off Greystones or somewhere. Sure, he'd forget he put her in the boot till she exploded."

"Who knows what they'd do if they killed someone?"

"It's too clever."

"I don't want it to be Alan myself, but I can't agree that he's an idiot, Talulla."

"Briege, we know him."

"I've a terrible feeling about this."

"A 'three' feeling?"

Briege nodded, dumb.

Chapter Eighteen

They washed the few plates together, subdued. The cat went to the door, mewed to get out, wanted to get in again immediately. "I'm like him," said Briege. "Don't know if I'm coming or going."

"Let's go."

"Where?"

"The beach. You know you need your 'fix'."

Briege smiled a little. She had such a habit now of going to White Rock in the mornings that she seemed lost when she missed a day. "I wonder what Emma's doing now," she said quietly. "Will we ask her to come, Talulla?"

Talulla hugged her. "If she's read the papers . . ."

"Poor little goat."

"You haven't called Emma that for years."

"Well, off with us. The air'll do her good. It'll be about the only thing that can."

Thorn Grove was a small cul-de-sac, similar to Thorn Crest except that the houses were built a few years later. They were subtly smaller and better-designed than the semis in Thorn Crest, and their red brick and pebbledash exteriors looked more stylish. They too enjoyed glimpses of the bay. Emma's house was on the side whose back gardens verged on Granny's Wood.

Emma opened her upstairs window to peer down at them, her long, dark hair tumbling over her shoulder. All she lacked was a prince in the front garden, begging to be allowed up. Her eyes, however, were huge and sad, and in that moment Talulla remembered that she had always envied Emma a little – sometimes a lot – and Emma was not to be envied at all. She never had been.

As if to bear this out, there was a rushing noise at the corner, then a screeching of tyres. A small black BMW slewed to a stop beside them. The curtain of the house opposite twitched and stilled.

"Perfect timing!" Briege said, but her voice trembled.

Emma's husband, Declan James, got out of the car. He was a big man, very big, and good-looking in a fair-haired, rugby-playing sort of way.

"He's had a skinful!" Briege whispered.

"Come to see the show, have you?" He

slammed the car door behind him with a flick of his hand.

Talulla remembered the odd angle of Emma's arm last New Year's Eve and felt cold. "You mustn't break your barring order, Declan," she said, hurrying after him. "Come on, now."

His face, which was designed to be ruddy and pleasant-looking, twisted. "Am I in the house? Am I? Am I in the – Jesus! She's shut the window." He pushed past Talulla and staggered up to the hall door. Talulla followed. "She's shut the window. Emma!" he yelled at the house. "Come out here!"

"Declan, you're not supposed –" Talulla found herself sitting on the ground. Declan hurled himself at the door, hitting it with a horrible thump of his shoulder. Emma screamed at him from inside.

"Is he in there? Is he in there with you, whore?"

"Oh, my God."

"It's all right, Briege. The guards are coming. Listen."

"Come out, de Burca! Send him out, you –"

Briege put her hands over her ears.

"Go over to Mrs Appleby. Go now, Briege, you're in the way." Talulla pushed her aunt towards the neighbour from across the street, who was standing just inside her garden gate, clutching her cane. "Go!"

"Wait'll I get you, Emma. Emma! Send him out. Just him." The door made a splintering noise, but held. There was a glass panel beside it. Declan put his fist through it. Awkwardly, he began to pull shards of glass away from the frame. They could hear Emma crying.

A garda car pulled up behind Declan's. "Declan James," Talulla told the men who got out of it. "Breaking his barring order." She was shaking.

"You don't go near him," said the guard. While he checked in on the radio, the other man approached Declan. "Mr James. Declan."

They'd a rough time of it until the second car arrived moments later. It took four of them to subdue Declan and take him away, streaming blood from a deep cut on his arm and finally tears, when Emma steadfastly refused to come out to him. All the time he shouted at her, his voice slurring more and more with drink and shock, the threats and insults appalling.

A woman garda, crisp in her uniform, strolled over to Talulla as Declan was finally manhandled into a car.

"Where's the van?" Talulla asked her.

"Full of kids. Eight or nine of them had a cider bash up the hill and didn't make it home. Well, you know. They started with cider. Someone must have brought, I don't know, the bit of E to liven things up." She grimaced. "I don't think they're even fifteen."

"Will they live?"

"Ach, well, probably. Eejits. What happened here?"

"Langers. Broke his barring order. He's just dangerous, um –?"

"Marian," the woman said in her calm voice. "Marian Quinn. You're Talulla, aren't you?"

"How'd you know?"

"You wouldn't forget that name, and then Aidan described you to me. After the shooting."

Marian Quinn's hair was too blonde but in a way that men, fools, would probably like. "Aidan described you to me." With that look. Right.

"You always think it'll happen when you're on duty, if it happens at all," Marian Quinn went on. "Not when you're meeting a girlfriend under Clery's clock."

Talulla knew she didn't intend it – and this made it worse – but "meeting a girlfriend under Clery's clock" seemed cringingly pathetic and gauche. So did being grazed by a shotgun pellet. "Better to have been killed meeting a man under it, I suppose," she muttered.

"Um, I don't know," Marian Quinn said, indicating the broken door with a devastating half-smile.

There was a sound of bolts straining, and the door yawed inward on its fractured hinges. Emma slipped out, looking very small. "I have to thank Mrs Appleby," she said. They watched her go across to the woman with the cane, who put her arm around her.

"That'll be the woman who phoned up," Marian said.

"She's a good neighbour. Emma's well-known here; that's her family home."

"He's the blow-in, so."

"Yeah."

"One they could have done without."

"I pity him a bit," Talulla said.

Marian gave her an incredulous look from under long lashes and strolled over to Briege. Out came the notebook. Well, thank you very much.

Talulla felt slightly sick now that it was over. What if Declan had got into the house? Could she have gone in after him?

She leaned her elbows on the garden wall, wincing at the faint pain in her side. "What's done can't be undone," said a voice in her mind. Her dad used to say that. It was sad. He always said it as if he had reason to know the truth of it.

Emma and Alan. What Alan had done to Emma, what Emma had done to Declan James: it wasn't right. It couldn't be undone. It just seemed to gather momentum, like something that couldn't be stopped.

Emma was back, throwing an abstracted look up the cul-de-sac as various neighbours melted back into their houses.

"They're charging him, thank God. How'd you know to come?"

"We wanted you to go to the beach."

"The beach! Oh. I'd have liked that." She sighed. "Mum has Iseult for the weekend. If she'd been here – !"

"We'll make a cup of tea," Briege said, taking her arm and patting it. "Who's going to fix the door?"

"They're contacting a man for me. They're very good. To think all this went on and half the force was beyond in Granny's." She motioned to them to go ahead of her through the front door, edging through it herself as if she couldn't bear to touch it or the door frame, shrinking away from the panel beside it with its stained shards. Declan's blood had pooled on the painted ledge at the bottom, splashed the brick, spattered the leaves of the pyracantha.

Talulla sat her at the kitchen table and boiled the kettle while Briege filled a basin with water and went out to wash the blood away. Emma put her head down and wept. Over and over again she cried, "It's all my fault!"

Chapter Nineteen

Down on the beach, Briege's face regained its normal ruddy glow. Outside Emma's it had been powdery-looking, and Talulla had been afraid. It was the same sense of dread she felt as a child, when she guessed that something she had done – being born, in this case – was a prelude to disaster. If she had waited a year, her parents' marriage might have "settled"; they might still be together.

Briege had told her it was Séamus's salary, not herself, that had caused the problem. "It wasn't that Hope was a gold-digger – she just needed millions of little cushions in life like she'd always had, and easy distractions – they didn't even own a telly, and she was thousands of miles from her friends." Talulla, unconvinced, tried to make a place in her mind where her parents were happy, a memory-place where she hovered shyly on the verge; but their time together was so short that her child's shadow seemed to loom right across it.

Briege leaned over and picked up a smooth, flat stone. It was dove-grey, with spidery white markings like mysterious writing. She popped it into her jacket pocket. The beach was a mantra for the senses, and Talulla, satisfied, could see her relaxing. Today there was a bright, sharp breeze off the sea, and drifts of cormorants floated just beyond the breakers, a promise of gales. The tide was out, so they scrunched along the firm sand just below the shingle.

"Should we have left her there with the carpenter?" Briege asked.

"She wanted to be on her own."

"Yes."

Talulla linked arms with her. "I'm always forgetting what a softie you are."

"Coward, more like! I nearly died when he pushed you down."

"It wasn't me he was after. Auntie-Mum!" Talulla said, stopping. "Are you crying?"

"No, it's the wind. I just –" Briege shrugged, then threw up her hands.

"It's a pity you can't be like Leila Cummings."

"Is it, now?"

"You could take great hope from all this." Talulla laughed at the look Briege gave her. "When the computer crashed in Harcourt Street last week, Mrs Cummings said she told Aidan that they must be very close to finding the Strangler, the devil was trying so hard to thwart them. There, now."

"Do you want to annoy me, or what?" Briege said, wiping her eyes, but starting to smile.

"No, but you might be preparing yourself for the Second Coming –"

"Will you stop, Talulla!" Briege looked shocked, but she laughed outright.

"Mur-na-ghan! It's really a tower block he's planning –"

"Oh, God, don't even mention him in this place!"

" – and then we'll have another corpse on our hands. The Angel Gabriel will do him in for us with a secret weapon hired from *An Taisce* –"

"Speak of the devil!" said Briege. She had spotted Gareth's tall figure at the other end of the beach. He was standing opposite the little cave, which was invisible from their angle, gazing out towards Dalkey Island.

"Look, we'll go and see your rock, and if he wants to meet us then he can. He'll escape if he doesn't," Talulla said.

Briege's pet stone was still lodged in its crevice in the massive outcrop which separated White Rock from Killiney Beach. Briege was fascinated by this stone. It was silk-smooth like its companions on the shingle but, although it was caught above the tide line in a pale gash in the granite, it had the glossy black sheen of an aubergine. Briege had tried to prise it out without success, and she always went to look at it. "It reminds me of life," she would say portentously. It was one of Briege's "departures," as Talulla called them.

"Why is the stone like life?" Talulla would tease her.

"Because . . . it's really grey. It only looks black and exotic because of where it is. Something keeps it wet." Another time she said, "It had to get there by terrific force, and only greater force can get it out again. But I don't think it'll ever come out."

Then Talulla had the sense to leave the subject alone. What Briege saw in it was important to her, if not quite clear.

The stone still glistened in its place. Even its shape was that of a very small aubergine, and Briege touched it lovingly. Its perfect smoothness resisted her fingers. There was an energy in its texture that slowed and held them while the granite, much coarser, bounced them along, releasing them. It was almost sinister, her dark trapped stone, and she loved it.

They heard the click of the shingle between waves and wind and, turning, they saw Gareth walking towards them.

"Have you any idea what was going on in Emma's?" he asked after they had greeted each other. "I slept it out. The sirens woke me. I called, but a workman answered the door."

Talulla gave him a somewhat scaled-down version of events, but he understood the full seriousness of what had happened. More than that, he was outraged.

Talulla wished he hadn't come down to the beach. She felt vaguely intimidated by him, as if she were still little and tongue-tied. It wasn't that Gareth was brilliant, she chided herself. In actual fact, he was socially awkward. Briege was offering him a cup of tea from their flask. Maybe she should wrap his cup in clingfilm when she got home and never wash it and make a little shrine around it or, better yet, post it to Lara.

Because of the freshness of the wind they drank their tea in the changing shelter, looking out its open front at the Island to the left and Bray Head and the Sugarloaf far away to the right. Talulla suddenly longed to get into the water, to confront the cold shock of its chill formidable life, but it was much too rough. The breakers were hoarse with sand and stones scraped from the sea's floor and flung as if catapulted; dislodged, then scattered like the small bones in their drift of earth in Granny's Wood.

The surf shifted around Dalkey Island like white fangs. Talulla wondered about everyone who had ever lived there, from the first people with their bits of stone to the monks and, finally, the soldiers. Not only had the soldiers survived the garrison's bleakness and cold, they had hung on there for forty years after the Battle of Waterloo. Someone forgot to disband them. They probably had to be prised off like limpets. Had anyone ever wanted to leave Dalkey?

Aidan was interested in all that. Lara said if he'd had enough money for university, he'd have become a historian or an archaeologist. Instead, he was stuck digging up facts about the living.

Gareth was saying, "No, I've too much sunk in this place. Anyway, I reckon my property value's about to plummet . . ."

"Murnaghan," Briege said, with a scowl.

"Oh, yes, if he gets the road. He keeps calling it an 'avenue.' We'll all lose from that, and the houses he's planning –" He shrugged contemptuously.

"More dratted town houses," Briege said.

He nodded. "Two up, two down, two cars."

"I think it's three. Three up," Talulla said. Gareth smiled at her politely.

"Any news from Aidan?" he asked.

"Not really."

Talulla felt Briege's curious look, but this was

no lie; the last news they'd had was from the
gardaí in Granny's.

She finished her tea before the other two and
strolled around near the cave, where the beach
became small and intimate, cluttered with
boulders and rocks between the cliff and the water.

It seemed so unfair to Briege, who had loved
and cared for her so faithfully, that Talulla felt
truly orphaned at this moment, but she did. She
would have given anything to see her father again,
just once. She closed her eyes, feeling the tears
squeeze out, getting those flickering, partial
glimpses of him – his proud glow when he didn't
think she was looking, the way he responded when
she asked him something unexpected: a slight
widening of the dark blue eyes, and a sense that he
was rushing into himself to reconnoitre, not in
some deliberate way but in a little fuss of country
reserve. And, oh yes, the pale hard abstracted look
of him when some Thursday or Friday he'd
suddenly announce that Talulla was to go to Aunt
Tessie's for the weekend, and Talulla could not
understand why Briege would be alternately
furious and pitying.

On one occasion, only one, Briege had refused
to send her off to Tessie: Talulla had been invited
to a birthday party on the Saturday, and she
wanted to go to it. Séamus went missing on the

Friday night, and Briege managed so well that Talulla never noticed anything until the Sunday – after all, he kept odd hours because of his work. Then she heard Briege on the phone to Jack Murphy, Séamus's great friend in the gardaí; and late Sunday night, rigid and listening in her bed, she heard the soft tap at the door and Briege going swiftly to answer it. Briege and Jack Murphy were whispering while her dad spoke, oblivious to their shushing, with the slurred, loud, complaining voice of a stranger.

Later that night he stumbled past her door to the toilet, fell heavily inside and got noisily, dreadfully sick. Something kept her from going to him and later – and this was the worst – she heard him crying in his room in an awful, stifled way. She put her head under the pillow, still able to hear Briege quietly close his door on him. Sometime towards morning, Briege crept up the stairs with a mop and bucket. She was in the toilet and bathroom for a long time. When Talulla got ready for school, they smelled of disinfectant and sweet, stale sick.

Talulla shut him out for a week. She turned away from his morning kiss and glared at him with stony amazement across the dinner table. He went into himself, diminishing and becoming so quietly distraught that, by the following Saturday, Briege

told her sharply, "That's enough, madame!"
Séamus, however, started going to meetings, and
there were only two or three more sudden trips to
Tessie's; one of them after an infanticide, a baby
girl found down a well. He made up for it in
cigarettes, of course.

"Daddy, Dad, what would you make of all this?"
And then the thing Talulla could say only to him,
a spirit on the wind: "Was it my mother in
Granny's? Did she come back for me?"

Briege and Gareth were still talking near the
bottom of the steps up to the railway bridge.
Killiney Beach curved away behind them, Bray
Head now softened to a sky-shadow in the
distance. Mist was moving in, softening and
smudging the lonely vista. Gareth's long figure
leaned confidingly. Briege's face turned up to his.
She nodded.

Why was it so sad? Talulla felt tears on her face.
Why was it all so sad?

Chapter Twenty

Aidan's first instinct was to turn the other way, but Alan de Burca had already seen him. He was across the road from the station, and Aidan suspected he was working up the nerve to come in. His face brightened as Aidan crossed to join him. Two things hadn't changed about Alan; his sense of timing and the trusting look in his eyes whenever he saw Aidan.

"Alan."

"I was on my way in," Alan said. He had got tougher-looking in Australia and it suited him. His hand when Aidan shook it was a man's hand, hardened and defined. His accent was unchanged, however. Interesting. In Aidan's experience, the vowels narrowed quickly when people emigrated to Australia. It was almost a sign they'd decided to stay.

"Were you on a stakeout?" Alan said, peering at him.

"Not exactly. Why?"

"Your eyes," Alan said.

"Can we start again here?"

"Oh. Right."

"Will we go for a coffee?"

"Yeah, great. Thanks. I can finally pay. Though I suppose that's a sore point. Fuck it!" Alan said, tugging at the hair above his ear, "It's back to square one. I nearly broke my neck on the moving stairs on the way to the baggage check, and I knew I was home. I've been putting my foot in it ever since."

Aidan would not let himself be won over. Alan had started to blink, which had always been a sign he was up to something. "Your arrival's coincided with some excitement," he said mildly.

Alan gave him a sharp look. "So I believe."

"In here?"

Alan's eyes widened. "Johnston and Mooney's?"

"I'm not sitting in the pub at this hour. What'll you have?"

"How's your mother?" Alan said, when they had sat down in the corner. The rest of the room was filled with women shoppers and mothers with small children.

"Asthma's a bit worse, but under control. She's fine otherwise."

"Lara?"

"Unchanged."

"Is she here?"

"She is not, thank God. She's tormenting the English. In London. She's a PA to some poor bloke. Doing very well, actually. Wants to quit the job, of course."

"Have you ever thought of emigrating?"

Aidan laughed. "I look that down, do I?"

"Well, yeah. You do."

"Say that again."

"What?"

"Say, 'yeah.'"

"Yeah," Alan said cautiously. Too anxious to please, Aidan thought.

"Sounded Aussie. Are you going back?"

"Depends. Will we get to the point?"

"Go on," Aidan said, impressed.

"Well, what about the corpse? What's being said?"

"'Corpse' makes you think of flesh, doesn't it?" Aidan said, watching him carefully. "Our friend beyond was skull and bones."

Alan turned pale but he didn't blink. "Nice. So who's it supposed to be?"

"Well, your mother at first. But now, your girlfriend."

Alan laughed outright. "Well, Mum's alive and well and living in Ealing with a fellow called Peregrine Bragg."

"You're joking."

"I'm not. 'Peregrine Bragg' is his real name."

"Jesus, Alan. How long did you know?"

"Five or six years. She got in touch with Dad a few weeks after she did the runner, but he didn't mention it. Herself and 'Perry' – he's not a bad old thing, it's just that his name's the only interesting thing about him – finally got married after Dad's death, so now it can be told." He shrugged, his face suddenly tired. "So. American teeth, right?"

"Right."

"Anyone reported missing?"

"That's the odd thing. There isn't," Aidan said.

"It isn't Ashling Leahy."

"Alan –"

"Aidan, it's not. I saw her last. She left Dalkey under her own steam."

"Do you know how we'd get in touch with her?"

"No. But I saw her last, Aidan, and that bitch was still living."

"Well, good. Sure, I suppose it'll be some poor Yank kidnapped from Omaha by aliens and dumped here after they'd had their way with her. Sure, most of us here in Ireland are alien discards, we just don't remember."

Alan's face was reddening.

"Well, ah guess our little lady's parachute jes' didn't open quick enough –" Aidan drawled.

"That is the most appalling take-off of an American accent I have ever heard. Even Ashling never sounded that bad."

" – and she jes' made herself a crater out in Granny's."

"Fuck off, Aidan."

"Alan. You get a solicitor. Today."

"I saw her leaving, Aidan. Just remember that. Do I really need a solicitor?"

"Your name's been mentioned."

"Don't move. I'd better go, like, hire my legal representative. I'm paying. Stay there. Please. Thanks, Aidan. I'll see you around."

Aidan watched him at the till. He looked more assured and determined than upset. But he was upset. He'd blinked like hell. When he insisted he was the last to see Ashling Leahy as she left Dalkey, he'd blinked. Which was the lie? That Ashling Leahy had left? Or that Alan was the last to see her? And who was the only person that Alan would ever endanger himself to protect? Emma.

"Oh, shit," Aidan sighed. Women at the table next to him gave him level looks. He left.

Chapter Twenty-One

Gareth had not been entirely truthful when he told Talulla that he had the house under control. When they spoke about it at the meeting, he had panicked for a moment. What if she offered to come and help him? She was a nice girl; it was entirely possible. He wouldn't have liked that. He loved settling in by himself and taking possession.

He was surveying the mess his Scots tenant had made of the scullery when the banger went off. The window rattled and a slotted spoon that was dangling from a nail beside it actually fell on the floor. He peered out the window, but his eyes were dazzled by the light in the room. In the thickening darkness outside, he could see only a flicker of white and a scuttle of movement as the children fled into Granny's. He opened the window and looked down. There was a strong stink of cordite. Where did they get such a brute? Smoke and mist drifted in around him, and he closed the window again, relocking it.

The slotted spoon was in no condition to be returned to the wall. He threw it into the sink with other grubby implements he'd found and put more water in the electric kettle.

He was almost himself again, his Beaulieu self. Usually it took only a day or so, but now the house was restless. Its old walls seemed almost porous, the way they soaked up the atmosphere of whatever was going on, then retained it like a sponge.

There must have been such ripples of unease in the house many times over the years as the land shrank and the Travers's fortunes diminished. His great-great-grandfather had sold the land on which de Burca's was built. That wasn't for money; he wanted his friends near him. They weren't a very healthy family, however, and after two generations the house was sold to a de Burca.

His own grandfather sold the land for Thorn Grove and Thorn Crest in 1955. Gareth didn't know why he did that; there was plenty of money even then. Or there would have been, had he not given Jonathan the farm. Dear Uncle Jonathan, Grandfather's pride and joy. He gave Jonathan the farm in Tipperary, and Jonathan sold it and went to America. Richard, Gareth's father, was the one who loved the house. He had wanted Gareth to grow up there too. But there was a sheen of acid over everything.

Jonathan got himself killed in Vietnam and Richard and Muriel carried on. Grandfather never knew Jonathan was dead. He outlived both his sons, but he didn't know about Jonathan.

The builders had been cleared to resume work on the de Burca site tomorrow. Hallowe'en. Great day for ghouls and goblins, for noise and uproar and men silhouetted in the dust like demons. They'd be finished with the little estate – "development", rather – by the end of next summer, just about the time his sabbatical was over and he'd be back exiled in London. Thank God for his promotion: that and a new tenant would help to pay the bills.

Perhaps at night, when the workmen had gone, the quiet fabric would reweave itself. Then he could gaze across the hill's darkness towards the bay and the glimmering shawl of the city, graceful shimmer of lights flung carelessly from the sea to the black horizon, and hear nothing except the night noises of the wood and the hill.

These latest disasters were almost a comfort. They confirmed the tradition of their lives, the Travers's, that all happiness was fleeting, incomplete and bitterly won. Wasn't the house itself a sign? Fix the roof, neglect the paintwork;

clear the gutters, throw out the carpet, the carpet his mother had bought years ago as a stopgap to be replaced with something elegant when there'd be money. He didn't mind: he liked the wide eighteenth-century floorboards, almost untouched by worm or dry rot. His footsteps on them at night resonated upon other steps, layer upon layer of possession that faded into the scuff of boots on flags, or of softer soles on rushes – for there were other houses before this one. His people had lived in them all. There should be a limpet on his family's coat of arms. Where they built they gripped, though some had joined the unending Irish diaspora.

The house was cold. Gareth's flat in London had central heating and, each time he came home, it was like re-entering a sterner, more resolute existence. He'd hated the cold when he was a child; it seemed to be part and parcel of his grandfather's meanness, until he was in de Burca's one day and heard Alan's mother complaining. Then he realised that old houses, even Victorian ones like de Burca's, resisted all attempts to warm them, and thousands would have to be spent to do so. "And then, Gareth," Mary de Burca had told him, "all the old furniture would crack and look even more hideous than it does now."

He had liked her. She talked to him as if he was

a person, but then she was very lonely. He was, too. His own mother believed that children weren't quite human – or at least weren't interesting – until they were nine or ten. "One's duty is to keep feeding them and hope for the best."

Mary de Burca let him play in her garden. He was seven, and Alan was a tiny baby. Mary noticed Gareth's chilblains and put Sudocreme on them, and that was why they'd been talking about the heating. She'd a big chilblain on her heel, she said. He wondered if he'd first been drawn to Emma because she'd long, glossy black hair like Mary de Burca's.

Gareth would have been surprised to know that people had ever connected Mary with the find in Granny's. He himself had seen her in London. It was only last year, but he'd have known her anywhere. Her hair was still dark, but when she put up her hand to take her ticket out of the machine – it was in a Tube station – he saw that her wrists had thickened. He hadn't remembered that she had thick wrists. Emma's wrists and ankles were supple and delicate. But Emma was never soft like Mary de Burca, not even when she was little. A delighted smile softened his face for a moment; then he looked at the small cold window beside him, now gone opaque, and he sighed.

Last night's residents' committee meeting had been sad. Gareth was glad he hadn't gone back inside; there was a sense of dissolution in the air. All those people had been kind to him while he was growing up. Reliable, uncomplicated – not like his own family. Now they were easily agitated and old. Even Briege O'Neill seemed shaken, and that had surprised him. His grandfather, cold bastard that he was, couldn't have cared a fig who was dug up in Granny's. For the first time that seemed almost a virtue. *Cast a cold eye on life, on death.* Somehow he doubted that Grandfather was quite what Yeats had in mind.

All the same, Gareth thought the committee had dismissed the Wicklow Strangler a bit too quickly. He decided to ask Aidan about that when he came.

Chapter Twenty-Two

Talulla saw Alan de Burca before he saw her. He was standing at the bar with his back to her, moodily glancing at his watch. Something was different, but what? He had always been dark, but now he was tanned as well. He was fabulous-looking, but that wasn't new. He and Emma had been the stars of their little group for years. It was inevitable. It wasn't just their looks; their intensity had set them apart.

She still held back, appraising, uneasy. If he were a stranger – if she hadn't known him for years – what would she see? A tall man, young and slim, almost Spanish-looking. His shoulders were a bit higher in the tweed jacket than before, as if he had learned that life's crosses might fall on them. His face, when he turned around, had changed the most: the dark eyes were quieter, almost dull, and there was a strained, patient look round his mouth. Talulla was reminded of Emma's face at her window that morning, and how small and beaten she had looked slipping out of her broken door.

Talulla ordered a Coke, Alan a pint, and they sat in the corner. Now he'd a feverish sparkle in his eyes, and she reckoned he hadn't changed as much as she thought.

"I'm sorry just to have phoned you up like that, Tully. Not even passing the time of day. I'm sorry about your dad."

Talulla was only able to nod.

"Really, I am. I – you're still upset. Of course. Are you sure you won't have a drink?"

She shook her head. "I'd love one, but I can't. I've still got to take the odd pain-killer."

"Pain-killers wreck you. What for?"

She told him, but briefly. That wasn't what he was here for.

"You didn't mind coming to The Druid's Chair?" he asked. "I couldn't face the middle of Dalkey again."

"I like it here. Good view. All that's fine. You needn't be polite, Alan. I know you want to talk about Emma. It's OK."

He had been turning a cardboard beer-mat over and over in his hands, and now it snapped. "God," he said, looking at it. "Yes."

When he looked up at her, his eyes were glistening. "I've been trying to get on to her all day. I phoned her in the morning. She wouldn't answer. I know she was there: the phone was engaged right after. Then I went to the house. She was gone, only a carpenter putting up a new door. It would, like, do for the outer gates of Dublin Castle. Did you know about this, Tully?"

"We were there for it."

"What happened? Was it Declan?"

"It was, but she's all right. He never got in."

Alan's eyes went black with rage. Tully wondered if it was possible to crush a pint glass in your fingers, but, to her relief, he carefully put it down and flexed his hand. "I crawled over to The Hag Appleby," he said.

"She's been very good to Emma."

"She told me shag all."

"Well, she protects Emma, Alan! She got the gardaí this morning, the minute Declan drove up she was on the phone. She can't just be telling Emma's business to – to –"

"To just anyone? Well, she knows me!"

Talulla shrugged, cautious. They fell silent. After a moment, Alan picked up his pint and sipped from it. Talulla found herself scrutinising him again.

"Did she ever say anything all this while, Tully? To you? Why she never answered any of my letters? She hung up any time I tried to phone her."

"You phoned her from Australia?" Talulla asked.

"I phoned her from every bloody place. London. Australia. She just put the phone down every time. That marriage made no difference to me. She knew that. I understood she was angry. Even too angry to tell me she was pregnant. I understood all that, but . . . why did she go on with it! She never loved Declan James for a single day."

"There's a streak in Emma. Remember the time she broke Lara's tooth?"

"The time she pushed Lara on to the footpath? Oh, yeah." He laughed.

"It wasn't funny at the time, Alan! Lara was really hurt. Over your famous ice lolly. Come on!" she said, to his confused look. "You bought two, remember? I'd bought my own, but it got down to which one of them would get your second ice lolly."

"Jesus, I wouldn't mind, it was only one of the orangey ones."

"And Emma never apologised to Lara, but she didn't eat or wash herself for three days, remember? Lara was furious. I mean, Emma did end up getting all the attention, with Lara at home with her tooth destroyed and her lip almost out the window, and a pint of her blood on the footpath, but the point was, Emma was genuine. She thought she'd ruined Lara. She was devastated."

"Real little self-punisher," Alan said. Talulla saw suddenly how drawn he looked. "So. She goes off and marries her adoring tyrannosaur. I told her that fellow was mad. Would nobody else – ?"

"Sure, we were all gobsmacked. It wasn't fair on him, you know."

"When was Emma fair on anybody?"

Talulla opened her mouth, outraged.

"I know I was wrong," Alan said, "but I told her – I broke it off with Ashling –"

"After you'd humiliated Emma totally!"

"We were so bloody young, Tully! It had gone on and on, sure we were fourteen when – Emma didn't understand. She was so loyal, she just didn't realise – I'd never known any other girl but her, and . . . Jesus, you find out what matters."

"Well, Emma's changed. If you can get her back now, more power to you, but she's grown up. Even if she did marry that idiot Declan when she was already pregnant, she's just about paid her dues. You should see the way she cares for Iseult. If you haven't grown up yourself, Alan, leave her alone."

Three years ago, Alan would have told Talulla what to do with herself after this remark. Now, he simply nodded. He took another sip of his pint.

"I saw Iseult," he said.

"Where?"

"I went to see Mrs Morrissey today when I was looking for Emma."

Talulla stared at him. "You took on her mother?"

"Before she slammed the door in my face, I saw Iseult."

"She's gorgeous, isn't she? Oh, Alan –"

The barman was at their sides, clearing Talulla's empty glass. "Same again, please," Alan said. When the man moved away, Alan looked at Talulla reflectively. "You've been a mate to concentrate on my problems like this when there's so much else going on."

"Interesting that you're steering the conversation in this direction." Talulla was cross with herself. She had begun to get maudlin, on Coca-Cola, no less.

"I'll bet. Do you share Aidan's opinion that the remains in Granny's belong to A. L.?"

"Whose else could they be?"

"Your mother's?"

Talulla gasped. "My mother left before we even moved to Dalkey!"

"Would you mind a lot if it was her?"

"I certainly would mind! My own father would have had to've done her in!"

Alan fidgeted with the torn bits of the coaster. "Sorry," he said abruptly. "I've another thing to ask you."

"Go on."

"Well, you saw Ashling."

Talulla nodded. If Ashling Leahy had been on your side of any mountain, you'd have seen her. She was almost six feet tall and had blonde hair like a beacon, and she was well-endowed with it.

"You've had all this garda training, haven't you, Tully? Self-defence and all that?"

"Only starting, Alan."

He laughed. "Will you hang on! What do you think I'm asking you? Look. If you'd fought our Ashling, like, the week before you were shot – could you have won?"

"I see what you mean."

"I'm not sure I could have overpowered her myself," he said seriously. "She was a self-defence nut."

"Well, you would know, Alan. Having been in such close contact with her."

"Thank you, Talulla."

"But . . ."

"What?" he asked, scowling.

"There's nothing like the old element of surprise, me boy. That's how the Strangler catches up with the women he kills."

159

Talulla ignored the black look Alan gave her.

"I want to get Emma out of here," he said abruptly, "but I take it I'll be a suspect as long as they think they've got Ashling Leahy in the morgue. That fellow will be at Emma again and again. He's another one I mightn't be able to beat. Funny. I don't even remember him that well. Must be some psychological block-out. Rugger-bugger type . . . blondy hair, blue eyes."

"No. Brown eyes. Rather piggy."

"Why couldn't he have met Ashling before I did?" Alan said after a moment. "Weren't they made for each other?"

He excused himself to make a phone call and Talulla, watching him move away, became aware that she was being watched herself.

Aidan was standing at the bar. Who was he with? She couldn't see. He raised his glass a fraction to her, and she felt her face go hot.

Then Alan was back.

"Still not answering?"

"Not our Emma. Do you mind if we go now, Tully? I've got a late meeting with my solicitor. His nibs there told me to get one." He nodded in Aidan's direction. Aidan's back was turned. He was speaking to the man next to him.

Outside, they threaded their way through the cars that seemed to have hurtled to a stop all together in the pub's tiny carpark. The air was keen. They could smell the sea, and the night smells off the hill opposite. Down to their right, the road sank away through mist and soft lights to Shanganagh.

Alan gave a long, long sigh.

"Do you have to go back to Australia?"

"Yes," he said simply. "And soon."

Chapter Twenty-Three

Where the drive curved round towards the front of the house, Aidan paused. He always did, just here. Beaulieu was a distraction. When you were in front of it, it was too lovely to be ignored. Aidan preferred to look out at the bay, his imagination scudding over the sparkling city to the black countryside miles beyond. Always it comforted him that it was there, with its measured lives and quieter rhythms. For a moment he could almost hear the slow, ritual breathing of the cattle out on the land.

The sharpening air stirred the night smells on the hill. Traces of pine and eucalyptus all the way from Knock-na-Cree mingled with the smells of the Chinese takeaways in the bag he was carrying. Beyond Gareth's dim scraggy lawn, its stone wall and gate, Granny's stretched darkly downwards, only its upper branches distinguishable against the invisible sea and the restless glitter of Dublin's lights. From here they seemed almost to merge but Aidan, tired, reflected that his work lay more and more in the widening darkness between them, in the thousands of lost spaces between light and light.

Darkness cloaked the devastation in de Burca's on his left. The high stone wall and a line of beech trees separated it and Travers's at the moment but, if Aidan knew Gareth, there would be a forest there as soon as he could grow one. Poor old Gareth. His oldest, most uncomfortable, most peculiar friend. Standing here with the looming side of the great house on his right and the fortress of darkness stretching down between him and the city and the sea, Aidan understood Gareth. He understood him when he reached the front of the house, which needed a carpenter and a few hundred coats of paint on door and window-frames, but which still managed to stun the eye through sheer, simple proportion, like a beautiful woman without any make-up. (Here Aidan pushed his thoughts from Talulla, pallid and perfect as he'd seen her in the hospital, actually shaking his head as he did so.)

"Deciding to keep all that to yourself?"

"Jesus, Gareth – ! Would you ever put in a security light, so we'll know when you're creeping around?"

Gareth laughed and took the bag with the beer in it. "You'd like that, wouldn't you? A spotlight right here?"

"Like a hole in the head, but you need something," Aidan said, as they went inside. "Sorry I'm late – I got a bit held up in the pub. Wait now, wait now. Gareth – what's this?"

"You told me to get a mortise-lock."

"This is crap. What are you doing, looking to collect on the insurance?"

"Insurance for what? The mortise-lock?"

"Wait now, don't tell me."

Gareth smiled faintly, waiting, while Aidan, stock-still, surveyed the entrance hall. It had its usual chilly fragrance of stone and old wood – of age, really. The oak stairs rose in front of them, angled gracefully towards the lofty first-floor landing on the right. The marble fireplace on his left was never used, but its brass implements still rested behind the ornate guard. On his right, where the oak chest had once stood beside the drawing-room door, Gareth's muddy wellingtons were flung against the wall. The rest of the great space was bare. Only the panelled doors and heavy pictures relieved its austerity.

"High time you did some gardening. Your grass is a disgrace," Aidan said, nodding at the wellingtons.

"Grass is bourgeois."

"You bastard!" Aidan cried suddenly.

"You never objected to such remarks before." Gareth, delighted, laughed outright.

"You've flogged the clock!"

"Not flogged."

"Ah, no."

"The clock . . . is being repaired!"

They put down their respective bags and slapped hands like Americans.

"The chest is gone."

"To pay for the clock," Gareth said.

"Good trade. I don't know what it was about that chest."

"I didn't like it, either," Gareth said abruptly.

There was steam on the kitchen window downstairs. Aidan had always liked the kitchen and tonight, for the first time, he realised that this was because Gareth's grandfather had never frequented it. That strange old man had cast his shadow on all the other rooms. Aidan's childhood dread had been that Mr Travers would emerge from the study while Aidan and Gareth were in the hall, but the focus of his fears had been the massive chest beside the door.

In the early days of their friendship, when the boys were six or seven, Aidan had got the notion that the chest was the secret entrance to the dungeons Mr O'Toole suggested were under the house. Then, one day, Gareth had heaved up the carved, heavy lid and showed Aidan the contents – a collection of threadbare rugs which released a cloud of dust and camphor. "It's a place for all the things you don't want," he'd said, as he let it down again with an awful crash.

The kitchen was a long, tiled room with the old range still in it. Aidan noted that Gareth had blacked it. Beside it was the gnarled-looking gas cooker which itself was almost an antique. The deal table – the thing Aidan liked best in the room – was scrubbed white. Gareth took great care of all these things.

They assembled the cartons of food and the beer at one end and sat down to eat.

"This is great."

"Sweet-and-sour," Aidan said.

"Thanks. Here." Gareth pushed chicken chop suey towards Aidan, who dumped some on his plate. "There's a takeaway beside me in London. It's not a patch on this."

"Would you come back here for good?"

"Sure, if someone will have me. I applied to Trinity when you sent the advertisement – thanks again, by the way – but they don't really need anyone in Medieval. I haven't enough published to overcome their good sense. Yet."

"What are you working on now?"

Gareth flushed. "I'm interested in the MacSweeneys. You know – well, maybe you don't. Galloglasses. Brought over by Donal óg O'Donnell. Oh, there's a bit more to be done there."

"Why galloglasses?"

Gareth shrugged, but he couldn't hide his enthusiasm. "They're just very interesting. Outsiders. As mercenaries, they thread through everything. They stitch back and forth between the Irish, the Scots, the Old Norse. Marvellous fighting men. I'd have liked to've seen them in action," he added with a faraway look.

"Sure, the tradition lives on. Come down to Store Street if you're starved for that. What's got you so bloodthirsty, anyway?"

"I'm fed up with saints and scholars. The truth is that everything in this island has been gained or held through force. There's nothing worth having here that hasn't got blood on it."

"Plus quite a lot not worth having," Aidan said. He realised he'd lost his appetite and stared at his plate, puzzled.

"Anyway," Gareth went on, "it's the men of action that interest me now." He sighed. "I'll work away . . . *silence the envy in my thought*." He began to eat again, rather hesitant, as if he had forgotten what sort of food it was. Aidan reflected that he probably had.

"Sounds like you've enough to be dealing with yourself, at the moment," Gareth said. "I hardly expected to see you this soon."

"Ah, it's only my own bit of research. It's the day-to-day stuff and the paperwork that take most of my time." Aidan kneaded the back of his neck, then stretched. "Has Boyle been round to see you yet, by the way, or any of the lads?"

"Boyle?"

"From Dalkey. The man who came up, you know. The sergeant, Gareth. They'll have to question everyone about your one in Granny's. Do a survey round."

"And you?"

"It looks like too long a shot for the Strangler. If it was him, we'd probably never be able to prove it."

"Bit of a problem for us, then, isn't it? Ireland's first serial killer. Safely impersonal. Would have settled things here, at least. Won't you take the rest of that?"

Aidan shook his head. His stomach was turning a little from the smell of the sweet-and-sour. He moved it closer to Gareth. "Did you ever meet Ashling Leahy yourself?" he asked.

"Indeed and I did. Well, saw, not met. Not one

of nature's victims, I'd have thought. She was here before I left for England. I saw her from afar. She was impressive. A sort of golden Amazon. I don't think I ever heard her speak. Apparently that was her weak point. Alan took her into Granny's, I know that. Bloody insensitive of him, but what's new?"

"Did you ever see them in Granny's?"

"No. Just heard about them. And where were you?"

"In France. Fine time to pick," Aidan said.

"Ah, yes! Whatever happened to that girl you went with? Curly hair?"

"Eileen? Didn't like her."

"'Didn't like her?' You went to France with her!" Gareth said, his eyebrows quirked.

"It was in France we realised we hated each other. Stranger things have happened. I haven't thought of Eileen since that time. Well, sent her a wedding present a year ago. Funny you remembering." On the eve of his and Eileen's departure for France, Talulla, who was in second year English at the time, had been visiting Lara. Eileen had noticed the way Aidan looked at her; it was as simple as that. He hadn't even been aware of it until Eileen pointed it out while they sweltered by the side of the road outside Chartres, waiting for a tow truck to come for the car.

"Who told you Alan and Ashling Leahy were out in Granny's?" he asked Gareth, recollecting himself.

"Poor Brendan O'Toole," Gareth said. "He went out there to grieve one day, after Frances's death, and he was shocked to his boots."

"He never mentioned that before, did he?"

"He wouldn't. It was only after, when Emma . . . he was saying last night he nearly blamed himself. He's not in great form, is he?"

"No, he isn't. You'd know he'd no kids of his own. When I think of the scrapes Lara used get into, and we never took our eyes off her. Some things you can't stop."

"Well, they're not kids any more," Gareth said. He gave Aidan a shrewd, melancholy look. "You're not eating much."

"May try a bit of the spring roll in a while."

Gareth pushed another beer at him. "Tell us about your friend."

"The 'Strangler'?"

"Of course."

"About everything I can tell is already in the papers," Aidan said.

"And why haven't you caught him?"

"Your questions are so original. The short answer is, he's been lucky. He's an opportunist, so he's unpredictable. He's primed to murder any female who's alone and vulnerable. But why we haven't caught him . . . He doesn't leave much evidence. Doesn't rape them." He sighed. "He'll be human wallpaper, Gareth. Some unlikely sod who gets around the highways and byways as part of his work. He'll be gone often enough that nobody says, 'Bingo! Our Sean's been down the country to visit Aunt Mary on the exact dates of all those murders, and she already dead these forty years!' He'll be some respectable-looking gobshite who mows the grass every Saturday. Or a priest would be perfect; would have been. I don't know about now." He sighed. "Grass-mowing and the priesthood eliminate you, anyway."

Gareth paused for a moment, then said, "You get too upset, you know. This isn't your line of work, Aidan, it isn't. Go back and do archaeology! Do your investigating when it's all had a chance to cool, as it were?"

Aidan laughed. "You wouldn't throw me to the piranhas of academe?"

"Look into a roomful of academics any time. It's not piranhas you'll see. We're gentle souls, most of us. You've missed your calling, definitely. You were in your element on Dalkey Island and around the place, scratching for flints." This was one of Gareth's pet theories when he'd had a few beers. Aidan the archaeologist.

Aidan looked at him indulgently, then sighed. "This Strangler case, even what has happened here, isn't what I think of as my work, Gareth. Murders – we've more of them now, to be sure, but they're still the least of what we're about. Jesus, I hope so. As long as we can keep the guns under control, we've some hope."

"Dog licences and pinched bicycles?"

"My favourite things. But sure . . . there are aspects of hunting this fellow that I like. Seeing how the lads around the country are working. What they know. How they know it. Learning better ways. Meeting, pooling the info, the bit of *craic* – what I don't like . . ."

"What?" Gareth's eyes were as remote and sad as a doctor's.

" – is dipping into this fellow's mind. Wondering how a creature who has all the empathy of a mollusc is able to cause so much pain. He's a fucker, Gareth. I hate him. I know who he'll pick. He's got me looking at women in a new way. They're vulnerable! They're light. A tap would finish them. It's not like domestic violence, that's bad, it's terrible, but – this man sizes them up. A little girl, well, sixteen, but – he squeezed out her life without a qualm. Sorry. You're too good a listener. I don't often analyse this stuff. Too busy."

"Go on," Gareth said.

"No – it's crass. I forget. You've just had a corpse dug up on your doorstep. Sorry, Gareth. Unless it's the food?"

Gareth, who had gone white, waved his hand. "It's the heat." He got up and turned down the Dimplex. Aidan watched regretfully. "As for corpses . . . please have a thought for my own field of study. Admittedly, this latest is a bit – proximate, what what what?"

"I'm not looking forward to finding out the who who who and the why why why on this one," Aidan said, but he couldn't help grinning. "Have you noticed that any time we meet we have a gloomy conversation?"

"Only the first one."

"I have corpses and you have girlfriends."

"Had."

"'Had'?"

"Nancy . . . has departed."

Aidan burst out laughing. "Sorry," he said to Gareth's nettled look, "it was just the toilet paper, remember?"

"Last time I'll invite you to use my flat."

"Four in the morning and the toilet paper under lock and key!"

"Nancy was, I admit, an economical person–"

"Did she take the wallpaper with her?"

"Not precisely. Sod off, Cummings! She did remove a small runner we had just inside the flat and, yes, some brass tacks with which it was secured to the floor . . ."

"I thought you were doomed that time," Aidan said, "doomed."

"She'd have organised all this," Gareth said.

"She wanted to," Aidan said shortly. "What happened, anyway?"

"The Trinity post falling through. She was only ever interested in living here. I'm not sorry. She was very fond of dried flowers. Great sex. But that doesn't go on forever, does it?"

"Dried flowers do. Right."

"Right. How's Talulla O'Neill?"

"Talulla?"

"Yeah."

"She's all right, I gather."

"I didn't like to ask her outright. She was down at White Rock today with Briege."

Aidan shrugged, ignoring the glint in Gareth's eyes. "The injury she got wasn't that bad. A graze – sore, and she'll have a scar or two, but . . . it was too soon after Séamus's death. Briege is devastated."

"The Tank. I thought she was a bit rattled, all right."

"The Tank is rattled. The word on the street is that she's even stopped giving out loans."

"Pity she wasn't dealing with Murnaghan, then."

Aidan fended off Gareth's efforts to steer the conversation back to Talulla, and they talked in a desultory way about Aidan's family, Mr O'Toole's drinking, the neighbourhood in general. Aidan felt there was an aura of guardianship in their talk as he filled Gareth in on the goings-on. It was almost as if their neighbourhood was a shared responsibility. His face flushed with annoyance. Gareth looked at him inquiringly, but Aidan shook his head. "A passing atavistic thought. Funny you seeing Mary de Burca and never saying," he went on.

"It just never occurred to me that anyone would think she was dead. Anyone who escaped from old de Burca was only beginning to live, in my opinion. Always going on at her. What a bastard."

"She nearly spent the roof over his head, Gareth," Aidan said mildly, "but I know that's no excuse."

"I heard him out in the garden one day," Gareth went on. "Anyone could have heard it. 'This is what I get for marrying low!' The bastard said that. To her."

"You were Mary's pet, sure."

"Oh, she liked you, too. But yes. I was her pet. I

175

was mad about her. She wasn't a snob, a fucking snob. God, we were rotten with that here."

"You were never like that."

"You remember Grandfather. Few could forget him. Sure, my mother was almost as bad."

"Ah, she was in a strange country, Gareth. And living in the same house with your grandfather? Couldn't have been easy. I was scared rigid of him."

Gareth laughed. It was a dry sound. "I was, too. So was my father. I don't think my mother was. He led her a dog's life, but she always had the comfort of knowing she was English." He shook his head. "An English Catholic, to boot! That made her rather special over there. She never got the picture. Grandfather despised the English, in a friendly sort of way. There was nothing friendly about the way he despised my mother."

"I liked her," Aidan said carefully, because Gareth's family was a taboo subject unless Gareth introduced it. "You always knew where you stood with her." Leila Cummings had always referred to Gareth's mother as "poor Muriel."

"She wasn't so bad."

There was a little silence. Aidan drummed his fingers, thoughtful. "Any ideas who the American lassie could be, if it isn't Ashling Leahy?"

"One. But I don't want to entertain it."

Aidan nodded slowly. "Neither do I," he said. "Neither do I."

Gareth said goodbye at the door and, as he closed it, Aidan felt a sharp stab of pity for him. He almost loved Gareth's house, its spaciousness, its fine textures and its tranquil beauty of proportion, but he was always relieved to get out of it and to be in the open air again. Perhaps it was a special strength Gareth had, to be able to tolerate so much emptiness under such weights of masonry and time. Perhaps it was a kind of madness.

For a moment, Aidan felt the cloying chill he remembered from long ago. That was another fantasy from his childhood, the feeling that Gareth's grandfather was standing at the window, watching him leave. Later, he realised that Mr Travers was indifferent to such small departures. He had already suffered the only one that mattered to him, his eldest son Jonathan's emigration to America. He had never been interested in Richard, Gareth's father, and he could hardly bring himself to speak to Gareth's mother Muriel, the middle-class English Catholic who insisted on bringing up Gareth in her own religion. They had all lived together under Beaulieu's graceful roof. Gareth called it the "household from hell." Now he was the only one left.

Aidan gazed at the cut-stone expanse of the frontage, at the arched ground-floor windows and the symmetrical oblongs above. Moonlight shimmered on their delicate, slightly uneven surfaces. The warmer glow behind the fanlight disappeared. Gareth had gone upstairs to bed. That was the odd feeling he'd had in the kitchen; that he was a tribesman or kinsman talking to his chieftain, who had been away. A great insight, he thought, for someone who voted Democratic Left.

Aidan pulled up the collar of his jacket. Dr McQuaid had been right. He was getting a cold. The wind stirred, and the darkness in Granny's shifted. He imagined that Granny's felt bereft of the dead woman, that she had become a part of the place and it wanted her back. "Who were you?" he said aloud. There was movement in the darkness, the trees only, but suddenly the place seemed to menace with meaning and Aidan, cursing his overactive imagination, half-stumbled back to the bright road outside and his car.

When he arrived at his flat, bone-weary, there were two messages on his machine. One was from Jimmy Meagher; the other was from Detective Esmé Dunne in Wicklow.

Chapter Twenty-Four

That night the wind whipped along the coast, testing harbour walls and trees and slates and all that could be shifted. Hanging baskets left from summer jounced on their brackets, and deciduous trees were stripped of their last leaves and scoured into their winter's sleep. Briege got up when the dustbin overturned, rolling and crashing like some Hallowe'en trick of the Minogues's. When she opened the back door, the skirts of her dressing-gown whirled behind her as if frightened by the trees' roaring and the wind's sudden whistle. In the side passage, the bin bucked and clattered, and a plastic wrapper lodged in her hair for a moment like a sticky bat. Shuddering, she locked the bin into the garage and went back to bed.

In Castle Street, the wind followed its route of seven hundred years. It flattened itself against the churches, new and old, honing the slabs above in

Begnet's so they'd be thinner than cornflakes on the Last Day, and the saint could hurl them into the brightness like confetti. It massaged the little castles' stony shoulders yet again, whispering to them of relations near and far, those who still slept, seamed, on the hill or near Carnsore; those who, hacked and oblonged, formed the Harbour at Dún Laoghaire and the Thames Embankment where, with human exiles, they endured.

Charlie MacDevitt dreamed that, instead of the costume she'd planned, she was wearing her friend's. Kevin Minogue kept saying, "But you're really beautiful!" over and over again, but suddenly she was in another costume with huge black wings like a bird's. At first she was disgusted, but then she found they worked and she flew over the hill and watched her shadow on the beach and the waves, with Kevin running below shouting, "Charlie! Charlie, come down!"

Leila Cummings simply woke up. She lay in bed listening to the wind, and prayed quietly because she felt afraid – but of what, she didn't quite know.

Gareth dreamed that his grandfather stalked ahead of him through the house, shutting doors and locking them because he had taken Uncle Jonathan's portrait from the hall.

Talulla woke up for a few moments when the wind dropped. It was the difference that disturbed her. She felt empty and tearful. Aidan Cummings. In her dream he held her, and she leaned her head on his shoulder. She touched his hair and it was dry and coarse, and that was how she knew it wasn't really Aidan at all.

Aidan, still shivering a little in the warm flat, made himself a flask of tea. It was so late that even Castle Street was empty, bits of paper tumbling through the apricot lighting in a frantic chase with their shadows. He took two Disprin, then slunk downstairs. The car drew up just as he stepped out on the footpath. O'Hare was driving. He pushed open the passenger door. "Looks like you were right," he said.

Emma checked all the locks and windows yet again and finally, exhausted, settled the chair against her bedroom door and drifted into sleep.

Chapter Twenty-Five

O'Hare was a good driver and he knew when to talk and when to keep quiet. He told Aidan what he knew: a woman's body had been found at a lay-by, on the road between the Sally Gap and Roundwood in County Wicklow, at around half past eleven. "Eejit left the pub with his girlfriend, and his driving gave her cause for alarm." Aidan could well understand this: the road was bad enough when you were sober.

"They got to the outlook there and she persuaded him to stop," O'Hare went on. "Then he persuaded her to get out of the car altogether and go for a canoodle in the sheltered spot behind, and didn't they discover the unfortunate woman there dead. That put an end to romance, anyway."

"Anything else?"

"McQuaid's on her way, effing and blinding."

Aidan smiled a little, wondering who had drawn the short straw. McQuaid preferred working in the daytime, and her comments on being woken up were as pointed as they were unrehearsed. He dozed a little, then woke as the car lurched out of a pothole.

"Bugger," O'Hare muttered, trimming his speed. He had taken a long route out of Glencree through the Sally Gap, a convergence of rounded mountains whose slopes were further softened by layers of blanket bog. The headlights glared on gorse and boulders in the desolation of scrub on either side of the twisting road, and the only thing blacker than the sky was the land itself and the gusts that caught them from time to time like great hands pushing them sideways. To their right only a low stone wall stood between them and a precipice, and Aidan had just begun to realise that he was tensing his muscles to keep the car on the road when he saw the brightness ahead.

Around the curve, the lights seemed almost nuclear after the dark landscape behind them. O'Hare slowed to a crawl, keeping as close to the side of the road as he could. He began a tortuous process of turning the car around, then stopped. "You can walk on if you want, sir," he told Aidan. "I'll back up as near as I can."

"Right."

"I'll wait."

"Thanks, Colm."

Aidan stood quietly for a moment, watching
O'Hare manoeuvre the car. Then, with flagging
steps, he approached the light. There were a
number of cars parked along the road facing
towards Dublin. He recognised the unmarked
black Corsa favoured by Jimmy Meagher and Dr
McQuaid's brown Volvo. A guard materialised out
of a shadow beside the ambulance and asked for
identification, which Aidan showed him.

There was a wide, gravelled semicircle ahead
on the left-hand side of the road. Tapes fluttered
all around it, but the main force of the wind was
muted here. Jimmy Meagher stood near the
ambulance with Chief Superintendent Murphy
from Dún Laoghaire and Superintendent Kilroy
from Wicklow. Esmé Dunne was there too, along
with a number of uniformed guards and detectives
whom Aidan didn't know. They were like figures
on a stage, somehow diminished by the glare.
Small motes of light flashed and glimmered
through the dark stand of trees behind them.
Aidan could hear snatches of Samantha
McQuaid's crisp voice instructing the technicians.

Everyone looked shaken, even Murphy. All the
other investigations had taken place during the
day. Nobody had ever come upon one of the
Strangler's victims at night, and Aidan felt an
unpleasant throb of excitement, as if he had

stumbled on the cave of a rogue animal and stood at its mouth, staring into darkness. To be so close and to see nothing. He could almost smell the bastard and he knew the others felt the same. They were staying away from the hollow where the body lay; the soft ground would almost certainly contain evidence.

Esmé Dunne, the first detective to arrive, had picked her way along the verge with plastic bags on her feet, her hands clasped behind her back. The dead woman, more girl than woman, lay fully-clothed in the hollow of grass among the trees, her legs straightened, her hands folded on her breast. Under them was a red crisp wrapper of some sort, crumpled tightly to resemble a flower. Her thick blonde hair was arranged around her head like a sunburst.

"I saw her this morning up the town," Esme told Aidan. He realised that she was trembling. It was almost imperceptible; a mixture of adrenaline and shock. "She's a traveller. Her family's in a couple of caravans just outside –" She stopped a moment.

"You knew her?"

"A bit. Aidan," she said intensely, "what is it about this man? He – mocks them. I'd have staked my life that poor Margaret would be – that she, of all people, would sense if someone wanted to hurt her." She stopped, on the verge of tears. "Jesus, I'll probably have to tell her family!"

They turned to watch as lights flared on the track behind them. It was the photographers, stepping carefully. They went over to Superintendent Kilroy.

"She's got two babies, Aidan. She keeps them beautiful. She's eighteen and the husband's over in England working and sending back money. Sure, he's only a kid himself. They want – shit! They wanted to live there and better themselves. In the meantime . . ."

A small procession was coming down the track. Two ambulancemen carried a stretcher with a black body-bag that seemed too big for the slight form within. The guards and detectives fell quiet. The stretcher was lifted into the glowing interior of the ambulance. One of the uniformed guards who had answered the call got in. In a moment it moved off, silent; only a great lump of a van, Aidan thought, without its flashing lights and klaxon. No terror, no hope.

"In the meantime," Esme whispered, her voice wavering, "she was living beside her parents. They're the worst pair of drunks in all Wicklow – they probably sent her out for a bottle. There's no other reason she'd be out at night. Fuck it!"

"Fuck it, for sure."

McQuaid plodded back along the verge, followed by a technician in a white boiler suit who loomed behind her like a tame polar bear. She carried her black bag in one hand and clutched a man's walking-stick in the other. "Bloody damp," she muttered, brandishing the stick.

Aidan and Esmé rejoined the others as McQuaid approached. "Well, gentlemen. And women," she added, seeing Esmé. "When was it you got the call? Half eleven?"

"Eleven forty-two," Kilroy said. "The couple who found her reckoned they arrived here at about twenty past. They lost their heads a bit — bolted off together in the car and never stopped till they got to Roundwood. From the way they described the scene, though, I believe it was not disturbed again until we got here."

"No. Probably not," McQuaid said heavily. "Your couple might have arrived quite soon after your murderer. The woman was almost certainly dead when he brought her here; there's not much lividity, but what there is is on her buttocks and the backs of her thighs and the soles of her feet. We found that with Una Ivory, remember. And the Bermingham woman. It's chilly, so . . ." She sighed. "Some tightness round the jaw. Temperature . . ." She shrugged, then looked at her watch. "What time is it now? Two. I suspect he

187

did it between nine and eleven. She'd almost certainly have been in a warm car, followed by her time in the cold here. I can't be sure. But, if you bring someone in, we'll have DNA aplenty for you. She's blood under her nails. And we've this as well."

On cue, the technician held up a small plastic bag. A man's earring was in it, smeared with red. "We're looking for a bloke with a very sore ear," he said. "Caught on her jumper. He wouldn't have seen it in the dark."

They all stared at it. Aidan felt suddenly powerful, his hands hollow with desire. His adversary's blood; jewellery that had passed through his skin.

The superintendent was assigning duties. Investigations would resume at first light; two guards would remain to protect the scene. Dr McQuaid presented herself at Aidan's side. "Aha! Detective Cummings. How's the flu?" She pointed her stick at him, then moved away towards the road.

Jimmy Meagher walked over to him. "Will we have a word in the morning?" Aidan nodded. He gave Esmé Dunne a quiet squeeze on the shoulder as he left, and she tapped his elbow with her fist. She looked better.

He dozed in the car on the way home, O'Hare

driving silently, respecting his need for sleep. Aidan had not seen the dead woman so he could only imagine her, her golden hair fanning round her ruined young face. He slept fitfully, waking briefly when O'Hare seemed to be heading straight for a stone wall. When he rounded the curve safely, Aidan began drifting again. It was not the murder he had just visited but the one in Granny's that grasped him now. He rubbed his hand across his forehead.

Boyle would go to see Alan de Burca in the morning. A Mrs Thomas had phoned up about Ashling Leahy. She owned the bed and breakfast where Ashling had stayed. Mrs Thomas took in summer visitors; she'd a nice double room "en suite." Three years ago, "the American girl," Ashling Leahy, had left without paying her bill. Her backpack was gone, yes, and the girls owed her for five days –they were to pay her at the end of the week – and then Ashling quarrelled with her boyfriend, or so Mrs Thomas heard afterwards.

Mrs Thomas wasn't that sorry to see the backs of them, even though they had cost her. The other one wasn't so boisterous, though Mrs Thomas actually liked Ashling the better of the two. They were divils for coming in late, and she didn't like that – Ashling was, anyway. The other girl, Janet, was more the tourist, going into the Genealogical

Office, taking walks – Ashling loved the pubs, she loved them. Mrs Thomas had sent bills to her home in the US (Ohio), and to the other girl's, Winton was her last name; but there was no response from either.

Boyle was a wicked mimic, and he had Mrs Thomas's breathless delivery off pat. Aidan hoped he hadn't noticed that his news was being taken badly. Well, one thing was interesting: nobody had ever mentioned that Ashling Leahy was travelling with another girl. Aidan leaned his head on his hand. If Ashling had gone missing, why had the other girl said nothing?

Mrs Thomas would search through her "old rubbish and receipts" to see if she still had Ashling Leahy's address. She was sure the girls had only scarpered, but anyway . . . Mrs Thomas had returned home from the cinema and a cup of tea at her friend's and, when she finally had a look at the paper, she had phoned Boyle. He would follow it up in the morning.

Aidan got to bed at four; still he lay awake, hearing the bookshop sign squeak next door and the toilet door on his landing click open and shut as it always did in a gale. When he dreamed, it was of the day he stumbled on Alan and Emma preparing a bonfire in Granny's, but in the dream they were in a house where everything creaked and moved. Something was coming, but they laughed at his warnings and when he, in his fear, pushed them ahead of him into the great carved chest to hide, he found himself alone and falling through a sightless labyrinth with walls he could sense but never touch as they closed above him.

Chapter Twenty-Six

Emma was in the hall when the soft tapping started. It was seven in the morning and still dark. She put her flask of tea down very gently on the carpet so that it wouldn't make a sound. She had turned the light on in the kitchen for a few minutes while she boiled the kettle. That was her mistake. He must have seen. Silently, she took off her slippers and crept barefoot towards the phone on the hall table. The tapping stopped. She froze and held her breath to listen, but she could hear no footsteps going away. Then she blundered against the umbrella-stand.

To her horror, she could hear the flap on the letterbox squeak open. A glimmer of street lighting was immediately obscured by black shadow, and something moving. A hand.

"Emma, let me in."

"You!"

"Emma . . ."

"No!"

"Coward."

She found her slipper and threw it. Hard.

The flap reopened. "Emma."

She hesitated, then approached the door. Instead of unlatching it, she sat down on the floor and leaned against it, sighing. Out of sight of the letterbox, her hand played across the wood silently, like a caress.

"Emma?"

"Go away, Alan."

"Only if you come with me. And Iseult."

"I can't."

"I'll stay out here then, till you do."

"You want me killed."

"I want to get you out! Let me in, Em."

"No."

"He's locked up, for Christ's sake!"

"He's not. He's out. Since last night. I'd keep looking over my shoulder there, if I were you."

There was a pause.

Emma, her mouth drooping, pressed her cheek, then her palm against the door as if it were something living.

"Emma, I'm freezing my arse off here. I have to stick it out so far to lean into your bloody letterbox that my coat won't even cover it! Look –"

"Go away, Alan." She started to cry but

silently, forehead and both palms against the door.

"Emma!" She could hear the rustle of his clothes inches away from her, and she felt the wood reverberate a little as he pressed against the other side. "I know about Iseult," he whispered. "I don't mind. I don't mind about anything, but we've got to talk! Em, I know everything, and I don't give a flying fuck – !"

She opened the door so quickly that he staggered. "Lock it!" she whispered, and then she flew up the stairs.

Charlie MacDevitt woke up that morning in her parents' bed. It was the perfect place to remember what she had dreamed and what she had seen the night before. Safe in the lingering warmth and loving smells, she relived the power of her flight and ignored its strangeness; something in her wasn't ready for the cold freedom that was part and parcel of the joy.

It wasn't the dream that had sent her scuttling to her parents' room, however, but what she had seen from her window when O'Neill's bins had taken off like the hammers of hell and she had plummeted into wakefulness as, beneath the very shadows of her wings, the boulders hurtled down the side of Dalkey Hill. The round dial of the clock beside her bed had glowed like a pale green jack-o'-lantern: it was four am and already Hallowe'en.

Shivering a little, Charlie crept to her window. Most of the clouds had blown away, and the sky was faintly moonlit. The hill, so friendly in daytime, now loomed too near, like a huge featureless beast; and mist, discernible only as a faint blur on the darkness, still clung among the dishevelled black shadows in Granny's. It was then, just as she was congratulating herself on being the first child awake on Hallowe'en, that Charlie saw the light. It was no more than a faint gold glimmer far back in the wood, like the eye of a great cat. While she watched, it disappeared, obscured perhaps by some tossing branch. Then it winked as if to say, "I too am awake. Watching."

Hairs prickling on her neck, Charlie had looked neither left nor right as she sped to the safety of her parents' room. As she snuggled between them, she remembered again the grotesque sorrow of the skull in Granny's, its leaning jaw and hollow eyes. It was a long while before the gentle snores on either side rebuilt the ramparts against the unknown.

Briege woke around five, wondering how she had slept at all. Alan had meant well, phoning her like that; she was sure of it. But what was she to do? He was right. She should tell Talulla. If Alan knew, others would. But how could she do it, how could she put it so that Talulla wouldn't be devastated?

Talulla gazed into Aidan's eyes. So it was true. He did love her. He had kissed her scar.

He giggled.

"Lara!"

"You don't half snore," said Lara Cummings. She was perched at the end of Talulla's bed like an expensive leprechaun.

"That's the pain-killers. What in the name of God did you do to your hair?"

"You like?"

"Sort of. No."

"You're right, it's a bit much." Lara stretched to look in the mirror, raising the top, sleek layer of her hair, which was frankly ultraviolet. "Prezzie." She tossed a small, oblong box near Talulla's hand.

"*Dune!* Oh, I love *Dune.*"

"It's too old for you, but –"

"It's gorgeous. Thanks. I thought you'd never get here. Why'd you come?"

"Why'd I come? Well, we don't want our Alan in stir for the Leahy tart, do we?"

"If you do your cockney accent, I'll go back to sleep," Talulla said, pulling at the duvet.

Lara looked at her closely. Her wide-eyed, unrelenting scrutiny reminded Talulla of a Persian kitten she'd once had and she laughed.

"You still look weeshy," Lara said, accusing.

"Well, I'm not. I'm back to work tomorrow. You don't look at all weeshy yourself. I love the suit."

Lara beamed. "It's a fourteen. I'm wearing it for Murnaghan. It's sexy, isn't it?"

"Extremely. You're on to everything, Lar. The road and the corpse. How'd you find out? I tried to phone . . ."

"The evening paper, followed by a phone call to Mum, who is wheezing like a sheep. I just dug it out of her. Shielding her precious Aidan from my presence, as usual. I wasn't going to say a word about his miserable investigation." She drew a long breath. "Joking aside, what's going on? How much do they know?"

"Nobody's saying, but I think they may know just about everything. Mr O'Toole has pinpointed a time. He says nothing could have happened in Granny's that he wouldn't have noticed, except around the time his wife died. And you know it's almost definite she was American?"

"But did they hear about the fight? Did anyone besides Mum and myself hear it, I mean? You see, I don't think Mum ever mentioned it to Aidan."

"*What?*"

"I know," Lara said. "It's unthinkable that Mum could see a spot of mud on her toe without running to tell Aidan about it, never mind a screaming row virtually in the back garden, but apparently she didn't. Not the whole thing, anyway." Lara hesitated and then said, "I suppose there's no way in the wide world it could've been your mother in the grave? Not meaning to be tactless."

"Not tactless, I never met the woman. No, if our Hope gets the chop, it'll be in a more elegant spot than Granny's Wood, honey. It'll be Cannes or Martha's Vineyard or the Concorde loo."

"I'll bet you're just like her."

Talulla's shriek brought Briege bounding up the stairs. She gaped when she saw Lara. "How'd you get in?"

"The key, of course. Under the flowerpot. I adore the security arrangements favoured by the gardaí. Mum goes for the plastic stone beside the step."

"Well, disregard my first greeting, dear," Briege told her, "there's nobody in this world I'd rather see." She went away again, promising to make tea and to search the freezer for bread.

"She looks desperate," Lara said when she'd shut the door.

"I'm worried about her."

"Do you believe Alan did it?"

"No."

"Um . . . ?" Lara raised her eyebrows and made squeezing motions with her hands.

"Not him, either. It's not his form, apparently. But I think they've given up on the Strangler much too quickly, Lara. So she was buried, and he doesn't bury people now. What if she was his first? And the first one we do know about was in Sandycove, hardly a mile away. He almost has to be local; he knows this area. In the meantime we'll be turned inside out, it's inevitable, and it'll all be dragged up again about Emma and Alan and – "

"Wonder Woman, right," Lara said.

They sat quietly, glum. Lara pinched at the duvet cover. She made three tiny pleats, then let them go. "Problem is . . ."

"Yeah."

"Our Em has been right on course for the past three years, hasn't she? It would explain her marrying Declan, everything," Lara said.

"A three-year guilt trip."

"A guilt *saga*," Lara said. "I just don't see where Alan fits in, or doesn't. Because how could she have managed without him? Sure, her parents were there, she was still at home, the place was crawling."

"I don't know."

"This leaves you in a bad spot, doesn't it?"

"I'm not involved in this investigation at all," Talulla said, reddening.

"Come on!"

"I'm not! If I found out anything certain I'd have to pass it on, but there's nothing certain, and that's that." She glared at Lara.

"Well, Tully, just so you know that if I find out anything certain myself, I won't be passing it on to you or to Aidan," Lara said thoughtfully.

She picked up the little atomiser she had brought Talulla and sprayed it into the air. *Dune* eddied around them, powdery, sweet and reassuring. Talulla thought it was like sniffing a perfect mother-child relationship. She reached out and sprayed it on her wrists and her hair.

Chapter Twenty-Seven

Aidan was surprised when he looked in the mirror that morning. Instead of the whiskery red face he expected, based on the inexplicable heat of his bed, a wan self looked back at him with glittering blue eyes, smudged underneath. "West of Ireland eyes," his mother called them.

Everything felt more real: the hot and cold drops in the shower spray more separate than usual, and the drag of the razor across his face particularly sensuous, dangerous and long. It didn't suit him to think that Alan de Burca could be a murderer. Well, he didn't think it; yet the idea of Alan even "helping with enquiries" appalled him. Aidan had once pushed Alan's pram around de Burca's yard while Mary de Burca, dressed for some party or other, teetered along the clothes-line in her knee-high platform boots, grabbing at the sheets before it could rain. Alan was tiny then, laughing and crowing in the pram, not like Lara at home who screeched like a banshee half the night. Aidan shoved a box of Disprin into his pocket as he left his flat.

He got to Dún Laoghaire just in time for Lorcan White's phone call from Wicklow.

Lorcan was waiting for him in a green Corsa outside the station in Wicklow town. The wind was whipping along the Murrough, chopping the water into unfriendly grey waves. The swans were nowhere to be seen.

There were a few rough edges to Lorcan's driving. He had been at his brother's wedding until six that morning. "I'm at me greatest, but not at me best," he said, snipping past a lorry. The interview could be a bit tricky, he explained, so would Aidan mind conducting it?

"Will I live to?"

"Arragh, you poor pet!" But he swerved on to the shoulder and stopped beside a gate. The sheep in the pasture beyond drifted towards the hedge.

"Right," Lorcan said. He rubbed his eyes. "Mr O'Riordan phoned an hour ago. They're all in a state, that's himself and his wife and their daughter. It happened yesterday evening, but they didn't phone us then because the girl was too upset. I know, it's unbelievable, she bit the fella and all. Then she scrubbed out her nails. They couldn't stop her. They were all three of them distraught. You'll see why.

"Marie's their youngest," he went on. "She's the only one left at home. She's a little bit backward, apparently. I don't know in what way. We'll see. She works over in the supermarket – Blake's – packing bags. When her dad went to collect her yesterday, she'd already gone. She took off on a few other occasions – told young people she knew that she needed a lift, just for the bit of chat – so he wasn't worried. She's, like, well-known."

"So was Vinny Ruane."

"Well, right! He was so confident that she was OK that he even did his own shopping before he went home. His wife couldn't believe it when he arrived back late and no Marie. That's probably what really upset the girl – she falls in the gate two minutes after her da, and sees her quiet little mother clawing the ears off him and calling him every name in the book. So that's them back in their shells –they're 'not that kind of people', right? – and the girl's in her own little shell because she knows what she did caused the ructions."

"They waited till this morning to get in touch with anybody at all?" Aidan asked.

"They had the doctor in last night. They've got a woman GP, and they got her to ascertain that Marie wasn't raped or badly hurt. The thing is, the

GP's visit upset her so much that she took a little fit – nothing serious – but they weren't about to add us to the mix. That's the suss. Now."

"If it's our man, he's been hyperactive to say the least."

"Third time lucky, if it was. Esmé phoned me this morning at seven. My wife wasn't too pleased. Couldn't even speak. Passed it over to me."

"Esmé was a bit shook."

"Jesus, can you blame her."

Lorcan threw the car into gear, and once more they hurtled over little roads, rounding blind corners at a speed that made Aidan sweat, and he was relieved when they pulled up at a neat bungalow about three miles outside the town.

Aidan reckoned that it dated from the nineteen-fifties. It was solidly built with a tile roof, its walls finished with white pebbledash. Both the house and the garden wall had been recently painted. The windows had been replaced with aluminium double-glazing, and a tiny double-glazed porch jutted coldly from the front door. The overall effect, enhanced by the borderless square of grass in front, was of chilly, dutiful care.

Mrs O'Riordan answered the door. Her expression was subdued. Aidan thought its main ingredient was shame. He was reminded of an expression of his grandmother's: Mrs O'Riordan felt she had "let herself down."

She brought them into the sitting-room, which was furnished much as he would expect with a sofa and two chairs, a rather heavy oak coffee table and a couple of small occasional tables with cheap but tasteful lamps on them. The dining area was in the other half of the long, double room. Its large window looked out on a line of conifers which did not quite manage to obscure the view of the mountain beyond. Sideboard, table with a centre leaf, six chairs, all in a light, yellowish veneer. There was a good thick carpet throughout, a dusky pink colour that came from a more modern era than the furniture. Everything clashed in a stifled way, and Aidan remembered growing up in a house of many children and not quite enough money, where everything was a bargain from the auction rooms or the summer sales. The effect in his own house had been cheerful; the clashes produced a kind of energy. He found these rooms draining until the picture on the far wall caught his eye.

It was a riot of primary colours, wild, generous blobs and circles sprayed across the paper. It was abstract, but it observed its own laws of proportion and rhythm. Yellows, oranges, turquoises, sapphires, greens, exploded from left to right in a shimmer of joy. It seemed to have every colour in it but red. The picture had been framed expensively and with great care.

Lorcan cleared his throat. Aidan realised that he had missed his introduction. "I'm sorry. I was admiring the picture," he said foolishly. Fine start!

As it happened, it was. The slight figure beside the door into the hallway relaxed a little. Marie O'Riordan had been hovering as if poised for flight. Mr O'Riordan stood next to her, his expression grim.

Mrs O'Riordan murmured for them to sit down, and they ended up with all three O'Riordans on the sofa together like hostages and Lorcan and Aidan across from them in the huge upholstered chairs.

Marie had a round, tear-stained face, bobbed brown hair and the rather childlike shoes and clothing that parents sometimes choose for vulnerable people, to signal to the world to be gentle. Unfortunately not everyone read it like that, Aidan thought, and wondered if the girl would be as well off in Doc Martens and a mini. Maybe not a mini.

The parents, hangdog, were still avoiding one another's eyes. Their great fear for Marie had almost materialised, and they, in their own minds at least, had been found wanting.

Mr O'Riordan cleared his throat and said formally, "Marie may be able to help you and she may not. She's been very upset. We all have." He then made a little speech that both Lorcan and Aidan understood was more for Marie's benefit than theirs.

Mr O'Riordan had a disillusioned look that Aidan found familiar. He had seen it in some Dublin *gaelgoirí*, and his eyes were drawn again to the lovely picture on the wall.

Mrs O'Riordan fished out cigarettes and offered them round while her husband was still speaking. She wasn't as mouse-like as Aidan had first supposed; "impassive" was a better word. She had the stubborn look of a reliable but uninspired head girl. The cigarettes, he guessed, were her response to life's unfairness and unpredictability. The parents were like two book-ends, holding Marie in place on the sofa. Had the tear-stained blue eyes a gleam of rebellion in them?

"And what age are you, Marie?" he asked softly.

"Twenty." And dressed for twelve, he thought. Sure, even Charlie MacDevitt wouldn't be caught dead in that gear. The parents moved restlessly. "And do you never wear Doc Martens? Or trainers?"

Marie favoured him with a sudden broad, collusive smile as her mother drew in her breath with a hiss. "Mam doesn't like them," she said.

207

"Do you get a bit fed up from time to time, Marie?"

"No! I've a job. I'm not fed up."

"The job's important to you, is it?"

The girl burst into tears.

"What's this got to do with any bloody thing?" said Mr O'Riordan.

"I want to go to Blake's!" the girl wailed.

"That's where Marie works?"

"How can we trust her again?" Her mother stubbed out her cigarette with a wrench. "You got into the car with a man! You promised you'd never do that."

Marie seemed to shrink. She put her head down and swayed a little, sniffing.

"Would you do that again, Marie?" asked Aidan gently. "Get in the car with some man?" She shook her head, grabbed a fold of her skirt and twisted it. "If he's the bloke we think, Marie may be only the second person who's got away from him. She only made the one mistake, and you won't make that one again, sure you won't, Marie?"

"No!"

Mr O'Riordan looked at his watch.

"Now, Marie – this man was in the supermarket last night? No? Had he ever been?" Aidan's heart was beginning to sink a little.

He'd a blue car. Aidan groaned inside. His hair?

Brown. He was bald, Marie remembered, glancing sideways at her father.

"Bald like your Dad? Or bald like Lorcan here?" Aidan asked, nodding at Lorcan's receding hairline.

"Bald like you!" said Marie, and pointed at Aidan. Her face cleared, and she gave a sudden infectious peal of laughter at her own joke.

"Bald like a black haystack, then," he said, biting his lip with disappointment.

"Look, you see the way it is," Mr O'Riordan said, sighing.

His wife shot him a glance that was worse than hatred, Aidan thought – it was simple dislike.

"Just a moment, if you don't mind, Mr O'Riordan." Aidan was insistent. "I think Marie's telling us something. Marie – how is it that the man is both bald and brown-haired, and yet he's got an ugly black mop on him like me?"

For a moment the girl's face flushed with confusion and effort, and then she made an unexpectedly graceful gesture with her hands as if lifting something off her head. "His mop came off!" she cried.

"Off with the mop. And underneath – bald and brown-haired, is that it?"

Marie nodded, laughing, and then her face crumpled.

"You were scared that time it came off?"

She nodded.

"Sure you were, but you did well. You were great to get away from him and come here. Better than any other girl who's met him. And you gave him a bit of your own, Marie? Scraped him, did you?"

Marie glanced at her mother, who, red-faced, gave her a little nod. "I washed my nails," Marie said sullenly. "But I didn't scrape him. I bit him."

"I understand. Sure, you wouldn't want to be leaving the likes of him under your nails. But tell us, Marie, did you scrape or hit his face at all?"

The girl moved uneasily on the sofa. Her eyes filled with tears. "All right. You've done grand." Aidan reckoned it was her sheer volatility that had saved her.

Well, that was the wig; but a blue car, not a red one.

Aidan could tell from the way Lorcan was sitting that there was another question to be asked. Lorcan would not break the rapport by asking it himself. "Tell me, Marie," Aidan said slowly, "did you notice any numbers on the car at all?"

Lorcan seemed to relax.

Mrs O'Riordan wanted to say something, but Lorcan warned her with his eyes.

"I did."

"Get your foolscap and a pen, Marie," Mr O'Riordan said quietly. The girl got up and hurried out of the room. "She has to write them out herself." He looked at his wife. "Why we never thought . . . !" She shook her head slowly.

Marie returned with a rumpled pad of foolscap and a Biro. She took this in her left hand, hesitated a moment, then slowly drew large, scrawling numbers and letters. She paused, then on the bottom half of the page she wrote seven numbers. Aidan recognised the "85" prefix for the Dalkey area. She turned to the next page of foolscap and wrote a very long series of numbers, followed by two at the end which she added in tiny writing. Then, frowning, she wrote a letter and another two numbers, and shrugged. Sighing, she handed the pad to her father. "Good girl," he said. "Good girl."

Aidan knelt beside her, pointing at the first series. "These were outside the car. On the plates."

She nodded.

"And this?"

She drew her finger across the back of her hand and giggled.

"On his hand?"

She snatched up the Biro and wrote the same numbers on the back of her own hand, except they didn't all fit.

"Good. I understand. And this one?"

She frowned.

"I'd say that's his mileage," said Mr O'Riordan. "Was that on his speedometer, Marie? Behind the steering wheel?"

"Yeah. Dad, I couldn't see the other one."

"What one?"

"That." She jabbed her finger as if pointing at something in front of her and a little to the left.

"On the windscreen?"

"Yeah."

"She may remember those later," Mr O'Riordan said softly.

Mrs O'Riordan leaned forward, intense. "Will that man . . . ?" She nodded towards her daughter, who, oblivious and now serene, was writing the numbers more neatly on a third page of foolscap.

"I doubt there'll be any trouble like that," Aidan said. "In fact, with this sort of information he mightn't be loose to trouble anyone for long."

Lorcan said, "Keep her with you today, of course. You'd probably do that, anyway. But after that . . . wouldn't she be safer at work than climbing the walls at home?"

Marie tore off a page of foolscap and gave it to Aidan. A round, cartoon-like face. Above it, suspended, a dark, furry cloud. On the head itself, short tiny lines like stubble, with a clear expanse in the middle. An earring on the left ear. The shape of an arm was drawn at the side. In the middle of the forearm was a semicircle of little dashes: the bite. Before they could ask her more, Marie fled, blushing, into the back of the house.

As they left, Aidan saw Mrs O'Riordan put her arm through her husband's, just for a moment. If he had blinked, he'd have missed it.

Lorcan had phoned in the registration numbers at once, and as they drove back towards the town, the sea now a sharp dazzle below them, the news came back to them on the radio. The car, a blue Escort, was owned by a woman named Ailbhe MacBride. Nothing was known about her. She lived in Cabinteely.

The telephone number belonged to a marine outfitter's in Dalkey.

Chapter Twenty-Eight

Briege thought there must be better ways to spend your bank holiday Monday than trying to foil Jason "the Fleecer" Murnaghan. The gardaí had left Granny's and, holiday or not, the workmen were back on the site. Mr O'Toole and Mr Lawless had been out since daybreak blocking the gap in de Burca's wall. Mrs Lawless and Briege were phoning all the residents of Thorn Crest and Thorn Grove to establish a rota to block the digger bodily, if need be.

This had opened a Pandora's box of neighbourhood agendas and grievances. "If only there had been such immediate support when we'd all the trouble with the drains," was one reply. "No, I certainly won't be available!"

"Sure, why wouldn't he put in a road?" said another. "T'would root out the courting couples! Didn't I find two condoms just the other side of my wall?"

"Well, thanks be to God they're using them," Briege said.

"They were still in their little wrappers!" barked the neighbour. "I don't know what's worse, not knowing what's going on at all, or knowing they're not using their condoms. If that man does run a road through, I only hope he'll light it!"

"Surely a road through there would mean we could park at the back of our houses," said another thoughtfully. "One might even get permission for a mews house at the bottom of the garden. It could face out on the road."

The last of the refusals was the most telling. "The place has been a menace for years! Kids running wild. How, in the name of all that's holy, can we object to it being opened up? A woman was shagging murdered and buried in it, without a single one of us knowing! I think this is the tip of the iceberg," said the neighbour, and maintained that the entire area should be excavated and sifted for corpses.

"Holy God!" Briege said afterwards. "This has opened a right can of worms. Anyway, we've enough people to go on until it's dark. I hardly think even Murnaghan will have those men bashing around under arc-lights."

"And he's no planning permission at all?" Lara and Talulla were still sitting at the kitchen table, feeling guilty about not being more active for the cause.

"He understands Irish planning permission," Briege said. "It's called the *fait accompli*."

"I thought there was less of that now," Lara said.

"Well, there is, pet, but Murnaghan's old-fashioned. How's your mother this morning, Lara, is she all right?"

"She is, but I'll go and look in on her anyway."

Talulla went too. Briege didn't know how to stop her without being obvious, and besides, she still couldn't think how to tell her about Hope. As always with Talulla, the best thing was probably to come right out with it.

Briege went up to her room and knelt beside her bed. "I'm sorry I was superstitious," she said humbly. "It was a lack of trust. Please don't let this be number three. Just to mock me. Since threes don't exist." She blessed herself. "Except the Trinity. You can hardly blame – sorry," she added quickly. "Just please, please let Hope still be alive somewhere. Let her be all right."

Séamus was wicked not to let Hope see Talulla, never even to tell the girl she had come. It would have been three years ago. Talulla had been nineteen. She had the right to make her own mind up about such things.

He'd had their phone number changed overnight that summer. He claimed there had been a threat, and Briege had never questioned it. Hope must have tried to get in touch. Then she'd arrived.

Oh, sweet Jesus. Briege had no reason at all to disbelieve Alan about Séamus's threats. Alan had been out in Granny's sulking or fooling and he'd heard Hope and Séamus. It was a right shouting match, and the kitchen windows were wide open.

"I don't know how you found us here, Hope, but if you ever show your face – !"

"I'll be here for a week, Séamus, and I'm going to see my daughter," a cutting American voice replied.

"You're not." And then Séamus said almost casually, "I'd kill you first, Hope. No problem."

Alan raced through his own garden and around to get a look at Hope. He saw her go off in a taxi. She was the image of Talulla, and raging. Alan had said to himself, "She'll be back." He had deliberated about whether or not to tell Talulla, but it was just at that time that everything went wrong between himself and Emma.

"Anyone could have seen Talulla's mother, Briege, and thought nothing of it," he'd told her on the phone. "I'm probably the only one to have heard her and Séamus shouting. I'm only telling you so you won't get a surprise."

Briege had thanked him profusely, thinking as she did that she had underestimated him. Not telling Talulla at the time, or even now, showed a delicacy in him that surprised her. Poor lad, poor lad. Perhaps he simply understood what it was like to lose a mother in murky circumstances.

Briege had yet to contact Emma. She was needed for the rota, too. Her line had been engaged all morning. Life was strange. Briege had known her own brother and Alan and Emma all their lives and there had been moments during these last two and a half days that she had believed, however briefly, that any one of them could be a murderer. She wondered if that was because it was true.

Someone might even be thinking that she could be a murderer herself. With that thought, she picked up the phone.

Chapter Twenty-Nine

"You won't mind leaving here?" Alan nodded at the bedroom window and the delicate, tangled branches of the beech outside.

"With you and Iseult, no," Emma said.

"I'll have to see Aidan again."

Emma curled closer to him.

"It was being apart drove us mad, Emma."

"So Ashling's probably alive somewhere, the cow."

Alan stirred, restless. "Why wouldn't she be? Who else would have wanted to top her?"

"Anyone who met her?"

"Emma – !"

"Listen, you. Yesterday morning when I saw that – thing – I was certain it was Ashling, I'd wished her dead so often. I went down to the church and lit candles for her. To apologise. Well, maybe to appease her so she wouldn't pursue some kind of eternal vengeance, and you would never be caught. And I was only coming out of there and I met you. My hair should be white. Allow me a few catty comments. I've earned them."

"You're a better person than I am, Em."

"Yes."

"I'd never have lit a candle for her. She showed me I was a shite."

"Well, somebody had to."

"God, I've missed you. Are you very sore?" he asked hungrily, kissing her.

"Oh, I'll survive."

"Don't move. I'll be back." He threw Emma's dressing-gown over his back and padded down to the phone in the hall. His flatmate in Australia was just home from the pub. He finally found Alan's address book under his bed.

"I don't think I can read it. You've crossed it out."

"Run a pencil or something over the back of it, then. Just do some bloody thing!"

Alan's flatmate, breathing heavily, produced a US area code, a few numbers and most of an address in Columbus, Ohio. "What's going on?"

"Tell you later. Thanks."

"Bye."

Alan stood in the hall, with the strong impression that he had missed something. A change in the light? A car?

For a moment he was rooted to the spot, frightened that he was not where he was at all; that longing had fooled him into thinking he was home in Ireland, with Emma upstairs waiting to make love again. What if his hand on the phone became transparent, or if he woke up ?

There was a movement behind him. Emma sat on the top of the stairs watching him, her elbow on her knee, her chin cupped in her hand. Her long black hair tumbled curling around her shoulders, and his fingers tingled with the memory of how warm it was, how silky.

He looked up the number of Dún Laoghaire garda station in the phone book, hating the awkward dead weight of it in his hands when all he wanted to do was –

Aidan was gone for the day. Alan left Emma's number for him to call.

Before he was halfway up the stairs, he had forgotten the fleeting change in the light as someone passed the window, and the sound of a car being driven away.

Chapter Thirty

Ailbhe MacBride, the owner of the blue Escort, lived in Cabinteely. It was a suburb just west of Dalkey that Aidan had never liked. It wasn't up or down; it wasn't in sight of the sea. It had no river and little tillage as far as he knew, though it might have been good land before it was built over. "Síle's Cabin." The image that came to his mind when he thought of "Síle" was of a wide-faced woman with coal-black hair and hard eyes, leaning thick forearms over the half-door. Behind her, darkness. Mouldy thatch. The colonialist's picture of the Irish, but with power.

Ailbhe MacBride did not have black hair. Her hair, cropped close to her scalp, was the colour of rust, her face stone-pale with strong cheekbones. Aidan was impressed immediately by her large, pear-shaped breasts, which shifted under her curdled green jumper without restraint or joy. Her thighs, after her breasts' exuberance, were disappointingly ordinary. She wore tight, faded denims that were revealing but not welcoming. Nothing about Ailbhe MacBride was welcoming. Aidan reckoned she was in her mid-thirties.

She shared some attributes of Aidan's imaginary Síle. She was a large woman, almost as tall as himself, and a slattern: the thin grass in the square of front garden leaned sullenly away from the wind, exposing muddy partings. The house itself, a small semi on a street of others like it, had the blank, indefinably scarred look of property that is rented. Just inside the front door, a mirror hung crookedly. There was a smell of paint, oily, astringent and sweet at once.

MacBride's face was impassive as Jimmy told her who they were, and that they wanted to ask her about the blue car parked in front of the house. Her eyes, long, hazel goat's eyes, narrowed a little as he spoke. "Could we come inside?"

She pursed her lips. "No," she said indifferently, and waited.

"Would you prefer to come with us to the station?"

After a moment, in which she almost showed an expression, she shrugged and turned into the house, leaving the door open behind her. They followed. She exuded a musky odour, as if she slept in her loose jumper and it chafed the scent out of her. Aidan found that he disliked her intensely; at the same time, she fascinated him. He felt he couldn't leave the house until something was resolved.

She faced them in the sitting-room, arms akimbo. Aidan felt chilled. The air in that room had no life. There were two chairs and a sofa, a coffee table with plenty of blotches and rings, and a small television in the corner. Everything had a film of dust over it. There were ashes in the fireplace and a few clinkers, remnants of a fire that must have died a week ago.

Jimmy cleared his throat. "We've reason to believe your car might have been used in the commission of a crime, ah, Ms MacBride."

MacBride looked impatient, then sceptical. She scratched one white forearm. Her hands were wide, veined and muscular, the nails short like a man's and stained with traces of vermilion and umber that looked curiously beautiful against the pale flesh. Her skin's natural shadows were blue. Aidan felt her eyes on him.

"I didn't use the car yesterday."

"Did you notice it gone?" Jimmy said patiently.

"I was working."

"Where do you work?"

"Here."

Jimmy, who was married to a woman whose

idea of working at home was having the place spotless and attractive, couldn't stop his eyes from darting around the sitting-room. MacBride's full lips curled. With one strong movement, she parted the sliding doors that led to the dining-room.

Aidan stared into the eyes of a woman, a woman whose face was scarcely visible through the curling, clutching stems of convolvulus that crawled up her body, knotting hideously at her neck. He knew he was looking at something marvellous, but he swallowed and tasted bile. It was the woman's eyes: terror. Disbelief.

Smaller pictures leaned against the wall, one cropped in composition, of two male hands around a throat, the chin only a sliver at the top.

"That's my work," MacBride said, ignoring their silence. "What crime are you talking about?"

"An attempted abduction," Jimmy said.

MacBride said nothing. She put her fist on her hip and raised her eyebrows. It was all Jimmy could do not to take a step backwards.

"Do you really not know what crime?" Aidan asked her softly. He nodded at the pictures.

As her face was changing, they heard a door slam outside, and through the window Aidan saw the car: red. A key turned in the hall-door. MacBride hadn't moved, though she was scratching her arm again. Long red weals began to show on it.

Chapter Thirty-One

There was nothing about the man to suggest what he was, not even the look in his eyes. He had a receding hairline, just as Marie O'Riordan had suggested in her sketch, and his light brown hair was trimmed to fuzz. He looked to be in his early thirties. Aidan saw nothing about him to dislike except the way he adjusted the mirror in the hall. He used his hands in an odd way, as if they were valuable. That was all, except for the way he ran when he saw them reflected in the mirror, peering at him like three gargoyles through the open door of the sitting-room. Ailbhe MacBride had made no sign to warn him.

She was after him before they could move, springing like a panther on to his back when he was halfway to the car, shrieking and tearing. Aidan wanted nothing so much as a bucket of water, but it would have been no good. The lads who had been waiting around the corner moved in and helped separate them. Both were bleeding.

The man, panting, handcuffed, smiled at Ailbhe MacBride. Aidan's stomach turned. It was the saddest thing he had ever seen, and the most chilling.

"Bastard!" she wailed. "Monster!" Two guards still held her arms, but the strength had gone out of her. "Bastard . . . !" It was like keening. Aidan's skin prickled with horror. The man laughed at his lover; there was a queer tenderness in the mockery. Neither of them seemed to feel physical pain, though the man's face was scored with scratches. The splotches of blood on Ailbhe MacBride's green jumper looked black in the fading light.

They were both cautioned. Jimmy went with the man, whose name was Basil Hughes, and some uniformed guards to Cabinteely garda station. Aidan remained with the others and Ailbhe MacBride. He could have done with a more experienced woman garda, he was thinking, or even Talulla, with her quirky perceptions – no, he didn't want Talulla in this place. They brought MacBride back into the house. Garda Sarah Conlon, white-faced and quietly overwhelmed, stayed beside her. MacBride asked permission to wash and to change her jumper. Aidan made her wait until a second woman garda would arrive.

One between her and the window, and another to restrain her if need be. He sent lads up ahead to remove razors, glass.

When Sergeant Whelan arrived a few minutes later, she gave Aidan a shrewd look. "You should be home in your bed," she told him out of the corner of her mouth.

"What?" he said coldly.

Whelan, who was an old hand, simply threw up her eyes.

"You'll want to change that," she told Ailbhe MacBride, who had refused to sit down or move from the hall. "Better come now, don't you think? They've cautioned you? Come now, and we'll find a jumper. Have you anything that's just been through the wash?"

Ailbhe MacBride's face brightened; for a moment her expression was almost childlike. She led them to the kitchen, a room that, like the sitting-room, was tidy in its sheer sparseness. On a drying rack among other clothes, underwear mostly, was a jumper. She squeezed it with one hand, then stood silent and irresolute.

"Sure, that's sodden," Garda Whelan said. "Where's your hot press? On the landing?"

Ailbhe MacBride nodded. "There might be one there," she said. These were almost her first words since she had been dragged spitting and shrieking from Basil Hughes. Whelan trotted upstairs; Aidan and Conlon waited. MacBride seemed to forget about them. She went to the sink and splashed cold water over and over her face, washing the blood away from her nose, which had almost stopped bleeding. The water drummed drearily onto the stainless steel. She dried herself with a tea towel from the rack. Bruises were fanning around her eye, and her nose was mottled and swollen.

"I want to see my work," she said. Her queer, goatish eyes were alive again. Aidan and Conlon accompanied her past the guards in the hall and into the dining-room. Conlon gasped, but Aidan didn't see the palette-knife until it was too late. Ailbhe MacBride had slashed the small picture, the nearest, before he could stop her.

"You shouldn't do that," he said stupidly, and she sagged against him, silently crying, chest heaving under the dirty jumper. Garda Whelan, back with fresh clothes over her arm, caught her on the other side.

"The sooner you're out of here, the better," she told Ailbhe. "Do you think you can manage with the lads?" she asked Conlon, who was green, whether because of the fright or the pictures Aidan couldn't tell. Sitting-room and dining-room were suddenly full of gardaí. Whelan raked them with a sarcastic look. "You'd think one of those would notice a knife, wouldn't you?" she said.

"It had paint on it," Aidan muttered.

Whelan did not bother to reply to this. She gave the clean jumper and a coat she had found to Conlon, pressing them into her arms. A car drew up outside. "That'll probably be Chief Superintendent Murphy," she said. "Go home, Detective Cummings. You look like death."

And Aidan felt icy, indeed. But he felt it was from something he'd picked up in the house; from the distraught woman who had carried the knowledge in her hands and in her work.

Chapter Thirty-Two

They managed to hold off Murnaghan, but it was tedious sitting in Granny's after a while. "It's so boring waiting around out here when there's so much going on." Lara had snagged her suit and laddered her tights. This didn't bother her, she said. She was making plenty of money. Talulla was stiff and cold and longed for her pain-killers, now all gone.

It had been almost festive earlier in the day. The neighbours came on duty in groups of three for an hour at a time, but these arrangements quickly frayed. At four o'clock, only two people had shown up. Emma, who had finally begun answering the phone, was due to take over at six. Talulla volunteered to stay on with her. Soon after that it would get dark, and Murnaghan was hardly going to use arc-lights.

A raffish side of Murnaghan's character emerged: he was enjoying himself. He produced a ghetto-blaster in time for the five o'clock news on RTE, and it was then that Talulla and Lara heard that a man was helping the gardaí with their enquiries about the Strangler case. Earlier, Murnaghan had been out with a bowl of nuts and trick sweets, the peppery kind that smarted. "He's attracted to you all right," Talulla told Lara.

"Moth to the flame," Lara said serenely. She flexed her cold feet and blew her nose. They had come to terms with the scene they occupied and had made themselves comfortable on the trunk of the fallen rowan. They watched as the JCB operator wandered up to the wall, looked at them and then disappeared back into de Burca's. He did this every ten minutes or so.

"Idiot," Lara said to his back. "I'm sorry to desert you and Emma, Tully, I've just got to spend time with Mum. Aidan's obviously caught up in this mad case. I probably won't see him at all this weekend. He'll be running around flashing his badge and being officious."

"He can be as officious as he likes if he helps put this fellow away." She avoided Lara's bright look.

"Well, well," Lara said. "For the record, dear, I don't really think Aidan is beyond redemption. I'd stay your friend if you went out with him."

"Fat chance."

"Very fat, according to Mum."

"Oh, God!"

"No, it's all right, Tully. She'll never say a word to him. Prayer. Gives me the creeps."

"Ah, it doesn't, Lara! She's so sweet –"

"She gets what she prays for! It would make your hair stand up. Anyway. I don't want to put you off. I've my own reasons for encouraging this."

"Ah, no."

"I sit beside Gareth at the wedding table . . . I ply him with drink . . . I console him after."

"If you want to console Gareth, pay for a new roof for that bloodsucking house."

"Yeah . . . I might have to make do with Murno, after all."

They sat in silence for a while. Lara flexed her leg and rotated her ankle, watching the ladder in her tights. Her eyes clouded. "Do you think he was here? The Strangler?"

They looked around, sombre. The light had drained away from the land leaving only a frail lavender brightness above them. The trees seemed to move closer in the darkness like a crowd after an accident.

"It's sick."

"This was our place." Lara trailed her hand along the rowan's trunk. "Do you get a different feeling here now?"

Talulla nodded. "It'll put itself back together again if Murnaghan doesn't get his road. Sure, think of all the things that must have happened here."

"But do you think he was?"

"That's the thing I hate – if he was, it was like an invasion. Like it ruined it. But that's the best solution. And his first one being just down the Metals . . . she wasn't even properly hidden, but she was from Cabinteely. The house they raided was in Cabinteely. Well, he could have known Granny's –"

"And Ashling Leahy, three years ago?"

"We don't know for sure it was Ashling Leahy."

"Tully, I heard them." Lara looked at her watch, then dropped her voice. "That girl was out here screaming like an animal, and her language would have taken paint off a wall. It was all about if Alan was breaking it off, he had to give her the money he owed her immediately so she could leave, because she'd been robbed. And he didn't believe her and, of course, being Alan, he couldn't pay her back anyway, just like that. She walloped him," Lara said frowning, "there was this big, meaty 'whunk' – then he'd have pushed her because she was bawling that she'd mud all over her clothes –"

"Lara, where were you? You heard all this through your open window?"

"I didn't like to admit it at the time, Tully. I sneaked down the back garden. Well, they weren't making it private! I thought I could shout or intervene or something if it got worse."

"But when did your mum come out?"

"When we heard Emma. I went inside." Lara looked away. "Emma was crying in front of that wagon. If she ever knew I'd heard that, I'd lose her friendship, Tully. So I legged it. Your one Ashling was saying Emma could have Alan back, she'd used him up, he was crap. Oh, it was all rage and hurt but it was incredible. I ran. I even phoned Alan, but there was no reply. I was frightened. Not for Ashling Leahy, for Emma."

"But your mum went out?"

"She'd heard – she was out in the shed doing something with the freezer – I hadn't realised. I saw her come back in, white as a sheet and looking a hundred. She would only say that things seemed to have quietened down, and Gareth was comforting Emma."

"Gareth! You never said half this."

"I was a bit sore. He'd his eye on Emma when he thought it was over between her and Alan. All I ever wanted in my life was to be comforted by Gareth Travers –"

"Not again, Lara! No!"

" – but it was not to be."

"Well, be glad for that. He loves 'em and leaves 'em."

"Oh, he does. Aidan 'cautioned' me about Gareth. He says Gareth will never settle down."

"I thought he'd gone to England that time."

"He went the next day. The horrible thing is, I thought I heard Emma's voice out there even later, but I'm not sure. By that time Alan would have been down at the Dalkey Island Hotel. Remember, he'd that job."

"All that sounds good."

"What do you mean, it sounds 'good?' It sounds dreadful!"

"No, it doesn't. Hearing her later, that's good. Emma would have cooled down, don't you see? Gareth was with her. She couldn't have done it, and Alan's off the premises. And it couldn't have been my mother," said Talulla. And she burst into tears.

Chapter Thirty-Three

Lara wanted to stay with Talulla until Emma arrived, but Talulla sent her home at five. The JCB operator had not peered out at them for over half an hour. De Burca's was quiet, and only the security guard's car was still parked on the site. There was a dim light inside the Portakabin. That was all. Lara, fluffing her hair, announced that she was going to cut through Beaulieu and walk home on the road. "If Gareth challenges me," she said wistfully, "I can tell him I was too frightened to walk through Granny's on my own."

When she was gone, Talulla reviewed the conversation she'd had with Briege that afternoon. Just as she was going out the door to join Lara, Briege had pounced. Her voice trembling, she told Talulla about Hope's visit and the quarrel Alan had heard between her and Séamus.

"Couldn't Alan tell me himself, instead of leaving you to stew over it!" Talulla said, furious.

"I can't believe he walked out and telephoned you, and I sitting there!"

Briege was astonished. "He was only trying to save your feelings, Tully," she said.

"Well, I'm amazed at you, Auntie-Mum. This whole business has turned your head. Did you never even think?"

"What?" Briege said stupidly.

"Didn't you always tell me that Hope's family was stinking? Hope's rich!" Talulla yelled. "You're a bank manager, Auntie-Mum! Do rich people fall off the world without enquiries being made about them?"

"Séamus felt so strongly," Briege said falteringly. "I suppose I felt – I felt he could fix all that, somehow. Cover it up. Isn't it strange? I don't believe I'd have entertained it for a moment when he was alive."

Talulla put her arms about her. "I entertained it, too, Auntie-Mum. Yesterday when we were down at the beach, I missed him so much. It was like – you know how he held in his sadness, just held it, all his life. Now that he's – now, it's like his pain has got out. It's just everywhere. It's stronger than I'd ever realised, and – I don't know. Anyway, Daddy couldn't have killed Hope when she came here. They'd have been all over us, Auntie-Mum. Even Jack Murphy couldn't and wouldn't get Dad off a hook like that."

Briege was satisfied. When Talulla left, she was putting on the kettle.

So Hope had come back. She had. Bitch.

Talulla paced up and down the small clearing, avoiding the smoothed patch of empty earth. If that poor woman hadn't been murdered and buried practically under her feet, Talulla would never have known about Hope's visit. She would never have realised the intensity of her father's feelings, his hatred and pain.

While she waited, sorrowful and half-dreaming, mist drifted in. It coaxed branches and stones into distillations of line and mass that got more haunted and indistinct minute by minute. The wood breathed quietly. The odd leaf fell; water dripped. Some small creature scampered here and there. There was no sign these days of the fox, never mind the badger, though Talulla imagined the fox must glide into de Burca's in the small hours, searching through the food and rubbish the men left behind.

Bit by bit, the noises from Hillview and the houses nearby were swallowed by the rapt quietness of the mist and trees. Talulla could no longer glimpse the bay, the sky had darkened so, but the light at the end of Dún Laoghaire pier winked, suspended, a blurred pin-prick. Perhaps places were sacred; perhaps they did retain people's love for them, or the chill of sad events. Talulla no longer believed Mr O'Toole's story about Granuaile's visit, but she knew there was something special about this place, about Dalkey, about Ireland, for that matter. It was a remembering sort of place, like that spot in Galway where a tradition of haunting was recalled. The tradition itself was a relic of tales passed down of a prehistoric battle. The dead were buried there, after all. The archaeologists had listened; then they found them.

She didn't know what made her turn around. The cloaked figure was utterly silent. Talulla recorded every vague fold in the black hood, the impression of lightness round the chin and, lighter still, the hand that secured the cloak in front, a woman's hand. Too fine a hand, surely, to be Granuaile's.

Talulla put one foot in front of the other. Stretched out her arm.

"Trick or treat!" screamed the apparition. "I thought you'd never look!"

"You wagon!"

Emma, laughing uncontrollably, cavorted and flapped like a dreadful crow.

"Bitch cow! You will die for this, Emma Morrissey, you may look over your shoulder for the rest of your life, because I will be there!"

Emma's laughter was near tears.

"Em, you eejit, are you all right?"

Emma leaned against a tree, gasping. "Yes. I'm all right. Finally. Finally!" She looked around. "I take it we're the only ones here?"

"We're not needed. Let's go in. Look, stay with us tonight, in case –"

Emma's breathing quieted. "Oh, Tully, thanks. That would be good, actually."

"Come on, so. Even without you here, it was getting spooky. I was thinking all sorts of things."

"I'll stay out here for a while, Tully. I love it so much."

"Emma, it's dark, it's freezing!"

But Emma made her feel the cloak – "A Kinsale cloak! Touristy thing. Mum bought it years ago. But warm. I'm all set, Tully. I want to stay out, just a while. It may be the last . . ." Her eyes sparkled. "Do you remember the time we planned to stay here all night on Hallowe'en?"

"Oh, yeah!"

"I'd like to do it now. Not all night. Just for a bit. Next year this could be gone, Tully. And I'll probably be gone before that. Tonight I have to be on my own here, Tully."

"In your hat."

"In my cloak, you mean," Emma insisted, her chin jutting.

"Don't be ridiculous. I mean it, Emma, I'm not going." Talulla zipped her jacket up farther and crossed her arms.

"You're joking!"

"I certainly am not."

"Excuse me, you were here yourself on your own –"

"Waiting for you! Forget it, Emma."

They stood silent, glaring at each other. The darkness was almost complete. "I suppose I know what to expect when you get that yeomanlike look on your face, Talulla," Emma said crossly.

Talulla simply shifted her weight to the other foot.

"Tully, this is stupid!"

Talulla didn't move.

"Oh, all right!" Emma grabbed Talulla's shoulders and gave them a little shake. "I'll go home. I'll get organised and come over to you later. Really. Now go away, Tully. Save me some sweeties."

Talulla waited until she heard Emma thrashing over her garden wall. Then she went to the wall herself and looked over. A light went on in Emma's kitchen. Then there was a glow from the landing. She felt uncomfortable, remembering how Emma sometimes padded around the house in the dark so that Declan would think she wasn't home. Maybe she was safer in Granny's after all. No. That was a mad thought. There was a movement at the back bedroom window, a pale flick of a hand. Emma had shut the curtains. The light went on.

Talulla waited until she was sure Emma would not come out again. It was too dark to go back through Granny's so she, like Lara, slipped through Beaulieu. The house was silent. She picked her way along the side of it, a little deflated by its sheer size and the weight of its stone walls. Beaulieu was like a magnet to attract you and an anvil to fall on you all at once.

There was a clutch of small apparitions on the footpath outside de Burca's, a fairy, a ghost, a pussycat and a ghoul. The older girl in charge of them pointed inside the gate, while their bags of nuts rattled with nerves. "In there," she whispered. "The skeleton!" The ghost was anxious, but the fairy took its hand and they hurried on towards Thorn Grove.

There was a big bowl of nuts, sweets and apples ready in the hall. Talulla could hear Briege upstairs calling the cat. She put her head over the railings and said, "There's one of you accounted for, anyway!"

"I'll look for him," Talulla said. It was no night for cats to be out. She stood by the stile in the back garden, rattling his box of dried food, calling him. Even here, yards from her back door, the wood exerted its silence. Talulla glanced back at the house. The gold light from the kitchen window shone out, reassuring. It was like the perfect home-haven of fairytales; but then, it was just that illusion of normality that meant danger in so many of them.

How well could you know anybody? You knew a little and thought you knew everything. There was a sudden movement at her shoulder, and Talulla's heart flew into her mouth. The cat's eyes were refracted light as he pushed his head against her. He had been fighting again. Little tufts of fur like pin-feathers came away as she stroked him, and his tail was still prickly and wide. "You'll be innocent as a kitten when you get inside again, won't you?" she said. He only mewed, and flexed his claws.

Chapter Thirty-Four

Aidan blinked at Alan. He felt as if he'd gone stupid. All he could think of was that Alan was the one who usually did the blinking and, since Alan wasn't blinking, he must be telling the truth. "But why didn't you bring this to Boyle?" Aidan asked him. "I mean, to Dalkey?"

"I thought you were doing it."

"No, this belongs to Dalkey. I was only there because of the other inquiry."

Alan's face fell. "We need to know."

"Oh, do you?"

"I've got to take Emma back with me before Declan James gets to her."

"Will you go over to the yoke there, and get me a drink of water? Please."

Aidan looked at the numbers Alan had scribbled out. They were faintly blurred. He swallowed two Disprin with the water. "We'll just see," he said. "She wouldn't be implicated, would she?"

"In what?"

"You said she was with another girl who supposedly took her money and did a runner?"

"Yeah, but the girl was gone. Ashling was going around looking for her."

"Think, Alan."

Alan shook his head. "No way."

"Just as long as Ashling will be around when Boyle wants to eliminate her officially. All right. You'll call her, I'll listen and maybe come in on the conversation."

"She'll ring off on me," Alan said nervously.

"That'll prove who she is, unless you've annoyed the whole continent."

The US operator was able to give them the number in Columbus, Ohio, when Alan told her the name of the street. They waited while the phone in Ashling Leahy's family home gave its long, drawling purr. There was a metallic click: a voice said, "Hello?"

Alan nodded at Aidan, who picked up the phone on the adjoining desk.

"Ashling?"

"Who's this?"

"Ashling, this is Alan –"

"Oh, shit! How'd you have the nerve to call me, you son of a bitch?"

"Ashling, I can pay you back –"

"Oh yeah, sure, you bastard, and I'll bet you're in some bus station ready to depart for Columbus, Ohio. No way!

"Ashling, I'm going to pay you back, but that's not why I'm calling."

"Well, you can't stay here. My mom's sick."

"I'm in Ireland, Ashling. You're all right."

"Thank God. I thought you were in the phone booth down the street. What do you want?"

"Just checking to see if you're still alive."

"Yeah. I'm alive. I'm sure you've been dying to know that for the past three years. Anything else?"

"That girl you were with. The one who took your money. Ashling?"

"What about her?"

"Look, we think she might – would you mind talking to Detective Cummings?" Alan put his hand over the mouthpiece and grimaced at Aidan.

"Wait! What does this guy want? Is he listening? Is this about the fucking hotel bill?"

"Well, it isn't, Ash, but if I pay your bill will you call it quits?"

"Yeah, sure, and I'll want a receipt, but what does this detective want with me?"

"He wants to know about that girl you were with," Alan said.

"Oh, shit."

"Hello, Ashling? Detective Cummings here."

"Hello."

"We're relieved to speak to you, Ashling. We were worried."

"Oh."

"Ashling, could you please tell me all you can about the girl you were travelling with? Janet Winton? Is that right?"

"Yeah. That's – that's –" She said something indistinguishable.

"I'm sorry? Ashling?"

"Did something happen? Why are you calling now?"

He told her.

"I knew it!" said Ashling Leahy. "God, I just knew it!"

"Knew what?"

"That something happened to her. I knew that guy must have been talking to somebody else."

"What guy?"

"This English guy. I met him in the pub. The day after Janet went. He said he'd met this American girl the day before and she was going over to England that night on the boat. So I mean, she was gone, she had my money, she'd already borrowed six pounds and she'd stolen my lipstick and my socks, so how was I to know? Shit! It mustn't have been her that guy met. It's just that he described her, you know?" Ashling burst into tears. Then she quieted and told Aidan everything she remembered.

Afterwards Aidan and Alan sat looking at one another. "I'll have to go to Dalkey," Aidan said. He gathered his notes. His hands shook.

"Look, Aidan, you should be home. There's something wrong with you."

"It's just the way I look. Actually, it's flu."

"I'll get you home," Alan said.

"How'd you come here, Alan?"

"Taxi."

Aidan handed him his keys. "We'll go in my car," he said. "To the station. Thanks, Alan."

Chapter Thirty-Five

The children's voices were thrown up on the gusts of wind like stray notes of a song. Emma snuggled on the little nest she had made for herself beside the rowan tree. She had brought out a flask of tea, but her best resource was the Kinsale cloak. With its gathered hood and black, voluminous folds it provided warm shelter from the mist and cold.

She had told Alan she wanted one last night without him.

"But what if Declan comes?"

"He won't," she said.

"Come with me, Em, it's safer."

"I'll go to Talulla," she said. It was very hard to let go of Alan, but Emma did it.

Here in Granny's she wanted to touch everything around her, to sniff and taste like an animal. She and Alan and Iseult would live under strange constellations from now on but, when she slept, her dreams would bring her back to this wood, this hill, this sky.

She wondered if Iseult, leaving so young, would remember it only in her dreams. Her face softened and her arms ached to hold her child. Her poor parents, they would be so upset. They would miss Iseult desperately.

Luckily, Emma heard the giggle before the explosion. It was so close she could smell the cordite. "Minogues!" she cried. "Come out!"

There was a scrabble in the bushes. Three faces appeared, pale blobs in the darkness. Two had odd-shaped bodies; they were revealed as a robot and Mrs Doubtfire when Kevin Minogue shone his torch on them. He himself was a recreation of Greenman the rock star, with a bright green mop on his head and a pale green face with dark, sinister eyes. The robot pushed a button on the box he was carrying, and Greenman's song "Samhain" suddenly threaded around them. Emma had heard it often and quite liked it, with its haunting flute and mandolin accompaniment, but Kevin switched off his torch again, and the atmosphere became uncanny. Just as she was going to demand that he turn it on, he did. Emma screamed.

There was a chorus of giggles and cheers. Finally, Emma said, "I suppose it serves me right. I've given one fright tonight and now I've had one for myself." She touched Charlie MacDevitt's decomposing face. "Latex?"

"It took me all afternoon to put it on," Charlie said shyly.

"Mind you don't just pop out at people, Charlie. It's utterly brilliant. You're all terrific. You shouldn't be here, though."

"You shouldn't either, by yourself, Mrs Morrissey. There's a ghost."

"Grace O'Malley's?"

"No, the one Charlie saw this morning when it was dark."

"A greeny-gold light, like a big eye."

"Where?"

"Over there some place."

"Probably the gardaí," Emma said firmly, and hooshed them.

It seemed too quiet when they were gone, but quiet was what she wanted. She wanted to see the pirate queen before she left. It was Emma's last chance to humour her superstitions. The Australian sun, even happiness itself, might burn them away.

Everyone knew that Grace O'Malley had gone to visit Elizabeth in 1575. They'd got on well together and chatted in Latin and Grace O'Malley, very satisfied with the visit, had dropped anchor in Dalkey sound on her way back to her stronghold in Clew Bay. Emma smiled to herself. She could never think of this story without hearing it as Mr O'Toole had told it when they were children.

Before she was settled, however Granuaile called in to Howth Castle, where she expected a decent welcome; but, instead of being handed a hot dinner and asked for the news, she was told that the family were already at table and she needn't wait. She went back to the strand in a rage; and, when she saw the heir happily playing there, she plunked him into her boat and made off with him.

A fierce game of tag went on in Dublin Bay, watched with great interest by William Travers from his vantage point on Dalkey Hill. The Lawrences finally secured their heir after profuse apologies and the promise that, as long as they existed, they would set an extra place at table for any stranger who might call.

What followed would never be proved, though Emma believed it. It certainly stood up as an early example of Travers' opportunism. William Travers, who never missed a trick, and was an eccentric even by sixteenth-century standards, had an enormous dinner prepared. Then he rowed out to Granuaile and inveigled her to share it. He brought horses to carry Granuaile and her kinsmen, but, as they approached the house, she dismounted, saying she wanted to walk the rest of the way.

There was still a little light in the sky and on the sea, which had gone tranquil and luminous. All around them the woodland up and down the hill was dark and gently breathing, and Granuaile said to Travers, *Is breá é bheith in Éirinn arís*, or something like it. "That was the second point she made that day," Mr O'Toole would tell them.

"She was saying she was in Ireland, the way she understood Ireland, though Dalkey was an outpost of the English Pale, and everything on Travers's table would have come from his fortified warehouse down below in the town – fortified against the likes of her! And the O'Tooles," he would add modestly. "We were hill pirates, ourselves."

Travers loved the hill so much that he had built well outside the town walls, which suggested how lost to common sense he was, despite his business acumen. The whole higgledy pile was torched to the cellars a few years later by the Byrnes, whom he'd annoyed.

Years ago when they were eleven, Talulla, Lara, Alan and herself had made a pact that they'd spend the night in Granny's on Hallowe'en. They'd all pretend to go to sleep and then sneak out again at midnight and meet behind de Burca's. Then they'd sit holding hands in a circle and wait to see Granuaile with her little group of Galway men walking up the avenue towards Travers's.

Lara was trapped inside because her older brothers and sisters sat downstairs talking until three that morning, and Talulla simply fell asleep. In the end, it was only Emma and Alan waiting in their sleeping bags. Curled up beside each other they finally slept, but not before they had a sense of the secret life of Granny's and the hill which set them apart somehow from the others. Emma woke slowly while it was still dark and sensed that someone else had been there, very close. In her child's heart, she knew it wasn't Granuaile. She woke Alan, and they crept back to her house. Alan went home at first light, but not through Granny's.

The tree beside Emma creaked as the wind picked up, and she put her hand on it in sympathy. She felt safe here now: here in this narrow band between past and future, this no-man's-land – she laughed to herself – Gráinne's Wood, at Samhain.

The moon rose glimmering above the trees, playing through the mist and edging the black hilltop beyond. Travers's light went out, leaving a grey spot in the web of branches like some small, defeated ghost dissipating on the air.

Gathering the warm cloak around her, Emma picked her way through the trees, touching one, then another as she passed, winding wraithlike down the rough slope until, much later, she saw the iron gates ahead of her. Beyond them cars coursed along Thorn Avenue, as alien as particles from some other galaxy. She turned away and slowly, joyously, began her stroll back up in the darkness.

Chapter Thirty-Six

Detective Chief Superintendent Murphy was already in Dalkey, attended by Sergeant Boyle and Detective Inspector Neligan. The station was quietly teeming, with extra guards on duty to cope with the fallout from Hallowe'en – bonfires and cider-drinkers, mainly. Neligan remarked that it was "quiet enough"; the pubs were still open and nothing serious had been reported.

The news about Basil Hughes's arrest had arrived and been absorbed and Aidan fielded smiles and quiet nods as they passed through the warren of small rooms. Neligan led him upstairs.

Murphy sat behind a scarred oak table in the interview room, a telephone at his elbow. He told Neligan he didn't need him and Boyle yet. Then he congratulated Aidan for his part in Basil Hughes's arrest and stretched out his hand for his notes.

Aidan sat quietly, gazing around while Murphy

read the notes he had taken during his conversation with Ashling Leahy. This room had once been a bedroom. It was still domestic, with its Victorian fireplace and its thick, quiet walls. Then there were the bars outside the window. The room was a bit like Murphy himself, solid, unpretentious, traditional – and somehow disturbing. Like him, it had seen much.

Surprised, Aidan realised that the fear he sensed in the room was his own. He felt Murphy's eyes on him and had a sudden urge to laugh; it died immediately.

Murphy spread the three pages across the table where he could see them all at once. Then he brought his own pad in front of him. "Now," he said. "Long day, Sergeant?" His face was kind, his eyebrows slightly raised.

Murphy had picked up his unease.

"They should all be long, so," Aidan said quietly.

"Indeed. The streets would be quiet and the jails would be full. It was a good job. A very good job." Murphy paused.

"This part's a bit close to home," Aidan ventured.

"Yes," Murphy said. He waited. When Aidan said nothing more, he became brisk. "There's been another development, Aidan, though I doubt it's related. But first I take it that we're no longer looking for an Ashling Leahy, but a Janet Winton?"

"That's right, sir."

"Well, I intend to 'reach out', as the Americans say, to my cousin in Albany, Aidan. To see if we can speed things up." He punched in a streel of numbers then scanned Aidan's notes, frowning, while the phone slurred briefly at the other end. Aidan could hear the staccato voice that answered from where he was sitting.

"'Away from his desk'? Go get him! Tell him this is cousin Jack." Murphy gave a shark-like smile that seemed to impact on the other side of the Atlantic, for the number was taken with loud reassurances that, "The Chief will call back right away, sir."

"Are there other developments, sir?" Aidan asked him, when he put down the phone.

"Do you know Tom MacDevitt?"

"I do, yes. They moved into Thorn Crest a year or so ago."

"Excitable?"

To be thought of as "excitable" by Murphy was a shame past bearing.

"No . . . a little, perhaps, but he's sound," Aidan said.

"He phoned here just before you arrived to say

that his daughter Charlie's gone missing. She was last seen going into the wooded area behind Thorn Grove –"

"Granny's Wood," Aidan prompted him.

"The children she was with said she left them to retrieve a banger she'd hidden there. They waited, she didn't come out. She'd told them there was a light out there at four this morning. The other children noticed signs of digging in the area between –" he glanced at his pad – "Hynes's and Morrissey's." He raised his eyebrows. "There was nothing like that when the team left yesterday, according to Boyle."

"Kids?" Aidan asked.

"Any ideas who?"

"I haven't kept up with them much lately. Stapletons in Thorn Crest have teenagers, and there's a couple of families in the Grove. They're quiet enough, but sure . . . And Charlie's not been found?"

"No. Naturally MacDevitt crashed around looking for her before he phoned, and the neighbours will be out, too, trampling all around and wrecking the place and locating her, please God," Murphy said. He sighed. "The digging – ?"

His hand was back on the phone before it finished ringing. "Bosco. Right, man, where'll it be? Lahinch or Portmarnock?" He laughed.

"What's the handicap? . . . Oh, we'll see, we'll see. Bosco, we believe we've just dug up one of yours. A young girl, Janet Winton, W-i-n-t-o-n. She was supposed to turn up in Ithaca for college – Cornell. Yes – well, we'd like to eliminate her from . . . August '93 . . . No, not yet. Dental work. The girl she was travelling with said she was on a grant. 'Scholarship'. Right." He drummed his fingers.

"The other girl, Leahy, is from Ohio. She thought Winton stole her money, Bosco. That's why she didn't report her missing. She even threw out Janet Winton's backpack full of her clothes . . . Indeed and she's sorry now! She phoned Cornell University that autumn, still looking for her money – do they think of nothing else over there? – and they told her Janet Winton had never arrived. Leahy panicked and put down the phone before they could ask her anything."

There was an explosive rattle of comment at the other end, and Murphy laughed. "More hair than wit, yeah, and a bad conscience. She scarpered from here without paying for the guest house . . . Look, Janet Winton was on a full, er, scholarship . . . yeah, exactly. Our lassie says she wouldn't have passed up a penny on a cowpat, never mind a full scholarship."

They spoke a little longer, and, after a parting

golf threat, Murphy rang off. "Well, now," he said. "We'll see how long it takes Cousin Bosco to run this down. It's not his own patch, so I give him an hour. Are you feeling all right, Aidan?"

Aidan wasn't, but he nodded.

Murphy looked at him steadily as he went on. "Just to be clear, then. These two American girls meet here in Ireland and decide to share accommodation to save money. It's wearing a bit thin after two weeks, as Ashling thinks Janet Winton is leeching off her a bit?"

"Yes, sir."

"But she still gives Janet her money to change at the bank. That's strange, considering, isn't it? Then, according to Ashling, Janet disappears with her cash that afternoon. She doesn't return to the guest-house that night and Ashling never sees her again. Ashling has her aeroplane ticket and just enough traveller's cheques to get home. And what's this about a loan?"

"It was to Alan de Burca. He's a local lad she got off with. Twenty pounds," Aidan said.

"Do you know him?"

"Pushed his pram," Aidan said.

"I see."

"He didn't have it when she wanted it back," Aidan said steadily, "so they had a barney. He'd just broken off with her as well, so it was fairly heated."

"So our lass goes back to the guest-house in a temper and chucks Winton's backpack into a skip?"

"So she says," said Aidan.

"Could she have kept the lot for herself?"

"Well, she said she threw in the backpack, she said nothing about the contents," Aidan said.

Murphy shook his head, smiling a little. "What do you think," he asked, "about Ashling's story about the Englishman she met?"

"It's not much, sir. Some English bloke she picked up in The Arches."

Murphy stroked his chin, sighing. "It's a bit neat, isn't it? You talked to her, Aidan." He gave him a searching look.

"I believed her, actually."

"An English fellow in the pub who said he'd met Janet the night before, the night she didn't return to the guest-house, on her way to the Sealink. 'Travelling light.' End of search by Miss Leahy," said Murphy, his light eyes intent.

"It'd be nice if she'd described him as a slim fellow with a wig and an earring," Aidan said.

Murphy did not smile. "It'd be nice if she'd described him at all, Aidan. Was Ashling in the country long?"

"Only about a month."

"Would she have known the difference

between an English accent and a 'West British' one, say?"

"I doubt it." Aidan swallowed. His throat hurt.

"Fellow she met, if she did meet him, might have been local," Murphy mused. "I'd like to know more about Janet Winton's last hours here. No harm surveying the locals down the pubs."

"A long shot," Aidan murmured.

"After three years it is, Aidan. Very. But, at least, this Ashling seems to be a memorable young one. Did you ask her for a photo?"

Aidan shook his head, chastened.

Murphy looked irritated.

Boyle tapped on the door, came in and sat down at Murphy's nodded invitation. "No sign yet of the child," he said.

Aidan excused himself and went downstairs for a drink of water. The desk sergeant had Panadol in her drawer, a box confiscated from a would-be suicide, then forgotten. He put them in his pocket.

Dr McQuaid had been right, Aidan reflected. He did have flu. Half the hauntings in Ireland probably originated with flu, this deathly chill followed by despair. He leaned for a moment against the newel post. It had penetrated him. Flu dissolved all the membranes formed by common sense, those barriers that kept associations and thoughts in their proper relationship, barriers which in his own brain had crumbled. His mind was full of suspicion and dread. He knew what he couldn't know.

Aidan went back upstairs. Murphy was talking on the phone again, firing questions at the Dean of Women from Cornell University and writing furiously on his pad. As he repeated the full name, Boyle's and Aidan's eyes met. "Jesus," said Boyle. Someone was running lightly up the stairs.

The child from Thorn Crest had not been found, the sergeant, a bit breathless, told them, but a young woman had been discovered battered and unconscious. "Morrissey."

Boyle's face bleached with rage. "Morrissey? Thorn Grove? That James bastard again?"

Murphy excused himself for a moment, put his hand over the phone and nodded at Boyle. "Carry on. We'll sort this in the morning. Check back with me when you're organised, Peter, will you?" Boyle, livid, was out of the room almost before he stopped talking.

"Isn't it a strange thing, Aidan?" Murphy said. "This lady at Cornell, the Dean of Women? She says nobody at all was interested in the whereabouts of Janet Winton, only herself. And she'd never met her."

"May I leave, sir?" Aidan asked. "I've got flu."

"Mind yourself, Aidan," Murphy said.

Aidan could feel his eyes following him as he left the room. As he stepped carefully back down the stairs, he realised how much he missed Séamus O'Neill. At the same time, he wondered if he could have confided his thoughts of this night even to him.

Aidan rested his forehead on the steering wheel of his car. He wanted to walk the few yards to Castle Street, fall into bed in his flat and sleep for a lifetime. Instead, he threaded the car past the narrow row of cottages, looped through Sorrento and up towards Hillview. Three words. All the way from America. Janet Winton's full name.

All the lost children. Where had Charlie MacDevitt got to? With any luck she'd be found under her own bed, hiding from Tom's wrath over the banger, but Aidan did not believe it. The world had overbalanced. Trees toppled, houses fell. In the emptiness, a million dusty moments of neglect and loss rose and, fusing like atoms, released this searing moment of clarity where ghosts and killers walked in black light and became visible.

. . . *nobody at all was interested in the whereabouts of Janet Winton, only herself. And she'd never met her.*

Dublin was only a rusty smudge on the mist when Aidan reached Beaulieu. The house seemed to hover lightly on the blurred air, its perfect proportions more striking than ever. All was dark and silent in front, but down the side of the house he discerned a light. Kneeling in the grass beside the kitchen window, he recognised the dim bulb over the gas cooker. A carton of some frozen food softened on the table in a pool of water. Slowly he straightened. Walking carefully but confidently on this familiar ground, he made his way across the road and on to the hill.

Chapter Thirty-Seven

Charlie MacDevitt hadn't been in Granny's five minutes before she started to feel frightened. It was one thing to be there with the others, quite another to be crouched in the dark on her own, unable to hear properly because of the wind. She touched her face carefully, then drew her hand away again. She frightened herself, to be honest.

Oh, that Mrs Blakeney! She'd told Charlie's father about the banger they'd set off under Travers's window, and Tom replied that he would ground Charlie the moment he caught up with her. He'd sounded furious.

"I thought you'd want to know. It is hard, with certain little influences running wild, isn't it, Tom?" Mrs Blakeney had said in her horrid, confiding way. "I don't know how parents manage these days . . . those that try, that is . . . Fingers crossed, Tom, the next Minogue will be female."

The children had heard it all. They'd been hiding behind the hedge with their bags, getting ready to leap up and call "trick or treat."

"Margaret-Thatcher-dog-kisser-Blakeney'll get a trick, so she will," Kevin Minogue had promised after they had crept away to safety.

Charlie felt the banger and box of matches in her skirt pocket. The banger, enormous, one of Kevin's best, gave her a sense of badness and power with which to confront the wood at night; but even this possession was no proof against the sudden swish and darkness that was Emma, walking back up in her cloak. The child gave a yelp of terror.

"Who's that?" demanded the familiar voice.

"Mrs James!"

Emma leaned down to her. "Charlie! Where are the others?"

"In the Crest. I'm to meet them."

"But, Charlie, what are you doing here ?"

They froze. During the second or two that the wind dropped, they both heard a chink of metal on stone. The faint gusts and rustlings resumed, but still they waited, motionless.

"It's the ghost," Charlie whispered, wringing the ends of the shawl she was wearing. Branches creaked in the darkness.

"Is that what you saw?" Emma shook Charlie's

arm, pointed. Just for a moment, far away behind the trees, there was a flicker of gold.

"Run!" the child whispered. "Let's run!"

"It's almost behind my garden!"

"Mrs James – please!"

"Go home now, Charlie. Go on! Don't worry. I just want to see –I'll follow you in a second. I'll catch up with you. Hurry!" She gave the child a little shake and a push. Reluctant and relieved at once, Charlie began to shuffle off. "Hurry!"

Twigs snapped as Emma moved swiftly through the trees towards the light. Charlie paused a moment and then, heart pounding, she turned back and followed her, taking care not to be heard.

She glimpsed the man, lean, black-coated, with his spade, just as he saw Emma. The torch bounced on the grass as he gave a soft, weird cry. The light glanced green up the spade's haft as he raised it, then brought it down hard.

Charlie ran. She ran without breathing as the trees reached for her. She darted straight through de Burca's and across Hillview without a pause. Only the wrenching moan of brakes and the bumper slewing beside her shocked her lungs into filling. The driver, misunderstanding her frantic gestures, shouted an obscenity at her and drove away. There was nobody else on the road. Not a car, not a soul.

It was so hard to see anything, the way the shadows moved. Charlie peered through the soft amber street light, trying to penetrate the blackness behind de Burca's gateway across the road from her. It was like a black cave. She could not even remember running through it. She gathered herself for the dash back over the road and past it, ready to run pell-mell for the turn into Thorn Crest and home. Then the shadows moved quickly in the dark mouth of the gateway. The long black figure of the spade-man formed on the night and Charlie, sobbing, turned and stumbled on to the path up Dalkey Hill.

Chapter Thirty-Eight

Talulla and Briege found Emma. She was almost invisible, crumpled under the black cloak in the dark, and they might not have found her at all that night if they hadn't stumbled over Charlie's bag of sweets and apples. It lay strewn a few yards from where Emma lay.

They had set out to hunt for Charlie after Tom MacDevitt came to the door looking for her. "I think she overheard me telling Mrs Blakeney I was going to ground her. Kevin says she didn't come out of Granny's when they called her. Wait till I find her – !"

"She wouldn't be over with that little one, what's-her-name, in Thorn Grove?" Briege asked.

"We've already phoned there," said Tom. He looked so miserable that they reassured him at once.

"We'll have a hunt round for her in our patch, Tom. She'd hear from your voice that you're annoyed."

"You know the way it is," he said.

"We do, Tom, and we'll tell her you've cooled down if we find her," Briege told him.

"Thanks, Briege, and we'll let you know if we find her, too," he said, and was gone.

That's how they came to be in Granny's calling out to Charlie like lunatics, until they stumbled on the plastic bag and the knobbly apples and saw something white in the grass ahead that was Emma's outstretched hand.

"Oh, Jesus." Talulla dropped to her knees beside Emma, searching for a pulse in her neck, her wrists, having to warm her own hands under her jacket and try again. How long had Emma been there? Her pulse when Talulla finally found it was no more than a flutter, so delicate that she felt she might destroy it by pressing too hard. Blood oozed horribly through her hair, stiffening it into a weighty mass, and there were clotting rivulets of blood on cheek and forehead, black in the weak light of the torch.

Briege shook Talulla's shoulder. "Is she alive?"

"Phone 999, Briege. Say nothing to anyone else, just get the guards and the ambulance here."

Briege was crashing back through the trees before she finished speaking. Talulla bent over Emma.

"You should have gone home with me, Em.

Emma? – You'll wake up out of this and tell me you've seen Granuaile, won't you, Granuaile and about half the stars in the universe. You're a holy show, do you know that? You've probably scared some poor bugger half out of his wits, he's probably still running. He'd want to be, wouldn't he, because when we catch up with him . . . Emma! Talk to me! God, you're freezing."

She took her jacket off and tucked it around Emma's body. She had never known anyone alive to be so coldly absent. Even her father when he was dying had seemed more aware, more present somehow. She kept talking, trying to keep her voice light, peering into Emma's face, which had begun to look transparently waxy and much too smooth. This sinister perfection was so frightening that Talulla found herself almost shouting; it seemed she must, to have any chance of getting through. "Don't leave us, Em! Don't cross! What will Iseult do? Or Alan?"

Someone approached noisily from the direction of Emma's garden, too noisily to be her attacker, surely, unless –

Declan James shambled into the beam of light. He was wearing a dark suit and looked incongruous in this wilderness, as incongruous as he had looked in Emma's life. He stopped.

"Would you move back, Declan? You've nearly killed her already."

"Killed who?" he said in a muffled voice.

"Would you move, Declan, if you fall – !"

He stepped back, staggering a little. "That's not Emma," he said, aggrieved.

"It's all you've left of her, you bastard!"

"What?"

"I said – !"

"That's not Emma?" He dropped to all fours like a huge dog and scrutinised Emma's face, breathing heavily.

"Don't touch her!"

His dark, slightly staring eyes met Talulla's, and she was afraid. "Sounds familiar," he said, his mouth twisting. "'Don't touch me!' A cracked falsetto. He knelt up, sighing, and gave Emma's still form a long, sombre look. There was blood on the front of his shirt. "Jesus." He stood, very carefully and slowly. "De Burca's in the passage," he said, nodding in the direction of Emma's garden. Then he wandered off into the darkness.

Talulla sensed that Emma had shrunk into herself in some indefinable way when Declan was nearby, and she began talking to her again, rattling on mawkishly, crooning, assuring her that he was gone.

Briege was back. "Has she revived at all?" She brought a flat bottle from her pocket.

"Briege, we can't give her that!"

"It's for us, girl," Briege said, and handed the brandy to Talulla. "There was someone crashing around near de Burca's, Tully, did you hear it? Don't bother wiping that, please, just give it to me."

"It's Declan James."

Briege stared, aghast.

Talulla put her finger to her lips, indicating Emma. "He's defused for the night. Oh, thank God! Listen to that, now. That'll be the ambulance." The sirens sounded faintly through the air. "They seem to be going very slow."

Briege picked up Emma's limp hand and stroked it, chafing the cold wrist. "The fog's got desperate. Look." When she angled the light of her torch, it flattened and dispersed immediately on the moist air.

"Did they find Charlie?"

Briege shook her head.

"Will you be all right here if I have a look round?"

Briege picked up Emma's other hand. "Some of them are organising a search here in Granny's," she said, dropping her voice. "And the MacDevitts are still phoning. One child she might have hooked up with is still out."

"You didn't tell them we found the bag, then."

Briege shook her head. "Fidelma MacDevitt's already hysterical. I only told the guards."

"I'm going up, Briege."

"Up – ?"

"The hill. I think – just to start calling, in case Charlie's hiding. She could be wandering around up there in the fog, frightened and freezing. The place'll be crawling with cider drinkers and God knows what."

"You shouldn't be up there yourself, for the same reason."

"I'll be fine."

"Go on then, so. The lads will know where to come." Briege turned back to Emma.

Talulla looked at her for a moment, surprised. Then she floundered through the trees towards de Burca's.

She paused when she got to the site. There were the cellars of the old house to fall into, and newly-dug foundations, and machinery. Like any building site, it was dangerous, and she prayed that Charlie had not already learned that to her cost. She picked her way through the gap in the wall and hesitated. Nothing. Then there was a brightening and a fading far in front of her, a car passing on Hillview, and she got her bearings. "Charlie!" she called softly. "Charlie!"

There was no answer. She threaded her way

forward, calling, using her torch where the mist thinned, finding nothing among the remote shapes and poignant desolation until she heard crying. It was Declan, sitting on the broken steps that were all that was left of the old house. She put her hand on his shoulder, but he didn't seem to feel it. "Declan, did you see a child?"

He did not respond.

"Declan?"

He shook his head.

"You should go home," she said, pitying him, but he pushed her away, hard. She left him and continued on her way. The cold blue lights of a garda car were pulsing through the fog as she crossed Hillview. She paused a moment to watch it turn into de Burca's. An ambulance followed. Talulla started up the hill.

Chapter Thirty-Nine

Alan stumbled into the little clearing just as the men strapped Emma to the stretcher. His face went blank when he saw her; his eyes got a blind look. "Take him with her," Briege told them. "He's closer to her than anyone, and look . . ."

He had difficulty climbing into the ambulance, and one of the guards muttered, "They wouldn't have done this to each other, would they?" Alan's face was swollen and starting to bruise, and there was blood down the front of his jacket.

Briege shook her head. "Where will you take her?" she asked the attendant.

"Vincent's."

She watched the ambulance trundle out of de Burca's and into the mist, its arctic blue signal strangely beautiful. Years ago, on the Dalkey Summer Project, Emma and Alan had gone for a ride in an ambulance. They'd talked about it for days; it was their favourite outing of all, transcending their visit to the Tea Time Express bakery.

Briege told the guards all she knew. She liked Detective Sergeant Boyle. He seemed to have just the right mixture of rage and competence. He would do all he could.

Mrs Morrissey, Emma's mother, answered the phone on the second ring, her voice breathless as if she expected something to be wrong.

"Emma's hurt, Dick. They're taking her to Vincent's," she whispered to her husband, who must have been beside her trying to listen in. Then, "Dick's going to phone our neighbour, Briege. She promised to come in and mind Iseult for us if anything – if Emma needed us. Oh, why wouldn't Emma stay with us! This is where her stubbornness has got her!" At this she broke down, and Mr Morrissey took the phone from her and said that they were leaving for St Vincent's at once.

Briege sat in the hall after ringing off, her hands in her lap. The house was silent; not even a floorboard creaked. She thought of the ambulance winding its way through the fog, and of Emma's parents setting out, both moving with the obstructed deliberation of nightmare, while Emma – she could not bear to think of what might be happening to Emma, the injury looked so terrible. And Talulla was up on the hill. She should have made Talulla wait for others to join the search. Why hadn't she stopped her?

She reached up and turned off the light. She did not want to be roused or summoned. One more person looking for Charlie MacDevitt would make no difference. Two hours ago, such a thought would not have crossed her mind: she'd have been in the thick of things, where she liked to be, where she felt in control. It was too late for that now.

The *still point*. Briege didn't know where the words came from; some poem she'd once known but forgotten. She would have liked to feel her rosary beads between her hands but couldn't stir herself to go and find them; she had to stay where she was. She felt as if moving would jeopardise some delicate balance. It was a little like the wait for the ambulance: you did all you could, and then you waited for the ambulance to come. You waited with all your heart and mind in the still point between life and death.

A car door slammed. Briege did not move. There was a step on the footpath, and the car drove off. She drew a long breath. Her precious Talulla was silhouetted in the glass of the front door, graceful, her hair a soft cloud with the street light behind it. She hesitated; then she rang the doorbell.

She'd lost her key! Wouldn't she take the one from under the flowerpot? But Talulla still stood outside, waiting. She half-turned, and hunched her shoulders, as if uncertain. Was there something odd about her? The hair prickled on Briege's neck. It was as if a changeling had arrived in Talulla's body, a changeling without a key or a memory. She rose and turned on the light. A slim hand tapped softly on the glass. Slowly, Briege opened the door.

She knew her immediately. For a mad moment she thought she hadn't grown a day older, like some woman out of a fairytale. Mutton dressed as lamb, only you couldn't even tell, because she looked like no forty-three-year-old that Briege had ever seen. Still the same soft, floating hair, though shorter now, the same pale face and haunted eyes. Talulla's eyes, only lighter.

"May I come in?"

Briege stepped back.

The woman came slowly into the hall. Her diffidence, Briege had forgotten it. She stopped near the door into the sitting-room. A photograph of Talulla and Séamus that Briege had taken was on the mantelpiece. They were out in the garden. It was summer; soft light coming through the trees in Granny's hid the harshest outlines of Séamus's face and camouflaged his illness. He looked young again and Talulla, beside him, was lovely. In that moment she had been the image of her mother. Briege turned quickly to the woman who stared at the picture so hungrily, turned and said, "Get out!"

Hope returned her look without insolence. "No," she said simply.

Talulla stopped on the path to listen. There was the usual concurrence of sounds, all masked by the wind: small scufflings in the undergrowth, night-smoothed hum of traffic and, louder now, the long, sighing breaths of the sea. She called Charlie's name again but there was no answer. The foggy darkness seemed to absorb everything, even her voice. She wondered if Charlie could even hear her from more than a few yards away.

Years ago, when they were all about thirteen, Emma had dared her and Lara to go up the hill at night on their own. It wasn't the darkness that stopped them, though that was bad enough; it was the noises.

Talulla felt a sudden strong wave of fear, and she tripped. Pain forked across her side where the shot had grazed her. Her heart thudded and flopped and the gorse beside her pricked at the back of her hand like little teeth. She jerked her hand away. The sudden movement seemed to free her.

She walked quietly, listening, longing for the strong fabric of her uniform and the comfort of her radio, the being part of a plan, of a project shared. "Charlie!" Her voice, cracked, sounded absurd.

The steps of the Cat's Ladder angled down the hill on her left to meet the Vico Road, and the sough of the sea was louder. There was a gold glow of light from a house midway down, and amber street lights threw up shadows from the road below. But the hill overwhelmed all this and converted it to confusion. The path smoothed; Talulla hurried along it, aware of the gorse and trees rising on her right, the tumble of boulders and rough scrub on her left. Could Charlie have scuttled into these like a little rabbit, was she only yards away? Talulla spoke her name quietly, then called it out.

She found that she was wringing her hands. The sheer hopelessness of finding the child in such conditions came home to her. She stopped. She could hear nothing but the slow, thin dripping of mist off gorse. Then, hardly more distinct than the call of a bird in the distance: was it her name? She was sure it was. "Charlie!" she shouted. "Charlie!" She waited, listening, but there was no response. She hurried on.

Chapter Forty

Charlie huddled in "den," shuddering at every sound in the darkness. Her arms and legs were scored with scratches. She was shivering; the knitted shawl she'd been wearing as part of her costume had caught on branches and been torn from her back, she wasn't even sure where. He would find it, sniff it perhaps, and know exactly where she was, like the man in the video she'd seen in Minogues's. If she turned her head he'd be standing there, silent and sudden like in the trees beside Mrs James, pale face, pale hands. She'd felt almost sorry for him for a second, he looked so frightened, but then his gaze had locked on her; then it was as if somebody held a rope and gave it a monstrous tug, jerking her straight through de Burca's and on to the hill, and her mother had told her never to go there alone even in daytime. Now he'd find her and kill her like Mrs James, and she hadn't been confirmed. A little explosion of breath escaped her at the thought of this and worse, far worse, her parents. Her mother. She clasped the rough, cool trunk of the fallen tree, her shelter, and pressed her forehead against it hard. Tears streamed from her eyes. A voice whispered near her: "Charlie?"

Talulla, sweating, was feeling the stitch in her side. She could see a little better here; the obelisk at the top of Killiney Hill was a few yards in front of her, gleaming faintly in the moonlight. The wind teased the grass and confused her hearing, roared in the trees around the clearing and mingled with the sound of surf on the shingle. She was sure she had heard her name called, and from this direction.

Help was approaching: sirens, their wails tossed and juggled, smothered then amplified by the wind, approached from all sides – from Thorn Avenue and Torca, from the Vico below and the Burma on the other side of the hill. Light-footed with relief, Talulla hurried towards the black crest of the wood, calling.

Charlie burrowed close to the earth like a little animal, clutching the trunk of the tree as if it could help her.

"Charlie?" It was so hard to tell with whispers but, no, if he were a good person he'd call out.

"Charlie . . ." in a more normal voice. "I've found your shawl. Aren't you cold?" The soft steps moved away a little, and Charlie knew he hadn't seen her. He just guessed she was somewhere nearby. Suddenly she felt she'd be mortified if he found her and realised she hadn't trusted him, it would seem so rude, but she still couldn't move. If he found her, she could say she didn't realise it was him. Or that she was waiting for her dad.

The wind angled through the fallen branches around her hide-away, but she was clammy all over. People did sweat, then, when they were afraid, no matter how cold they were. She held tightly to the tree, which rustled with some quiet safe dreaming of its own.

Pad, pad, he wandered here and there, invisible, but always close. Other steps approached, quick steps on the leaves. "Charlie?"

Talulla! Charlie almost stood up, but her arms, locked coldly around the tree, wouldn't obey her, nor would her voice when she heard the quick, sharp scuffle as the man pounced.

Chapter Forty-One

Briege moved around the kitchen like an automaton. She had settled the "impostor", as she called Talulla's mother in her mind, in the sitting-room. "She'll never resist her," she thought dully. This, then, among all the night's tragedies and debacles, was the "three." Hope, beautiful, rich and uncannily like her daughter, had finally come back to claim her. As if summoned by the thought, she appeared in the doorway.

For a moment she hovered there, watching Briege set out the cups. Then her eyes were drawn to the blank of the kitchen window. Briege felt there was something spooky and predatory in Hope's pose; the other woman gazed at the darkness as if she could penetrate it, her vision moving through the solid granite of the hill itself to find her daughter. When Hope turned back into the room, this impression was heightened; her face was a mask of longing. Briege wondered if her own was the same.

"There's something wrong," Hope said, accusing.

"Wasn't there always?"

"I mean now, Briege. Where is she?"

Briege felt her face burning. She bit her tongue. Hadn't she said herself that Séamus was wrong to send Hope away? "She's on the hill."

"Why?"

Briege told her. As she watched Hope, she remembered more and more about her. At the end of her recital, Hope's face bore an expression of patrician incredulity. "So she's just running around up there on her own?"

"Certainly not. Every guard in south Dublin will be up there with her. And she's twenty-three, you know. She's trained –"

"As a policewoman. Yes, I know," Hope said, her lips thinning.

"You knew that?"

"Yes, I did. I also know she was shot. Shot! What was it? A week after his death? Two?" Hope's face was red now, and Briege saw with satisfaction that it didn't suit her. Her eyes glittered. "You wouldn't even tell me that."

"Why would I? You never asked!"

"I asked Séamus. I asked Séamus in this very

room. I came here! You had no right to make Talulla – my God, what a name you gave her – you had no right to let her think I never cared about her."

"I only found out yesterday that you'd been here that time, as a matter of fact! Séamus never mentioned it. A neighbour told me. In case it was you they found in the wood."

"No such luck," Hope said. "It was a pretty close call, though. God, he changed."

"He changed, all right."

"He scared me to death." Hope stared at the window again. This time its blackness seemed to defeat her. "I've never had any more children. I did remarry." She shrugged. "Eighteen years. We don't have any kids."

"Talulla was all Séamus had, Hope."

"I wasn't going to take her away. I just wanted to see her. Did you even know about the divorce? Séamus could have got married again. I know other people here do."

Briege said nothing.

After a moment Hope said, "I know I messed up when Talulla was born." For the first time she looked like the weary, anxious middle-aged woman that she was.

"Ah . . . you were both too young. Too different, maybe."

"You raised her, didn't you?" Hope said shrewdly.

"I helped. Séamus was a good father to Talulla. He went to pieces at first — why wouldn't he? Well, that's how she got the name. You might have named her before you left, if you'd thought of it."

Hope gave a ghost of a smile. "Was there some unfortunate person in the family already named Talulla?"

"Named *Tuilelaith*?" Briege gave it its proper Irish pronunciation and had to smile as she saw Hope's lips move silently. "No — there was a virgin saint from Kilkenny named *Tuilelaith*. Séamus was drunk, and the priest they found was from Kilkenny. I think Tully is named after the priest's mother, to be honest."

"'Tully!'" Hope said, flinching. "God, that's worse. 'Tully,' it sounds like some name out of Popeye or Moby Dick. Say she's pretty, Briege. With a name like that, she'll need it."

"She's lovely. You saw the photo."

"May I go get it?"

Briege nodded; but when Hope put the framed photo on the kitchen table between them, she felt a chill of misgiving. It was like remembering the dead.

Aidan arrived in the car park just ahead of the posse. From his vantage point he could see blue lights flickering along the upper Glenageary Road and more coming up Saval Park. He hurried on to the path to Killiney Hill that would take him past the old meeting place.

Where had Gareth gone? Why wouldn't he wait? Maybe, of course, he was out. A party. But there was no party: there was an emergency. Gareth would die thrashing before he'd waste a frozen dinner. He stopped. Maybe he should have gone into the house to look for him; the mortise-lock, maryah. The place was like a sieve. There would be Gareth, napping under his bibliographies, shotgun at the ready for the casual intruder. Better to phone. And why hadn't he? Because he knew Gareth wasn't there. Hadn't he seen the dinner, pooling on Gareth's scrubbed table?

Aidan's feet knew the way, like the feet of an old horse going home. An old horse. Jesus, he was thirty-one! The mist again. He rattled his torch, which had begun to give off a sepia light. He'd borrowed it a few days ago from his mother; his own had gone missing. Good thing Jimmy Meagher couldn't see the state of him – he'd have his life.

Something ahead of him on the wind: a

woman's voice. Where the paths diverged, he heard it again from the trees on Killiney, two notes on the darkness. "Charlie . . ."

He felt a crawling on his spine and cursed his cousin for insisting all those years ago that it was bad luck to call a child's name out-of-doors at Samhain. The frail voice called again.

"Talulla!" he shouted. "Talulla!" He pelted along the path, his heart pounding with dread.

Chapter Forty-Two

Charlie pitied the child who was whimpering. The sound was a sad little ripple within the torrent of crashes and scuffles that threatened to crush her, then hurtled away. When Talulla cried out sharply, Charlie realised somehow that it was herself whimpering; the man was sobbing, but all the while he was holding Talulla, tearing at her, hurting her.

She hugged herself so tightly that the lumps in her pocket bruised the soft flesh of her arm like a reproach and, dragging out the banger and matches, she tried to strike one. Her hands shook and the wind snuffed it. Again. Nothing. The man and Talulla were only yards from her, and the sounds were unbearable. Charlie opened the box a little and shoved the next match into it. There was a sudden, white-gold explosion of light on the ground and, as she pushed the banger towards it, Charlie had the impression that the tree's slim branches were leaning over her, the man's pale, astounded face caught in them like the moon.

After the blast, Aidan heard the child wailing. At first he did not connect this with the small form hunched over Talulla, its face a ravaged blob in the weak moonlight. Some atavistic sense of recognition rooted him to the ground; the hairs stood at the back of his neck. Then he realised what he was seeing. "Charlie? Are you all right?" The child nodded, sobbing.

Aidan, his throat dry, ran his hands over Talulla's face, her neck. No real swellings or cuts on her head; she groaned when he touched her neck, but the pulse was strong and nothing seemed fractured or dangerously swollen. "Do you know did he kick her, hit her with anything? Had he a knife?"

"I don't know." The child's voice was a thread.

"It's all right, Charlie," he said gently. "I don't think she's too bad." He felt Talulla's hands – some blood on her fingers, but no cuts that he could find, no blood when he ran his hands quickly over her body.

"He didn't have the spade."

"The spade?"

"He hit Mrs James with . . . in Granny's." Charlie fell silent.

"Charlie?" The child was shaking. Aidan took his jacket off and wrapped it round her. Others were coming. Voices rustled on the wind and lights winked up the hill. Still he couldn't leave. "Let's wake her nibs here. Talulla! Get with it. You're upsetting the child."

"She's not." The child slipped out of Aidan's jacket and tucked it around Talulla with curiously motherly little gestures.

Talulla seemed to come to all at once. She hit out, wild-eyed, just missing Charlie, and then she was on her feet, reeling, before Aidan could stop her. He caught her as she fell. He was reminded of young animals trying to stand for the first time, whose legs wobble and splay. He soothed Talulla with the simplicity that he would have used on a colt or a calf. In a moment she recognised his voice, and she clung to him. It was all he could do to support her, but he would have died rather than let her go. "Could be my only chance," he muttered.

"What?"

"Nothing. You should sit down again. Keep your head down."

He stayed on his feet, marvelling at the way Talulla sat with her back against his legs. She leaned against him as if she owned him. She was warm. Absently, he stroked her hair. The heat from her hair seemed to travel up his arm. Every part of him that was not touching her was deathly cold.

Charlie watched them. "Will he come back?"

"No," Aidan said. "He won't come back. Look."

Many small fingers of light pricked the darkness. There was a fretwork of voices among the trees.

"Tell me, Charlie," Aidan said quietly. "Did he follow you up here?"

The child nodded. "He saw me. Then he found my shawl." Her face crumpled.

Aidan put his arm around her. "It's OK now, Charlie. Trust me?"

She nodded.

A bulky figure stumbled into the clearing; a powerful torch shone on them, then was waved in wild arcs at the sky. Its owner tottered towards them.

"Mr O'Toole."

Mr O'Toole stood hunched before them, panting. "Why wouldn't you call out?" he wheezed at last. He groped in his pocket.

It was like waiting for someone else to answer the phone, Aidan thought. None of them could be bothered. Charlie snuggled beside Talulla, and all three were as dumb as owls.

Mr O'Toole offered the flask, was declined, and took a strong tot himself. Then he hallooed and waved the torch. "Here! Here!"

When the lights and voices were converging nearby Aidan, heartsick, slipped away.

Chapter Forty-Three

After Mrs MacDevitt arrived, breathless and tearful, and bundled Charlie away home, Talulla wavered among the others for a while, trying to find a place at the edge of things where she could be quiet without being cut off.

It had been a night of shattering intimacies but very few certainties. She could not name her attacker; even Charlie, who had looked into his face, seemed to have been been dazzled by the light. Charlie mumbled that she thought it was Murnaghan, but Talulla felt the man was younger; why, she wasn't quite sure. Besides, Murnaghan would never involve himself in such an escapade. Later, she reckoned that they both knew who it was but simply refused to believe it, and she wondered if all detection was simply an assault on human trust and incredulity. The man's hands had been round her throat, and she still could not believe he had wanted to – to end her. She touched her neck. His destructiveness was on her, like a stain. But Aidan's touch afterwards – Talulla did not realise she was crying until Mr O'Toole, who had been quietly watching her, took her arm and led her down the hill towards home.

There was almost a carnival atmosphere in the car park on the other side of the hill. The van and three squad cars were parked there at careless angles; the area was fraught with wind-strewn conversations, the burr of radios and the odd squawk of drunken complaint. The shadowy activity seemed to centre on the van, which drew away as Aidan approached. He could hear Boyle on the opposite verge, talking to a man with a cultivated, indignant-sounding voice. Two uniformed men were chatting near the path. They turned when they heard Aidan's footsteps on the leaves.

"Any luck?" he asked them.

The taller of the two leaned towards him, seemed to recognise him, and laughed. "Sprats only," he said. "Five gobshites in the nip, slaughtering chickens. Lumps of dead bird all over the rock, themselves – Boyle's raging, some eejit put a couple of them in with the cider crowd and the lads puked up. The smell would haunt you, they never even plucked them. No sign of the other fella, anyway, sorry about that."

The man in dignified conversation with Boyle was wearing Nikes, socks and nothing else. His chest was smeared with blood in which little pin-feathers trembled like hostages. Behind him, on the low wall, sat a woman in a raincoat.

"On the contrary, Guard, I have a complaint," the man in Nikes was saying. "My partner has been bitten by an uncontrolled dog –"

"Some animals are upset by bizarre behaviour, sir."

"If the dog had been under control," the man pronounced, "his assessment of my behaviour would be immaterial, Guard."

"Unfortunately there are a few strays –" the guard began.

"No stray. No stray. The dog was trailing a lead. He –"

"It was a Jack Russell," the woman said, in a disgusted voice. She was English, Aidan noted.

"With respect," said the guard, "could it have been the chicken he was after?"

Aidan left them to it. The hill entertained all sorts, and it was still Hallowe'en, or Samhain, as Mr O'Toole would insist.

The place he was looking for wasn't easily seen from the path, even in daylight. It had been a great spot once upon a time. Someone, they never knew who, had attached a stout rope to the branch of an oak tree that gripped the side of the hill. They had spent days there, himself and Gareth Travers and Peter Lawless and a few of the lads from the Grove, swinging out above the incline and trying to reach the other side. The rope had perished by the time Lara and Talulla were let loose. It was Alan, in fact, who had broken it, or maybe Emma. Alan had never let Emma take the blame for anything.

The younger ones found the tree and the remains of the rope, but they never used the hiding-place farther on behind the rock. Gareth and Peter and himself never let on it was there.

Gareth went off to college then, Peter to Boston where he married an American, and himself to Templemore. All the same, it was here that Aidan had gone to find a distraught Gareth after his mother's death – eight years ago. As time went on, they had drifted apart. He had noticed Gareth going into himself a bit but they were both busy, and Gareth was in England most of the time. Then, one day, there were things they couldn't talk about. Like Gareth's obsession with Emma.

He stopped and rubbed his face, unsure where to find the small track in the darkness, no more than a runnel off the path. He was reluctant to use his torch. Stale as it was, it would be visible as the only flicker of light in the hill's blackness. Things were coming back to him, though: how the path rose and crooked a little just before the little crease in the undergrowth. Now he was on it, his feet on the slippery stones and the depression just beyond which was always moist.

It was in this gentle hiding-place, where everything was green and living, that Gareth had confided how he couldn't possibly believe in God, how his grandfather detested his parents and him and, yes, how the old man had made his will. The house, that beautiful, unspeakable burden of a house that Gareth was so passionate about, would be his only if his uncle Jonathan – an ocean-going shite, by all accounts – had no legitimate issue. But there was no question of that, no question at all until Janet Winton turned up in Dalkey looking for her Irish roots.

"Gareth?" Aidan picked his way across the slope, blindly sliding on leaves and stones that had gone frosty. "Gareth?"

There was nothing.

He reached out; his hands met the rock that jutted forward, hiding the level comfortable space behind. He smelled old pennies.

Gareth's forehead was cooling, his chest under the shirt and jumper still warm. He must have waited until the very last, Aidan thought, hoping he'd come. For a final chinwag. Gareth had some old-fashioned expressions he liked to use. "Chin-wag." Aidan sat there in Gareth's blood, holding the limp hand. It was quite cold, but it hadn't started to stiffen. Maybe the blood leaving all Gareth's body from just above the wrists meant the hands stayed supple longer, though Aidan doubted it. He'd have to ask McQuaid about that. "Jesus, Gareth," he said aloud, "you were a fucking murderer and you wouldn't even tell me. You wouldn't even tell me!"

Gareth was a great one for research. He'd researched the best way to slash your arms, that was for sure, but what in the name of God possessed him to bury Janet Winton's handbag in Granny's? The one thing Aidan could have advised him about, the one thing Gareth could never ask him.

When the dogs and the handlers found them, Aidan was still talking. The ambulancemen prised his hand from Gareth's and brought him to casualty at Vincent's (Loughlinstown was full). Gareth they brought to the morgue.

Chapter Forty-Four

It wasn't like Briege to be jittering at the front gate, old and stooped-looking all of a sudden. She was talking to someone there, some woman her body language proclaimed she neither liked nor knew well, and both of them were hugging themselves with the cold. Had no one told her that Talulla and Charlie were all right? Both women looked up, then at one another.

Briege moved tentatively on to the footpath. Talulla could see she was upset, and she felt a stab of childish anger. She wanted Briege to comfort and reassure her, not the other way round. The other woman pulled back towards the open hall-door. Light streamed around her without revealing her face, but even from that distance Talulla knew she wasn't one of the neighbours. A journalist!

Briege took Talulla by the arm. "Tully," she said, "I want to tell you before . . ."

"Why didn't you just tell her to get lost?"

"Just like that?" Briege seemed horrified.

"Well, of course!" Talulla said loudly. The woman in the doorway seemed to flinch for a moment, then stood fast.

"She came all this way to see you," Briege said, wringing her hands.

"For heaven's sake, it's not your one from Bosnia, is it?"

"From Bosnia?"

"What's-her-name! The journalist. No, it couldn't be. Of course not. She covers wars," Talulla said.

"What are you talking about?"

"Is that a journalist or isn't it? You didn't talk to her, did you, Briege?"

"It's your mother," Briege said quickly.

Talulla looked again at the figure beside the front door. Hair that waved like her own, the hall light behind, same figure, same way of standing when unsure, right hand massaging left elbow.

Something irresistible seemed to climb up inside Talulla's chest and expand. When it got to her neck she realised, too late, that it was hysteria. She laughed so hard she couldn't breathe. She laughed until she was weak.

Briege nodded to the lovely woman, Talulla's mother, to go inside. She waited while Talulla wiped her face on her sleeve. "I saw the MacDevitts going by. Is Charlie all right?"

"Great! What's two attempted murders to a child of ten?"

"I meant physically," her aunt said in a tight voice. "Will you come into the house?"

Talulla turned around to thank Mr O'Toole, but he had melted away into the darkness. "I can't, Auntie-Mum," she said in a small voice.

"Picks her times, doesn't she?" Briege said. She put her arm around Talulla's shoulders.

"Oh, God, couldn't she just come back tomorrow?"

"She will, of course. Just let her see you, Talulla. I think that's all she wants for now."

"What's she like?"

"Come and see. Pretty rattled, to be honest. It's hard for her, too."

Talulla linked her arm tightly through Briege's. "How do you feel, Auntie-Mum?"

"Rotten!" Briege said and, when Talulla walked into the bright hall and she saw her bruised, swollen face, "My God!"

Talulla hardly heard her. All she could think of was the woman in front of her, who couldn't look much different than she had twenty-three years ago on the day she abandoned her. Talulla had never even seen a photograph of her; Séamus had destroyed them all.

The woman's pale eyes filled with tears: her lips moved silently. Talulla suddenly saw herself in the hall mirror. Even with a black eye shutting and a crust of blood under her nose, she looked uncannily like her mother. She started to laugh. "Well – what do you think of me?"

For his sins, Aidan claimed afterwards, the first sight he saw in casualty was his mother, his sister Lara and Mrs Lawless sitting together on a bench.

"We were just saying a few little prayers for Emma," said his mother, in a whispery voice.

"Mum hasn't been put on the nebuliser yet," Lara said. "And now I suppose you'll be brought in ahead of her, too. Look, Mum – his clothes are destroyed."

Lara claimed this conversation never took place; he was raving when he was brought in, she said, and there were no benches in Vincent's. "And not only had Mum already been on the nebuliser, she had to go again after she saw the state of you!"

Aidan preferred his own recollection. That, and Charlie MacDevitt and her banger gave him his only bit of comfort from that night. And the way Talulla had leaned against his legs, as if she always would.

Charlie let herself be babied as the latex was stripped slowly from her face. It was a long, miserable process. She answered the woman garda's questions in between the peelings and tuggings. In a queer way she still felt it was all a mistake and, when morning came, Mr Murnaghan would be revealed as the real culprit. A new older self knew that wasn't true. There were deep seams and complications in life, and some sorrows past bearing.

Tom removed the last of the latex, the sorest bits caught in the fine hair at her temples, while Charlie sat on her mother's lap. Tomorrow would be time enough for her to assert herself. She'd have a few things to tell Kevin Minogue, not the least how his banger had saved Talulla's life. She couldn't quite think of her own life yet. She had seemed to go in and out of it in some way, almost to become someone else.

"Mum." The voice was very small. "Where is Mrs James?"

"Mrs James is in St Vincent's Hospital, darling. I think she'll be all right."

Charlie straightened up. "Oh, no!"

"What is it, darling? What is it?"

"I left my bag in Granny's!"

"We'll get you more sweeties, love."

"But Mr O'Toole's little bottle!" Charlie murmured, disconsolate.

Her mother's eyes widened. She opened her mouth to respond, then stopped. Tomorrow was another day.

"I just couldn't wait any longer to see you," Hope said simply. "I just couldn't." Her eyes reddened, then her nose. Very carefully, Talulla put her arms around her. Hope's hands rose, humble, and came to rest on her daughter's shoulders. Briege thought of tentacles.

Chapter Forty-Five

Hope stayed a week. After the first night, they persuaded her to leave Fitzpatrick's Hotel and stay in the house. Talulla had expected to start work again, avoiding some of the stickiness of the visit, but she was given an additional, compulsory week off until her bruises could fade. "Just be sure you're all right," Sergeant Whelan said firmly. Talulla could hear talk, doors slamming, all the endless activity of the station in the background of their conversation, and she was disconsolate when she put down the phone. At the same time, she was relieved. The terrible events of the weekend did not fit into the forms of the stories she swapped with her fellow recruits. There were different forms – languages, really – for different people, and the two who could understand about Hope and all that had happened were in hospital.

Aidan, in giving them all a fright, had got himself in bad odour with Inspector Jimmy

Meagher. Talulla met Jimmy on his way out of Aidan's small room on the ward. It was Thursday, the first day that Aidan was allowed visitors. Jimmy was resplendent as usual in a perfectly-cut tweed jacket, and there were knife-edge creases in his trousers. He looked cross, and Talulla scowled at him. He ignored this and, turning, raised his hand to Aidan in a curt gesture of farewell. The air around it seemed to arrange itself in little squares.

"Garda O'Neill," he nodded, pleasantly enough.

"Well enough to be scolded, is he?" Talulla gave him her most brilliant smile. Behind him, Aidan slid under the covers until nothing showed except a few limp tufts of black hair.

"Indeed and he is," said Jimmy Meagher, with a glinty assessment of her neck and her eye. "On sick leave yourself, are you? Well, now, take care."

Before she could answer him, he had swooped off.

Aidan was still hidden. She pulled the sheet away from his face, then sat down beside him. His lips parted a little as if he were about to speak, but he said nothing, only put out his hand and touched her hair. She held his hand – it was still too warm – and put it lightly against her "shiner", then her neck. He smiled at her with his eyes, that

312

seemed darker blue than ever and electric with fever.

Again he started to speak, but Talulla shook her head. "I'll kill that Jimmy Meagher!" she whispered. Aidan looked pleased. She kissed his poor knuckles but, in the moment she looked down, he fell asleep.

The next day she arrived before Jimmy and told him about the funeral. It had been a quiet affair, but very well attended. Gareth had left a will, along with a letter to Aidan, and he had specified that he wanted to be cremated. Talulla, paradoxically, found this a chilly end.

"Cremated! Typical." Aidan moved his feet under the covers, agitated.

"I don't like cremation, either, but it wasn't too bad, considering."

"Yeah," he said bleakly, "'Considering' . . . !"

"It was nice enough," she said. "Did you know he had relations down in Tipp?"

"They came?"

"The great-uncle and aunt."

"I don't believe it. No, I do." He sighed.

"There's lots of rumours going round about his will, Aidan."

"I'll bet."

"Anyway, this pair didn't say a word to anyone

except Barney Hitchcock, and then they left in a right snit."

"Good enough for them. His grandfather's brother. Like two peas in a pod. Gareth saw him once in his entire life, his dad pointed him out to him at Leopardstown. He breeds horses, or did. He must be a hundred."

"Well, he was spry, maybe a bit mummified-looking from all those morning gallops in the wind. She looked shook, of the two of them."

"So she would, being married to that. She's thought to be a flinty aul' shrew in her own right."

"It would have helped you to be there, Aidan."

"What, so I could 'accept that he's dead'? I know he's dead, Talulla."

"Yes, but –"

"I don't need to see him – packaged – in some fucking urn in the presence of those two, who only came to gloat over his disgrace and claim –"

Talulla put her fingers on his lips. "And with people who really liked him, loved him, and were sorry as well as shocked."

"I won't see him in a fucking urn," he said, his face white and set.

"Nobody saw him in anything, Aidan. The urn won't be ready for ages."

Aidan fell silent.

"Oh, Jesus," Talulla muttered. She picked at the blanket.

"'Oh, Jesus' what? What?"

"Don't get excited, Aidan –"

"Ah, no!"

"Look, it's all right –"

"He left me his ashes. He left me his fucking ashes, didn't he?"

"Well, he wrote to you, too. He –"

"Bastard!" he said, furious. His fists clenched.

"Oh, God, I don't know how to tell you. I'm sure he didn't mean –"

"Who's to know what Gareth meant?" He turned away, his face twisting. Talulla leant her head on his shoulder and, after a second or two, he wound his arms around her. "So bloody weak," he muttered. "Childish. Sorry."

Talulla wished he would let himself cry outright. She knew what happened when men didn't, but then Aidan wasn't her father, and she wasn't Hope. It had been a relief to find that out once and for all.

She snuggled her head on Aidan's shoulder, full of a new, weird confidence. It had been a surprise to find that she liked Hope, enough even to understand and to forgive her father's bitterness towards her. She was also surprised to find that she felt as ambivalent about Gareth Travers in death as she had in life. His attacks on Emma and her were the acts of a madman, and so was his terrible pursuit of Charlie on the hill. She pitied him, despite everything; there had always been something blinkered about him, something – as if his house and its past, even his studies were like hard, false limbs, without which he would crash to the ground.

It was his treatment of Aidan that enraged her. He had been as close to Aidan as he could be to anybody, but he hadn't any notion of what it would cost Aidan to be put in charge of his ashes. Not after Gareth had refused his help in life; not after he'd lied to him for years.

Aidan's breathing was quieting, but he did not loosen his arms. It was strange how they had never said anything. The crisis had intervened in all that. She had leaned against his legs, and he had stroked her hair. Even his leaving her, bruised and disorientated, while he went to find Gareth showed where they were with one another. It was a little frightening. Perhaps this was what her parents had felt, this inarticulate certainty; but then, they were different. And they had been too young. All the same, she shivered.

"Tell me about the letter," he said finally.

"It's for you. Sealed up. Barney Hitchcock has it and the will."

"Does the whole world know this?"

"Just me and Briege and your mother."

He sighed.

"Your mum's all right, Aidan. It's actually worked out well, my week off. I drop in on her a few times every day and stop her from rushing out into the cold."

"Thanks."

"Lara's coming this weekend . . . You really are sick, aren't you? You didn't moan."

"As long as she goes back on Sunday. After that, I'll be out of here."

"You won't go back to your flat. Not right away."

"I will go straight back to my flat. To my own bed." He held her tighter, and they were quiet for a while.

"You'd better give me your key, then, so I can have it ready for you. Your mum isn't up to it."

"If you're in it, it'll be ready for me. You're shaking, Tully. Are you all right?"

Chapter Forty-Six

Emma was out of intensive care. Talulla met Mrs Morrissey and Iseult in the corridor outside her room. Mrs Morrissey seemed to have recovered from the shocks of the weekend, or perhaps that was only her make-up. Iseult looked bewildered. She was wearing a new red dress and coat, shoes and little blue tights. Her pale gold hair was caught in two sleek pigtails that quirked like small question-marks on either side of her head. Talulla hunkered down beside her and tweaked them. Iseult brightened and began to giggle.

"Can I hug you, or are you too beautiful?"

"You can hug me," said the little girl, and stuck out her arms. Talulla picked her up.

"Mmm, lovely smells, Iseult. How's Emma, Mrs Morrissey?"

"Lucky," said her mother. Talulla tried not to stare. A delicate paleness around the dark eyes couldn't be hidden even by Estée Lauder; Mrs

Morrissey had certainly suffered, but she also had an air of suppressed excitement, even of glee.

"She isn't to move her head, or she's to move it as little as possible for another day or two, but they're delighted with her. The doctor says her skull is good Dalkey granite! And – " with even greater satisfaction, Talulla thought – "the scar won't show." Then her face fell. "She has some absurd idea about emigrating to Australia with Alan de Burca, Talulla. Absolute madness, especially –" She caught herself up. "I'm counting on you, dear, to talk some sense into her."

"'Alan'," Iseult said, pleased, rolling the name in her mouth.

Mrs Morrissey threw up her eyes. "Now," she said. "Granny will bring you to McDonald's." They left hand in hand, the child chatting eagerly and giving little skips.

"I heard all that," Emma said. She was sitting up against a mass of pillows, which were arranged behind and beside her like a wall of sandbags.

"You look like an idol," Talulla told her.

"Don't make me laugh! I thought you'd never come. I've been going mad. I mean, Mum and Iseult to top it off! Alan tried to sneak in pretending to be my husband, and then Mum blew the whistle on him. Good God! What happened to you?"

"How long have we got?"

"Oh, don't mind that. They keep coming in, but I'll just move my head if they annoy us. Tully, was it Gareth?"

"It was, actually. He couldn't help it."

"No," Emma said, "he couldn't. But nasty enough of him, all the same." She looked at her fingers, spread them and closed them, her face sad.

"What's this about Alan?" Talulla asked.

"Oh, he hasn't been allowed in since Monday night, and Mum has been intolerable! She won't speak about anything that would upset me, she says, which means that I know absolutely nothing about anything. She did deign to tell me that Charlie MacDevitt was all right, but not a word about you being involved. Then she arrives today with poor Iseult and starts rabbiting about builders and decorators –"

"Has she cracked? I thought she looked –"

"I'm cracking. She has me demented, Tully. I keep telling her that there is no way I will ever live in that house –"

"What? Your parents'? I thought you loved it!"

"No." Emma stared at her. "Gareth's! Beaulieu. Do you mean that people don't know?"

"Know what, Emma?"

"Gareth left Iseult Beaulieu in his will."

"*What?*"

Emma's face crumpled.

Talulla held her hand, helpless. A trolley rattled outside. A very young nurse arrived into the room, swishing. "Oh!" she said, when she saw Emma's tears. She left.

"I think she's gone for reinforcements," Talulla said.

"You look stunned."

"Try 'comatose.'"

"Yeah. I was so ashamed, I couldn't – now it'll all be out. Mum hasn't really grasped it yet, but Iseult will be much better off in Australia. She's Gareth's, Tully. He figured it out. That awful day, he couldn't take his eyes off her, that day we found the – Janet Winton. His cousin. It's unbelievable, isn't it . . . Gareth with a cousin. I couldn't wait to get Iseult away, remember? She reminded him of someone. The wheels were turning. He was counting, and he realised. Apparently he went straight from there to Hitchcock and changed his will. It was a matter of time before someone – Iseult couldn't be Alan's or Declan's, because they've both got dark eyes. Their parents, too, though Alan didn't realise that mattered. He just fell into the truth. Then he saw Iseult's likeness to Gareth immediately."

"I can't believe you and Gareth."

"Well, you're right. There wasn't any 'me and Gareth'."

"That day in Granny's!"

"The day of the long knives. Yes. After Gareth's night of the long shovel."

"Emma!"

"It was just the once. Well, twice. That terrible girl bawling all this muck about her and Alan. Out in Granny's. She went off and I found a piece of broken glass and dug at my wrist with it, only it snapped, and then Gareth appeared out of nowhere and stopped me. He really did look like the Angel Gabriel, and he was so upset, we just sort of – anyway, then he wouldn't let go of me. He wouldn't let go until he'd done it again. He was a little bit mad, you know? 'A little bit,' nothing. I was scared shitless, Tully! My parents were away, remember? He nearly wore down the door that weekend. Oh, God!"

"Shh . . . don't move, Emma, don't move!"

"Oh, Tully, I feel so sorry for him – Declan, too. But I see bits of Gareth in Iseult, and she's so sweet! They gave him a dog's life up in Beaulieu, or he'd never have been the way he was . . . but I couldn't. I just couldn't!"

"Now, ladies!" It was the ward sister, summoned by the student nurse. Emma, too drained to protest, was given a sedative in her drip.

"My chemical straitjacket," she complained. The Sister only smiled.

"See you tomorrow," Talulla said.

"Sorry," Emma mouthed.

"Don't be silly! But, Emma – one thing."

"What?"

"You won't sell it to Murnaghan, sure you won't?"

Emma gave a tearful snort, and the Sister said, "Out!"

Chapter Forty-Seven

By the end of the week, Talulla had almost come to terms with Hope's presence in her life. Tuesday, naturally, was spent in shock; Wednesday, they talked a little; Thursday, the floodgates opened, and they talked until their jaws pained them; and Friday, Hope prepared to go home. "Of all the times for me to come!" she said. "The week when everything happened!"

Talulla had her own ideas about that, and they were too superstitious to be shared. She supposed she got that from Briege. She reckoned she wasn't very like Hope at all; but then, Hope would get an expression, or make a gesture, and it was as if Talulla glimpsed herself in a mirror, glimpsed her real self out of the corner of her eye. She wondered how people managed who grew up with their real mothers.

"You're so Irish," Hope told her wonderingly. "I mean, look." She made Talulla stand next to her in front of the mirror in the hall. "We're really alike. But you'd know I was American, wouldn't you? And I would know you were Irish. Hm. You're part Cherokee, did you know that? There's a bit of Sioux as well," Hope said complacently.

"'Way back. And Irish. Mainly Scots . . . some German."

"American," Talulla said, weak.

"American," her mother agreed, looking at her with pale, smoky eyes. "I think we get our spirituality from the Irish and the Sioux," she added.

"After all the business about 'Irish identity' at college!" Talulla told Aidan. She had stopped in to see him after leaving Hope at Dublin Airport. "Post-colonial. How about ten per cent pre- and ninety per cent post-colonial?"

"Sounds like a parcel."

"Well, what kind of parcel? The woman's just told me I'm a menagerie!"

"You're Irish."

"Why?"

He looked at her long and consideringly.

"Aidan?" she said faintly.

"You just are. What else would you be?"

"German? Cherokee?"

"Jesus, girl, you learned Irish in the Irish schools!"

"It's the language then, is it?"

"Not at all. It's the oppression." His eyes sparkled. He wasn't touching her today, though she was throwing out tiny lures, like resting her hand close to his on the coverlet. She wondered how they had started playing these little games.

"You could at least take it seriously."

"I take you seriously. Let's get married."

She gaped at him. Her heart sank a little.

"All right," he said equably. "Let's not."

"It's too dangerous," she mumbled.

"Oh, it's dangerous, all right." He looked almost scornful. Then he relented. "I should cop myself on. You've been sorting out your mother, all week; I've had nothing to do but lie here thinking."

"You've had Jimmy Meagher every day. That's enough to be going on with."

"Ah, it's good of him. He's keeping me up to date. I'm actually caught up on my paperwork."

"And?'"

"We've got Basil Hughes cold. There's enough evidence in the boots of those two cars to put him away forever."

"What's he like?"

"Rat-grey eyes and a pair of hands."

She shuddered.

"Everything he is was in her pictures. Ailbhe MacBride's. Like a pollutant in the air; he doesn't actually appear. Only his hands, in one. She slashed that one. Jimmy thinks she knew: she didn't know. Her hands knew. She was all the time painting his portrait, every picture was him. A nothing. Just women being throttled. Hands. Plants. She's shattered, poor woman. She loved him."

"Were they any good?"

"Magnificent. But they're gallery stuff. You wouldn't want them on the wall at home."

"I'd like to see them."

"I wonder if she'll ever show them. As long as you never go in that house."

"Why?"

"It has a bad atmosphere," was all he would say.

Talulla hoped he would ask about Gareth's ashes, but he didn't. "The flat's all right", she said after a moment. "I aired it and dusted a little and threw some things out of your fridge."

"What things?"

"Don't know. Samantha McQuaid might."

"Oh. Right. Sorry."

"Well, at least you eat vegetables." She took his hand. It had been strange, being in his flat. It was orderly, much more so than her room at home. She couldn't touch his bed, that was much too intimate, somehow, but she picked up a pile of his clothes and put them in a bag of laundry she found in his wardrobe. He trusted her, letting her in like that, so she was careful. Under the window beside his bed was a small stack of magazines, *Archaeology Ireland*. They were well-thumbed.

"Penny for them?"

She blurted out something she hadn't been thinking of at all. "Aidan, I think I joined the Gardaí to please Dad . . . and, when he wasn't pleased . . ." she shook her head and burst into tears.

"You felt you had to show him. Who wouldn't?" He stroked her arm and looked earnestly into her eyes. "Look, Tully. I love the force. It suits me. But you're different. You're . . . I don't know how to put it. Your structures, the way you think, are different. You're – making adjustments all the time, or something."

She stared at him. "Making adjustments. That's exactly how I feel! But Aidan, I love it, too. I'll miss everyone horribly. And knowing things. And the power . . ."

"Sure you will, but you've got me."

Emma said that she would try not to sell Beaulieu – which now, mysteriously, began to be called 'Travers's' by all and sundry – to Murnaghan, but that she'd have to sell it to somebody. Declan, who had gone to a drying-out clinic, was angling for a share of the proceeds. "It'll assuage his pride

and get him off me, once and for all," she told
Talulla and Lara. Lara had thrown up her job in
London, to Aidan's disgust.

"But it's not his!" Lara cried.

"I owe him something, Lara," Emma said,
shrugging.

"You owe him a lawsuit for that broken arm."

"It's over, Emma, anyway. All of it," Talulla
said, frowning at Lara.

Charlie and the Minogues decided to exert their
own subtle influence on events. Kevin had
retained a few bangers for emergencies, and
there was a bit of latex in the bottom of
Charlie's tube. Their friend Francesca from
Thorn Crest had discovered a talent in herself
for looking vacant, and the little Minogues
simply didn't wash their faces. They hovered
near Travers's gates, impervious to the glares of the
auctioneers.

That particular Saturday, the smallest Minogue
was getting an earache. They were all cold and
discouraged, and it was only Charlie's and Kevin's
persistence that kept them there to witness what
happened next. A white stretch limousine drew
up, followed by two black ones. People emerged
from these like bees from a capsized hive, officious
people, all looking this way and that. Charlie

removed her woolly hat, displaying the spreading latex scab she had secured over her hair, but these people took no notice.

One of them opened the door of the white limo, and two large feet, shod in space-age trainers, thrust out. Then came the rest: skinny ankles, long legs in immaculate denims, three layers of shirts, oddly-textured and, finally, a pale face surrounded by a cascade of mousy hair interspersed with narrow chartreuse plaits and tiny flowers.

"Greenman," Kevin breathed. Charlie clapped on her hat, Francesca beamed, and the two little Minogues scrubbed their faces on their sleeves. Kevin, ever-inspired, stowed the banger back in his pocket and shouted, "Save the whales!"

Travers's was saved, and so was Granny's Wood, but there were prices to be paid. Greenman's security lights probed the hiding-places almost as far as O'Neill's, and his dogs prowled Travers's at night so that the children were always a little afraid. The great gates stayed tightly shut, though it was said that the house, extensively repaired and refurbished, was lovely. A swimming-pool stretched across the lawn where Aidan had loved to pause, feasting his imagination among rough grass and shadows. Who could say what became of Gareth's ashes, that Aidan finally scattered there at his request, or Janet Winton's, that were mixed with them? It seemed a kind of justice: her stepfather would not pay for her body to be brought back to the US.

Greenman, who was unassuming, though possessed of that strange protective lamination made up of a million gazes, met Aidan and Talulla in Castle Street one day outside the Exchange bookstore. "Do you remember an old chest that was in the house? In the hall?" he said. "Big, carved thing; one of those Victorian copies."

Aidan nodded.

"Why'd he get rid of it? Do you know? I've been offered it – I've been offered half Dublin, come to think of it – all this gaff people say was in the house. But this actually *was*, so you say . . . ?"

"Gareth hated it. Thought it was ugly," Aidan said. "If you brought that thing back, he'd probably – well, never mind."

"Haunt me?" said Greenman, with his fey smile.

Aidan gave his blank look as Talulla watched, interested.

"Just as well," said Greenman, after a moment. "This character wants a bomb for it. Says it has a story."

"Old things always have," Aidan agreed. "Some story or other."

"You don't want to sell me the clock?"

"No."

Later, Aidan told Talulla how he dreamed the chest was the opening to hell and how, for Gareth, in a way, it was. The chest had a story indeed.

Dear Aidan,

Sorry I didn't tell you this when it mattered. I still want to get by with it; what's done is done. You'll read this only if things don't work out.

The woman in Granny's is my first cousin, Janet Travers Winton. She was my uncle Jonathan's only child. She was like him; had their eyes, his and my grandfather's. She was one of us, all right, true Travers, unlucky. She didn't even know about the will, it was just something she said and those eyes – I flung out my hand and she cracked her head off the bloody fireguard. She would have got on to the will, Aidan. She saw my face when she said who she was. So I hid her in your favourite chest until it was dark. I lost the run of myself. But I don't want to pay for it, Aidan. Not paying is one up on grandfather.

Emma never loved me. She was too upset to care. It was just the once – sheer impulse, out in Granny's. She wasn't impressed, poor girl, but Iseult's mine. I know it. So I've left her everything but the clock. That's for you. It's still at the mender's – I've left the details with Barney Hitchcock.

You'll never read this. I'm going to find her bag out there, Aidan, it's the only thing that ties Janet Winton and me together. (Except blue eyes and the famous Travers luck.)

Gareth had folded the letter carefully and left it beside his will, but he hadn't signed it. Aidan wondered when he had written it. Was the letter upstairs, waiting to be read, the night they'd sat together talking?

Boyle kept the letter for evidence. He was welcome to it. Aidan felt Gareth had renounced their friendship in not letting him help, and he was saddened and sickened that, in the end, he had felt no remorse.

Now, peering into the bookstore window, Talulla said, "I've seen another one!" and she was back inside, heading for the review hardbacks on the shelf beside the door. While she was at the desk, oblivious, a toddler began to sift through the contents of her rucksack.

"Tear them up!" Aidan's mind whispered to the child, but she stuffed the ticket to Boston back in the bag. Then the traveller's cheques were scrutinised and tasted, but by this time Talulla had seen what was going on. She picked up the bag, laughing, and reassured the child's mortified mother.

Through the glass, her eyes and Aidan's met. Ghostly reflections of the traffic up and down Castle Street flitted between them. He would melt and disappear too from her thoughts when she was gone, gone to visit that woman who was like some figment from Tír na nÓg.

"I'm all set," she told him happily when she came out. Her bag, which he took from her, was a ton weight. "Two for going out. Three for while I'm there. Two for the way back. Aidan – ?"

He turned to her.

"What is it?"

He shook his head, smiling.

Chapter Forty-Eight

When she got back from taking Talulla to the airport, Briege went for a walk at White Rock. The day was cold and blustery. Wild storms during the last week of November had scraped drifts of sand from the sea's floor and distributed them on the shingle in new, clean configurations, smoothing it under her feet. Her eye was drawn by squabbling and shriekings high on the granite restraining wall below the railway, yet another domestic fracas among the resident gulls. A scruff of feathers emerged from a cleft; two great ungainly wings stretched, then teetered for balance. Claws, hidden, stubbornly clung. The scolding continued.

Briege picked her way through the tumble of boulders separating White Rock from Killiney beach. She searched twice, wondering if she was confused; but her queer black stone was gone. It seemed there were storms strong enough to shift anything.

She had come to a peaceful decision about her retirement. She would stay at the bank for at least another year; she would miss it far too much if she stopped now, with Talulla almost ready to move on. Talulla would never stay in America, but she might well marry Aidan or move in with him. Briege hoped it would be marriage; the more mortar in a relationship the better, as far as she was concerned. Whatever about that, one thing was clear: her Talulla had grown up. She was reared.

As she skipped a pebble across the waves, she realised that she was no longer alone on the beach. Brendan O'Toole, who had not seen her yet, was approaching from the Killiney train station. Behind her, Kevin Minogue and Charlie MacDevitt, with many loud, bossy proclamations, were escorting the two little Minogues down the steps. A sharp gust caught Kevin's green baseball cap, twirled it high in the air, then tossed it on to a wave that, cresting and spreading, left it safely back at his feet.